To Brian, Rachel

Hope you enjoy the ___

God Bless,

Henry C. Martin Beckett

10/15/11

Matthew 6:22-23

HILL OF GREAT DARKNESS

H. C. BECKERR

WestBow
PRESS
A DIVISION OF THOMAS NELSON

WestBow Press books may be ordered through booksellers or by contacting:

WestBow Press
A Division of Thomas Nelson
1663 Liberty Drive
Bloomington, IN 47403
www.westbowpress.com
1-(866) 928-1240

Because of the dynamic nature of the Internet, any web addresses or links contained in this book may have changed since publication and may no longer be valid. The views expressed in this work are solely those of the author and do not necessarily reflect the views of the publisher, and the publisher hereby disclaims any responsibility for them.

Any people depicted in stock imagery provided by Thinkstock are models, and such images are being used for illustrative purposes only.

Certain stock imagery © Thinkstock.

ISBN: 978-1-4497-1795-7 (sc)
ISBN: 978-1-4497-1797-1 (hc)
ISBN: 978-1-4497-1796-4 (e)

Library of Congress Control Number: 2011929577

Printed in the United States of America

WestBow Press rev. date: 6/23/2011

For Uncle Harry, who now sees his Creator face-to-face.

For Dorothy Holst, who took the time to show a little boy
the wonders of God's word.

For Pastor Fred Winters, whose wisdom guided this project
from its inception.

For the men and women of NASA, who put steel and flames
to mankind's dream of the stars.

But most of all, for the Lord Jesus Christ, who gives us eyes
to see, teachers to teach, hearts to seek wisdom, and dreams
to fulfill.

To God be all the glory.

"THE SECRET THINGS BELONG TO THE LORD OUR GOD"

—Ancient Hebrew Text

Gen. J. J. Smithton, DOD
Roger A. Hand, USAF (Ret.)
Michael Goldstein, NASA/JPL
Rear Admiral Richard Halbrande, US Navy

CLASSIFIED—CLASSIFIED—CLASSIFIED

U.S. DEPARTMENT OF DEFENSE

MEMORANDUM

APRIL 1, 2037

CLASSIFIED

In response to the events surrounding the tragic fate of the spacecraft Magellan and its crew, the president of the United States and the Department of Defense have issued the following statement concerning the unauthorized release of information on what is now to be referred to officially as the Magellan Incident:

1. No one is to disclose, on or off the record, any information concerning Magellan that has not already been officially disclosed up to the date of this memorandum.
2. No one is to discuss the deaths of the crewmembers of Magellan.
3. The apparent yield of the nuclear blast that occurred moments after the spacecraft's emergency crash landing on the moon is to remain HIGHLY CLASSIFIED until the DOD sees fit to reveal it to the public.
4. Any recorded conversations between Magellan and Earth (Houston Control or personal) that have not been released prior to this memorandum are to be considered CLASSIFIED.
5. Any and all references to Cahokia Mounds Historical Site are to be deleted from all recordings, reports, memos, hard drives, and/or software.

Failure To Comply With These Guidelines Completely Will Be Viewed As An Act Of Wartime Treason, Punishable With A Minimum Twenty-Five-Year Prison Sentence As Well As Forfiture Of All Personal Holdings, Property, Cash, American Rights, And Citizenship.

PART I: MAGELLAN

CHAPTER 1

INTROS AND EXITS

Yesterday's Twilight

He stood on the edge of the ancient precipice, the mighty river far beneath him, the dawn growing ever brighter behind him and engulfing the entire scene in a soft pinkish-orange glow, his eyes scanning the river north to south as if he were an eagle ready to dive from the cliff to catch a morning meal. Just as Kobi-nana turned around to face the tribe that had gathered to hear him, the sun broke free from the bonds of darkness and illuminated Kobi-nana's face with the brilliance of a thousand campfires. This was his land, these were his people, this was his day, and this was his moment. He slowly drew in a deep, mighty breath and then spoke with a voice that cut through the early morning fog like a peal of thunder.

"My warriors, my friends," he began, "today is a great day for our people, and it is a day that will be remembered long into tomorrow's tomorrow." As he spoke, he lifted the tribal chieftains' spear that had been in his family for generations high above his head with both hands.

He continued, "As you and your young ones know, where we stand is sacred ground. It is at this very spot alongside the great river of mud that our forefathers fought and overcame the fierce serpent-bird Pi-Awsa. It was with this very spear that I hold in my hands the fatal blow to the great and dreadful plague of our people was delivered." He started to pace left to right and back again as if to gain momentum in stride and in speech.

"Where we stand is the place from which Pi-Awsa made its final dive into the great river so far below." He continued with his hands outstretched, the

3

tribal spear now in his right hand with its hand-hewn stone point pointing upward.

"Our fathers watched as the river swallowed the death bird and then parted, carrying Pi-Awsa to the secret underground place. My people," he continued, his voice gaining fervor and momentum, "It was the Great Spirit himself that performed the feat, creating the little river that goes into the ground. To this day, that mysterious river flows silently into the Great Darkness that the god of the night-sky, Kayo-Kee-ya, placed by his very own hand underneath our mighty temple."

Tomorrow's Dawn

Long, sleek, and fast, *Magellan* majestically held her orbit above Earth at twenty-five thousand miles, silently asleep in near space, awaiting her re-awakening. The first ship of her kind, designed for use in experimental drive systems testing, *Magellan* looked more the part of an expensive sports car than a spacecraft. Just one week earlier she had taken her maiden test flight, using her own engines at less than one-half power, from Earth to lunar orbit and back in less than six hours, easily surpassing any and all expectations of the new twin ion-drive engine cannons.

With a crew of only three people on board for the test run and not a single glitch, *Magellan's* on-board propulsion system quickly earned the respect of her design team at the Jet Propulsion Laboratory in Pasadena.

Built without a single taxpayer dollar, this pinnacle of mankind's engineering once again awoke the imagination of every schoolboy and girl who dared to dream of space exploration—a dream that had been lying in dormant waste for far too long. It seemed as though every single television on planet Earth was tuned to one of the countless news channels, watching the constant reports and updates of *Magellan's* progress toward her first real mission: the testing of a radically new propulsion system, one based on gravity and numbers—not the old "slingshot" use of gravity as her predecessors knew, but the actual (at least theoretical) harnessing of one of nature's most powerful forces. Known simply as the IGS System, the formal name being Inverted Gravitational Sequencing, this propulsion device looked very promising indeed—at least on paper.

Magellan had been built entirely in space, right alongside the completely renovated International Space Station—at least the biggest part of her was. One thing that had caused some intense international worries was the fact that she was the first spacecraft to use a small nuclear power plant as her main source of power and propulsion. So, once the ship was ready to be powered-up for the very first time, the shuttle *Atlantis*, which had been purchased from NASA after her de-commissioning, had to tow her to her standardized twenty-five-thousand mile orbit, just in case.

The contrast in architecture and design was apparent as the aging space shuttle towed *Magellan*. It was almost like seeing a big, beautiful diamond being pulled by an old lump of coal. It was rather awkward-looking as well, with *Magellan* being almost five times as long as *Atlantis*, prompting one CNN reporter to remark, "Looks like the old tug in the harbor escorting out the newest cruise ship."

It was the Chinese orbiter *Yangtze* that was delegated to bring up the plutonium fuel rods as well as two of *Magellan's* crewmembers for this IGS test flight. Although much newer and smaller than her American orbiter counterparts, *Yangtze* still managed to wow earthbound viewers who were watching the live docking maneuvers with *Magellan* on video feed. *Yangtze* had come up from behind *Magellan* and flew over her. Then she cart wheeled into a perfect nose-to-nose position. After the usual space chatter about systems, green-lights, pressurizations, and equalizations, *Yangtze* slipped silently underneath *Magellan* by doing a forward flip and then docked belly-to-belly with the "Jewel of the Night;" almost immediately, the transfer of cargo and personnel began.

"Dr. Armone, welcome aboard *Flagship Magellan*," came the beefy greeting from *Magellan's* commander Matt Moore. "I trust your flight was enjoyable, sir."

Dr. Jon Armone was the chief propulsion theorist from JPL as well as one of the top nuclear physicists in the world. "The flight?" Armone replied, "That was wonderful—it was the fancy maneuvers that have my innards all shook up." The last part of his statement seemed to be directed more toward *Yangtze's* pilot than to Commander Moore.

Dr. Armone was about to say something else when all attention was directed to the next arriving member of *Magellan's* team. Tripping over his tongue in all of the known dimensions of time and space, Commander Moore finally managed to greet and welcome the highly esteemed and strikingly beautiful Simone Sytte—See-yet-tea, as she would always find herself pronouncing for people as she displayed the charm and grace of a diplomat.

"And greetings to you as well, Miss Sytte. Welcome to the first truly interplanetary spacecraft."

"Thank you, Commander," she said.

It was Simone Sytte who had developed a highly reactive, but less dangerous, rechargeable fuel rod system to be used in space. Two years and some one hundred twenty-five million of her own dollars later, she had convinced most of the entire international community to allow nuclear power in space—that is, under certain restrictions. One of those conditions was the twenty-five thousand mile orbit, thus allowing all of Earth's communities to feel safe from any "accidents."

Cargo transfer from *Yangtze* to *Magellan* took less than an hour and was anything but exciting. With the transfer complete, *Yangtze*'s commander offered up his hopes for *Magellan's* success and then departed from them at a very dangerous speed.

"That man is a maniac," Armone said.

"That man, sir, is China's top fighter pilot," came Commander Moore's somewhat envious reply.

"I think he's cute," Simone said. "Short but cute."

"Next to you, Miss Sytte, everybody is short. Besides, he's not your type."

"Oh, and what is my type, Commander?" she said playfully.

"Well," he began slowly, as if he were trying to dig himself out of an extremely deep hole, "for starters, he—uh, uh, oh, never mind." Turning to Dr. Armone, he said, "Time to get to work," and made a hasty retreat to engineering with Jon following behind him, laughing all the way down the corridor.

CHAPTER 2

CLASSROOM ANTICS

Springtime in Illinois had always been a favorite time of year for Professor Martin Sherfy because teaching archaeology inside of a classroom while the winter snow was piling up on the outside was, by any stretch of the imagination, no adventure in learning whatsoever. He stood looking out the giant window in his classroom, searching for the signs of spring that the calendar date was proclaiming; then, checking his wristwatch, he walked over to his desk and started shuffling through his notes for his next class.

"Good afternoon, Professor Sherfy," came the usual and obligatory greeting from the first few students who would straggle in. Usually, once there were four or five students in the classroom, the remaining students would enter the room without sensing the need for such pleasantries.

"Good afternoon, class. I trust you are all well-rested from your weekend. I would like to start this week with an announcement about a little field trip of sorts. Since we have been studying the Mississippian Indian culture, um, that's the 'Monks Mound Indians' for you people who have been napping in my class for the last six weeks, I thought we would take a short trip out to the mounds site and do a little investigation of their astronomical observations."

Seeing a hand going up toward the back of the room and instantly knowing to whom that hand belonged, Martin smiled inwardly and prepared for the usual comic game-play.

"Yes, Mr. Jones."

"Professor, we've been learning about these mounds that the Cahokians—"

"That's Mississippians, Mr. Jones."

"Oh, yeah, that's what I meant, the Mississippians—the mounds that they built all around the area. So, my question is, when did they have the time to study the stars?"

"At night, when they couldn't see to dig." The professor paused for a moment to let the chuckles die down before he continued, "Besides, Mr. Jones, the propagation of the human species was not the only nocturnal activity available to primitive cultures." With that, he turned his attention back to the entire class.

"Imagine, my young friends," he began, raising his hands high above his head and spreading them as wide as possible, "a night with no artificial light such as, oh, a streetlight or the distant glow of a nearby town and all of creation lighting the night sky before you."

He took a moment to let that thought sink in as he looked into the eyes of his students and then continued.

"Mankind's imagination knows no limits here; he sees just how small he is and how vast the universe before him is. He watches the seasons come and go, and he begins to notice specific times and events. Now that brings me to—" he paused for the effect to take root, "Woodhenge. As you may or may not know, next Monday is the Spring Equinox. Now Woodhenge is constructed so that the Spring Equinox positions the sun rising at the southern tip of Mound Thirty Eight, aka Monks Mound, and lines up with the center pole as well as two of the peripheral poles of the structure. I would like for us to be there on site by six a.m. I guarantee you guys a spectacular sunrise event—that is, as long as there are no clouds around to obstruct the view. Any questions?"

That oh-so-familiar hand raised itself in the back of the room. "Yes, Mr. Jones?"

"Will HAL be there, Professor Sherfy?"

Obviously caught off-guard by the question, Martin cautiously offered an, "Excuse me?"

"Oh, you know—'Open the pod bay doors, HAL.'"

"HAL 9000—now there's a name I haven't heard in years." He spoke almost to himself. Then, addressing the class, continued, *"2001: A Space Odyssey.* HAL 9000 was the schizophrenic computer that murdered all but one member of the spaceship *Discovery*'s crew."

"Yeah, and it all started with a sunrise, Professor."

"That's right, it did, Mr. Jones, but let me assure you all that this sunrise will be a blissfully tranquil event. Won't it, Mr. Jones?"

"Peaceful, yeah I'm sure. Oh, by the way, if I have a note from my mom—"

Before he could go any further, Martin interrupted and said with a smile, "This is a requirement for the course, Mr. Jones."

"A requirement?"

"A requirement."

"So, six a.m. at Cahokia Mounds?"

"At the Woodhenge site, Mr. Jones." Then he continued, "I expect to see you all there, class, no exceptions." Professor Sherfy spent the next ninety minutes going over the societal progress of the Mississippian culture of that time period and then saw that time was up for the day, so he dismissed the class. He couldn't help but notice the look that Katy Kulner gave Kevin Jones as he walked past her out of the room. It was quite evident that the young woman despised the young rebel/comedian.

"Katy?" the professor said as she passed by him.

"Yes, Professor Sherfy?" she answered with a *what now* attitude.

"You know that I tend to let individual personality traits be expressed in my classroom, so try not to let Mr. Jones upset you. He's just being himself."

"Yeah, I noticed," was all she said as she made her way to the door. Then she disappeared out into the hallway.

Martin pondered the attitude of the young woman and then sat down at his desk. He reached out and opened up the top drawer and pulled out an old, tattered, beaten, and worn-out leather book and began to read excitedly for at least the hundredth time: *"In the beginning God created ..."*

CHAPTER 3

QUESTIONS, QUESTIONS, QUESTIONS

Six days later …

The stage was simple enough: two high-back swivel chairs on a deceptively simple-looking soundstage underneath a plethora of lights. To the left of the stage, a door opened and a rather large, almost menacing-looking man walked in. The Jet Propulsion Laboratory's chief executive, Roger Hand, was always ready to walk into the limelight and explain or sell JPL's project of the year, day, or month. On this particular evening, Dr. Hand was especially excited about his first global appearance on live TV. Yes, tonight was the night that the entire world would learn exactly what JPL, and a small handful of scientists from all over the planet, had been up to for the last eighteen months. Make no mistake about it; the whole world was watching, wanting to learn about this top-secret rocket propulsion system that was about to be tested for the very first time with the help of the spacecraft *Magellan* and her crew.

Behind the stage, suspended magically in mid-air, it seemed, was the largest *3D* LGD screen monitor that Hand had ever seen. At least forty feet in length and some twelve or fifteen feet tall, this modern monster of high-def would soon link up *Magellan's* now-completed complement of crew members with himself, an interviewer, and the world. All of this would be live in real time.

"Ladies and gentlemen, we are on in five minutes," came the announcement over the house PA system. Instantly, Dr. Hand was surrounded by technicians and network advisors drilling him, wiring him, patting him with make-up, and prepping him for what could be the biggest night of his career.

"Dr. Hand, it is an honor to meet you, sir," came the voice from behind him. It was a certain female's voice that he did not expect to hear. Turning to face the woman who was approaching, he spoke with his usual charm.

"Ah, good evening, Miss Vandale."

"Ms. Vandale, if you don't mind, sir," she said, with a smile that could cause fusionary dysfunction in the sun itself. "Is there anything I can get for you, Doctor?"

"No, thank you, I'm fine. I, uh, I thought Rob Robbins was doing this gig tonight, Ms. Vandale," he said as he looked deeply into her big, green eyes.

"Network execs thought Jessica be a whole lot prettier for a global audience to look at, Mister."

"Now there's a voice I haven't heard in years, least, not in person, face-to-face." Roger was speaking as he turned around and met the gaze of Ralph Marlowe, the science editor for World News One, which was the host channel for the evening's event.

"So, how's space flight, Ralph?" Roger chuckled as he warmly shook his old friend's hand.

"Right where I like it, buddy, in the hands of someone else—anybody else, in fact," came the laughing response of the healthy, trim man.

"Aw, c'mon Ralph, no one can land a shuttle like you!"

"Yeah, I know. Good thing those babies can float."

"One minute; places everybody," came the stage director's voice, and Dr. Roger Hand found himself perched atop a ridiculously high glorified bar stool.

Jessica Vandale leaned over to her guest and said, "Remember, Dr. Hand, always speak to me or to the camera that has the red light on."

"Jessica, please—Roger's been in front of more cameras than you have—even in your dreams!"

Thanks a lot, Ralph; I bet she really tears into me now, Roger thought to himself as he got all nice and comfy high atop Mt. Ridiculous.

"Ten seconds, people—five, four, three, two ..." Then a forefinger silently pointed to the anchor.

"Hello, planet Earth—"

Nice touch, Roger condescendingly thought.

"It is truly an honor to come into your towns, your homes, and your lives on this night, the eve of what could be one of mankind's greatest adventures." She continued on, "And with us here tonight in Studio Two is one of the people responsible for the *Magellan* project, Dr. Roger Hand." Then turning to Roger, she said, "Dr. Hand, welcome to World News One."

Roger smiled at Jessica and said, "Thank you, Ms. Vandale; it is a pleasure to be here."

"Along with Dr. Hand here in the studio, we will be joined in just a few moments with the crew of the spaceship *Magellan*.

With that, the large-screen monitor behind her came to life with a live shot of *Magellan* floating in space a safe distance from Earth.

"Dr. Hand, could you tell us just what is so special about *Magellan?*"

Looking straight into the eye of the camera, and by extension he hoped the world, he began, *"Magellan* is the most advanced piece of human engineering that has ever been developed. She is fully automated and yet fully responsive to the human element. A baby could fly her," Dr. Hand said with a smile and then continued on. "Built entirely with private funds from international sources and donors, *Magellan* has been developed to further the peaceful exploration of our nearest neighbors in the solar system." He paused, turned to Jessica Vandale, and then added, *"Magellan* will truly live up to her name. She will be an explorer in the truest sense of the word."

Listening intently and staring deeply into his eyes, Jessica asked, "Could you please elaborate 'peaceful exploration,' Dr. Hand? Many people on the planet are concerned," then she turned to face the camera, "to put it mildly," and then turned back to Roger, "with the fact that there is a nuclear reactor on board, along with the nuclear fuel needed to power that reactor."

Roger Hand leaned forward, much like a friend who is sharing in an intimate conversation with a friend, and said, "I would like to assure all the people and nations on this planet of ours that the nuclear material on board *Magellan* is completely safe. For one, it is a type of fuel system that was developed exclusively for use in space exploration vehicles. Second, just to help make the people on Earth feel safer, *Magellan's* orbit is twenty-five-thousand miles high, and she orbits in a pole to pole trajectory. Now if—and I do mean if—there would be any kind of accident, there would be a very slim chance of anything ever reaching our atmosphere, let alone land or sea."

"Dr. Hand, isn't it true that tomorrow *Magellan* will be passing over Canada, and then North and South America? And all this while you are 'powering up' the new IGS drive system—is that really safe, sir?"

Unruffled and unwavering, Roger Hand replied, "Yes, Miss—I'm sorry, Ms. Vandale; it will be totally safe. In fact, we planned that trajectory specifically so that we would have a better view of the test firing of IGS. In reality, *Magellan* is an experimental vehicle designed to test new theories and then use those tests to take us to our nearest planetary neighbors—for example, Venus and Mars. Tomorrow the onboard nuclear reactor will only be at about twenty-seven percent output. That's only enough to supply power to life support, logistics, and diagnostics for the test. The IGS system actually powers itself using the Earth's gravity as its power supply. But that is one area I would rather have its designer and creator explain."

"And explain he will, I hope," Jessica said with a smile, "right after this break."

The Twilight

As the tribal leader continued his discourse before his people, he could see movement toward the rear of the gathering. It seemed as if someone was trying to position himself above the countless thousands.

"It is this very underground river that I plan to travel upon and enter with it into the Great Darkness. I believe in my very being that this is the secret way, the only way, into the presence of the Great Spirit, the one who leads us all, the one who cares for us all, the one who made us all."

It was then that a voice was heard speaking from the crowd. "And who is the one that has shown you such secret wisdom and counsel, Kobi-nana? Did the Great Spirit himself speak to you of these wondrous things?"

Kobi-nana looked and now knew who it was that had positioned himself above the crowd on a large rock in the center of the gathering, with his old and worn body clothed in deerskins dyed blood red. Standing firm on the formation, he could clearly be seen by all. It was the old one of the tribe, the wise one who could read the stars—the one who could see into tomorrow and tell of things unknown.

"Sometimes we are expected to use our minds and understand mysteries on our own, old one," the chief fired back.

"It seems to me that maybe you have too little understanding and possibly a little too much time on your hands to dream of such adventure, my chief," the old man said with a smile. "Do you forget the stories that our ancestors told

of the day that the Great Darkness came to our world?" The old one jumped down and now began to slowly make his way through the crowd that parted before him like the bow of a canoe parts the water upon which it glides and continued his history lesson. "Remember being told of the destruction, the death, the heavy darkness that threatened to swallow the very land itself? It was only by the mighty hand of Kayo-Kee-ya that our people found safety. **He** *placed the darkness in the ground;* **he** *showed us how to bury the darkness with copper and earth.* **He** *did this, Kobi-nana—not our fathers, not myself, and certainly not you. Only a god can wrestle with the great and terrible power of the Great Darkness, not a man and his warriors. What you desire to do is foolishness. It will undo your very being."*

Although he had great respect for the old one and his wisdom, Kobi-nana was quickly running out of patience.

"Every soul in this vast sea of people knows of your great wisdom, old one. However," he continued as his eyes, which now reflected the morning sun giving the appearance of glowing like two hot embers of fire, locked onto the eyes of the old one, "there comes the time when bravery must stand and wisdom must be seated and silent!"

The old one knew that this young, arrogant chief had overruled him. Bowing low to the ground and then stepping back gracefully, he disappeared once again into the massive throng of people. He could only hope and pray that no one else would follow this fool of a chief into the underground lair of the Great Darkness.

CHAPTER 4

SPACE CHATTER

The Dawn

On the other side of the world, in a dimly lit office room, ten men sat silently watching the televised interview with one man sitting apart from the others at the end of a long conference table.

"There is more here at stake than you may realize." He spoke softly as he flicked the ash from a rather large cigar and looked into the eyes of every man present.

"Do not listen to this broadcast with your ears alone, my brothers. Listen with your soul, with all that you are. There is much to be learned from these people, and there is much to be taken from them."

—

Walking up onto the stage with a glass of water in his hand, Ralph Marlowe looked at JPL's chief executive and complimented him on the opening segment.

"Nice touch, leaning into the view field like that," he said as he offered his friend the glass.

"Yeah, maybe," Roger replied as he looked around to see if anyone was around to listen in, "but I gotta admit, I just about slid out of that blasted barstool chair of yours." He took the glass and relished a long drink.

"Well, we could put some Velcro strips on them to hold you in place if you like."

"I'll pass on that one, buddy," Roger said as he started to shake the ice around in the now-empty glass. "So, tell me, Ralph," he said, stealing a glance over at the lady interviewer, who was busy primping and prettying herself in her handheld mirror, "is she really as tough as her demeanor would suggest?"

Eyeing his friend with one eyebrow raised in suspicion, he answered, "Jessica's a pro, and she's a tough kid. She definitely knows her stuff." He reached out and took the glass from Roger, who was finishing up chomping on the ice as Ralph continued.

"She's just not what I would call, um, outgoing.

"Fact is, she pretty much keeps to herself. She does have an attitude, but hey, you have to in this business."

"One minute," came the obnoxious loudspeaker's roar.

"Just play nice and don't take anything too personal that she throws your way. Oh, and by the way," Ralph leaned a little closer and lowered his voice, "if I were you, I'd be ready for anything."

"Oh great, don't tell me she found out about the squirrel and the swimming pool thing."

"I warned you; she's a pro," Ralph said with a playful glimmer in his eye as he turned to walk off stage.

"Ten seconds. Places, everybody, and three, two, go!"

"We are back, we are live, and we are not alone. Now joining Dr. Roger Hand and myself, ladies and gentlemen," she paused slightly for effect, "I give you the crew of the spaceship *Magellan.*"

Instantly the monitor above the stage changed from the shot of *Magellan*, with the beautiful blue orb of Earth in the background, to what seemed like any business executive's private office located anywhere here on Earth.

"Hello, *Magellan,*" offered the host pleasantly enough.

"Good evening to you, planet Earth," came the beefy response from *Magellan's* commander. "Please allow me to introduce *Magellan's* crew to you." *He has obviously been briefed on the show's protocol,* Roger thought. "First up is the co-designer of the IGS system and everyone's adopted dad or uncle on board, Dr. Jon Armone."

"Hello, Earth!" he said with a smile and a wave.

"Next to him," continued Commander Moore, "is one of the most well-known people in both the scientific and geo-political realms, Miss Simone Sytte."

"Good evening, my earthbound friends," Simone replied in her heavily accented voice.

Roger Hand (along with countless other human males) was always mesmerized by the very sensuous and deep, throaty voice of the "Princess of Uganda," as she had come to be known.

"Next, allow me to introduce our very capable pilot and favorite Texan, Captain Tom Williamson."

"Howdy, y'all!"

"Next in line is our mission specialist slash walking encyclopedia, Mike Beck."

"Hello," Mike said with a smile.

The commander did a double take on that one, obviously expecting more from the man and playfully not getting it.

"OK, folks, we continue on with our beautiful navigation systems engineer, Miss Deborah Dean."

"Hi, Earth!" Another big smile emanating from space.

"And this is our communications officer, Mr. Carl Lewis."

"Howdy!"

"Over hiding in the corner we have two very special members of *Magellan's* team. First is Kathy Parker, and then there is Charlie 'I can fix anything' Hodson."

"Hello," came the response from the two in perfect stereo.

"These two are up here to make sure that if we break anything, we can still get back home." Moore was making that last statement with a smile when a crashing metallic sound came from just out of camera view causing the entire crew (as well as a few earthbound folks) to jump.

"Oh, sorry y'all, I dropped my good luck charm," the Texan said as he bent down and retrieved an old horseshoe.

Then he looked back up at the camera and added, "Don't leave home without it," and promptly dropped the relic again.

"I'm just glad you didn't bring the whole horse," Dr. Armone said with a chuckle.

"I wanted to, but I couldn't get it past customs. No passport."

"OK, last and hopefully not least, I am Commander Matt Moore, and it is my job to keep all these folks," he took a quick look at the Texan, "and their horseshoes in line and out of trouble."

There was a short pause in action as the camera zoomed out of close-up mode and captured the whole group on screen.

"Thank you, Commander Moore." Then smiling at (or for) the camera, Jessica Vandale added, "You just might have a budding career ahead of you in television." Then, turning serious, she focused on Jon Armone.

"Dr. Armone, welcome to World News One, sir."

"Thank you, Jessica."

"We are all excited about the impending test of the IGS system, but I have to admit, we are all pretty much at a loss when it comes to knowing what it is. Could you tell us what it is? We have heard for weeks now about this new propulsion technology, and no one seems to have the slightest idea of what it is. Can you enlighten us, or is that part of *Magellan* still 'top secret'?"

Dr. Armone seemed to light up like a Christmas tree at the opportunity to share his newest toy with the world.

"I would love to tell you about the IGS system, Jessica." As he was talking, he walked over to a control console and leaning upon it, began to explain the propulsion device. "IGS stands for Inverted Gravitational Sequencing. It is a computer-initiated drive system that uses fields of gravity as its power, or more accurately, its fuel." He continued, "Using specially sequenced computer programs directing a nano-field plasma beam to tap into a gravity 'wave,' if you will, the spacecraft would then be propelled away from the source of gravity exponentially according to the power of the gravity wave."

Now that's a good way to mess up a person's mind, Hand was thinking to himself, and he evidently wasn't the only one thinking that way, because he heard little Ms. Vandale ask, "Can you tell us in common, everyday language what you just said, Dr. Armone?" Apologetically, she added, "So that even I can understand," with a chuckle and both hands raised in mock surrender.

"I am so sorry, Miss Vandale; I do tend to get carried away somewhat." The doctor was reforming his explanation. While he ran his hand through his pure white hair, one lock of hair kept falling down into his eyes. "Let's say that there is a transformer outside of your house, ah, you know, like the ones up on the poles where your electricity comes from—"

Not too childish, Jon, Roger silently pleaded with his top scientist.

"Now, take off all of the protective covering and expose the inner parts." The scientist was using his hands as if he was doing the actual work. "Now, walk over to your garden hose, select the high-pressure nozzle, turn on the water, and take aim at the transformer. Pull the trigger and *boom!* You're in the next county!"

For some reason, Jessica seemed thoroughly pleased with the explanation but less than enthusiastic about the outcome.

"My goodness, that doesn't seem like much of a smooth ride, Dr. Armone."

Jon Armone was grinning like a schoolboy when he admitted, "We're all hoping that it will be."

"So, let me get this right. You plan to point this laser at Earth and shoot. Is—I'm sorry for asking this—is this laser of yours nuclear?"

She really does have a thing about nukes, doesn't she? I wonder what's up with that ... Roger thought to himself, and somewhere back in his mind, a very small, imperceptible red flag began to wave. The sound of Jon Armone's laughter brought him back to the moment.

"Let me assure you, Ms. Vandale, as well as all of planet Earth, that what we will be aiming at the Earth is not radioactive, nor is it explosive in any way. It's more like two magnets repelling each other. IGS is very safe, very safe indeed. In the same way that a laser is simply amplified light, IGS is simply amplified gravity."

Roger Hand saw a small flashing blue light off stage, just out of the camera's field of view. Just as he noticed it, his hostess spoke up.

"Well, thank you, Dr. Armone," Jessica said convincingly enough and then turned to the camera. "I think you have answered one of the questions that the world wants to know on this night, the eve of what possibly could be mankind's next 'giant leap.'" She paused for effect and then smiled that incredible smile of hers and said, "We have to take a break; when we come back, we will turn our attention toward the power plant of *Magellan* and its designer, Miss Simone Sytte. Don't go away; World News One will be right back."

With that, all the cameras went into stand-by mode. Behind him, on screen-zilla, the shot of *Magellan* once again appeared.

"Hey, Ralph," Roger half-shouted to his friend as he was approaching the stage, "how are you getting that shot of *Magellan* anyway?" pointing back to it with his hand over his head.

"One of China's little secrets, buddy; *Yangtze* has a whole complement of over a hundred of the teeniest, tiniest space satellites in her hold at any given time." Then, prodding his friend, "You've got clearance; guess you missed that one, huh?"

"Must have"

"Anyhow, they popped one out last week when they dropped off Jon and Simone. Pretty cool stuff huh?"

"Pretty disturbing stuff, if you ask me. Never did trust certain elements of that regime."

"How 'bout every element of that regime?" Ralph said as he walked toward the edge of the stage. "Call me next week and I'll share some not-so-secret secrets with you."

"Deal," he said as he hopped down off of the four-story bar stool and simply took in the business around him. Roger loved to watch live television in progress. It was a living animal in its own domain rarely seen by outside folks.

"Thirty seconds, people." The announcement rudely interrupted his observations.

Mentally counting down, then focusing his attention on the stage director, he was only off by about a half second when he heard, "On in five, four, three," then only the silent hand count for two, one. Jessica Vandale had stealthily slipped up onto her chair (*Or was it her throne?* Roger thought) and was smiling as the cameras came to life.

That smile could stop a comet dead in its path, Roger was musing to himself when he realized that Jessica had already begun to speak to him.

"—know this genius of the twenty-first century, what can you tell us about Dr. Simone Sytte?"

Genius is the understatement of the day was what Roger Hand would have liked to say, but knowing his dear young friend was very modest, he began simply by saying, "Actually, Jessica," Roger was feeling much more at ease now—or as one from NASA or the Department of Defense would say, acclimatizing to the situation at hand—"Simone would probably prefer to be called Miss instead of Doctor." Thinking on the fly, he added, "In fact, just plain Simone would suit her just fine. She is a very special lady, bright and inquisitive."

As he spoke, the screen behind him began to morph from the now all-too-familiar shot of *Magellan* to the face of a lovely young woman—a lady in her early to mid-thirties or so, who obviously was not used to all the attention and accolades she was receiving from her friend and colleague.

Hand was now once again leaning into the near field reception of the camera as he spoke. He knew he had to soften the world's attitude toward nuclear power in space.

"This is going to be an important night—don't blow it for everybody," he remembered Dr. Armone warning him just over a week ago as they were meandering around Johnson Space Center checking up on all the last-minute details of the IGS test, as well as preparing for the live broadcast the night before the flight.

"No one has been as dedicated to making *Magellan* a safe and—how shall I say this—radically different type of space vehicle." He continued, now on a roll, "It was this ingenuous young scientist who first implemented the nano as well as the micro-molecular technology in the nuclear realm. It is this wonderful," *Not too campy, Roger,* he was warning himself, "young lady that has not just one or two, but sixteen patents on seven different nuclear field levels."

He continued with a slight chuckle, "I've got to admit to you, Jessica, and to our audience, that I am truly honored to know her as a fellow scientist and a very close personal friend as well." Having said all that, Roger leaned back to his formal position, then smiled as he looked over to Jessica Vandale.

Without skipping a beat, Jessica gave the introduction.

"Ladies and gentlemen I would like to introduce to you the nuclear specialist on board *Magellan*, as well as the co-designer of the IGS system, Miss Simone Sytte. Good evening, Miss Sytte."

"Good evening, Ms. Vandale," came the highly polished, even regal, Ugandan accent of the young scientist. "And how is planet Earth tonight?"

Nice touch, girl, Hand thought as he remembered just how talented this young lady was. She truly had earned the title of the "Princess of Uganda," and at six feet eight inches tall, Simone towered over the entire crew much like an oak tree in the middle of a field of prairie grass as they now sat semi-circle around a mini cam.

"Miss Sytte."

"Just Simone, please; that will do nicely."

"Very good then, Simone," Jessica cautiously and gently continued, "is *Magellan* really a safe, secure ship, or is that just what you astronauts are indoctrinated to say? I mean no disrespect, Dr. Sytte, but there is enough nuclear material on board to produce a number of weapons, should it fall into the wrong hands. Not to mention, heaven forbid, an accident on *Magellan* that could conceivably rain down nuclear terror on the Earth."

Rain down nuclear terror? I wonder if she actually writes her own lines. Roger's eyes were scanning beyond the stage lights to find Ralph.

"I speak for all of humanity when I say that we here on Earth are more than just a little bit nervous about a group of independent US citizens in charge of a flying nuclear laboratory. Could you help settle our nerves, Dr. Sytte?"

With a smile, Simone retaliated, "I am honored to be on your program, Ms. Vandale, but I truly doubt that you speak for all of humanity, for if that were the case, we probably would not even be having this discussion from on board this magnificent vessel. Let me assure you that the nuclear material on board is not even capable of being used in the manufacture of any weapons systems. It has been designed down to the molecular level to be completely un-excitable. That means that it cannot, by design," *Yeah, her design,* Hand thought to himself as he sat smiling ear-to-ear, "be manipulated into a volatile chain reaction level. On their own, these atoms are too slow to be used."

Careful how you say that, girl. Roger was getting nervous

"Too slow?"

She missed it, good. He relaxed.

"Yes, ma'am, too slow. For a chain reaction to occur, the atoms must be able to do what we now call 'swarming.'"

"Swarming?"

"Yes, swarming. You see, we have learned that when fissionable material reaches a critical stage, the uranium or plutonium atoms act much like an excited swarm of bees. These atoms have been re-arranged so that they cannot move fast enough to 'swarm.' By slowing their molecular structure down, they are safer to use in a peaceful way."

"Tell us, Dr. Sytte, how does one slow down an atom?"

"It sounds much easier than it actually is, but ..."

Simone reached over to a console and tapped a key, and instantly a floating hologram of a uranium atom appeared next to her.

School's in session. Roger was smiling again.

Simone continued, "The atom is basically three parts: The nucleus, which is made up of protons, with a positive charge, and neutrons, with no charge. Orbiting the nucleus like tiny little moons are electrons, which are negatively charged. On their own, these atoms can be deadly, but what we have done is to slightly alter the electrons by fusing multiple electrons together. They are still negatively charged but now what we call 'heavy'—thus slowing them down and—"

"Easier to control," Jessica finished the sentence, nodding in comprehension.

"Precisely, Ms. Vandale, and let me add this, with a heavier element, weaponizing is pretty much impossible."

Leave it at that, Simone, someone may be taking notes ... Roger was silently pleading. He also found himself smiling once again. He loved to listen to his scientists explain something so complicated and make it sound like child's play. They were always the best salesmen, and the best salesmen always make the best sales.

Simone continued, "By design, these slower, heavier uranium fuel rods can not only be completely depleted of their energy level fairly quickly, but they can also be recharged on board *Magellan*."

"Recharged?" Vandale responded incredulously.

"That's right, recharged. This makes it possible to power a vehicle the size of *Magellan* with only five fuel rods."

It was obvious to Roger that little Ms. V did not have the slightest idea of the implication of that last statement, and it must have been evident to Simone as well, because she added an explanation to her last statement without any prompting from the host;

"It would be like powering a small city of, oh say, ten thousand people with five double A batteries."

"Wow, that is impressive! So let me ask this; what about the danger of any kind of radiation leakage?"

"Again, by design, Miss, um, I mean Ms. Vandale—I truly am sorry, ma'am—"

"No, no, that's quite all right, Simone, please continue."

The hostess was absolutely mesmerized by this point.

I hope the world is listening as closely to this as she is, Roger thought.

"The only way these rods can be used and lose radiation is in what we call a 'containment field.'" Simone continued in her usual charming intellectual way, "A hyper-electro-magnetic field set up at a specific frequency that actually induces a nuclear power feed. This frequency is purposely mismatched to any known field on, or in, Earth. Actually a brilliant setup, if I do say so myself!" The young scientist was absolutely beaming now.

"And one last thing, Ms. Vandale. We are not a group of independent American civilians. We are explorers." Simone was looking around at her comrades as she spoke, her hands sweeping out to encompass them all in her statement. "We are scientists, humanitarians in the truest sense of the word, who seek a better tomorrow for all mankind. And besides that," with the coming statement Simone sat tall, erect, and proud, "I'm Ugandan."

I'm so glad she was smiling when she said that, Jon Armone thought as he sat in awe and watched this woman stand her ground better than any man could possibly hope to against a person like Jessica Vandale.

"Thank you, Dr. Sytte." Then turning to the camera, Ms. Vandale continued, "We are almost out of time, but when we come back, we'll take a short tour of the spaceship *Magellan*." She turned her head to look back at the monitor behind her and said, "Commander Moore, you up to it?"

"Yes ma'am, I sure am!"

"All right then, ladies and gentlemen, we'll be back right after this."

Pause mode in the studio, on *Magellan*, but certainly not in Roger Hand's mind. Something was bothering him, but he just couldn't put his finger on it. Yet.

The Twilight

Satisfied with the fact that the old one had said his piece and departed, Kobi-nana once again turned his full attention to the tribe. "When the sun is at high point in the sky today, I will enter the cave of running water in my canoe. Where it takes me once I get to the dark place I do not know for sure, but this I do know—if I do not go, I will never know the reason for the dark place." The chief paused for a moment, allowing the logic of his statement to sink in, his eyes scanning the tribe, looking for any type of response.

"My question to you, my tribe, the people of the great Kayo-Kee-ya, is there anyone who will come with me? I am fully prepared to go on my own with my family into the mighty place of darkness, but," he once again raised the tribal spear high above his head for all to see, "are there any of my great warriors who would like to be standing before the Great Spirit when the moon rises late tonight?"

A deafening roar now erupted from the mass of humanity before him, and he knew that he and his family would not go alone into the darkness. For a moment, Kobi-nana felt as if he were the ruler of the whole Earth. It seemed as if it were all his and his alone; all he had to do was to go and take it.

CHAPTER 5

INNER SANCTUM

The Dawn

It was at this very moment, as the cameras went momentarily dormant and one of the stage hands tossed him a hand towel, that Roger Hand realized two things. One was that he was sweating profusely, and the other, was that he was holding his breath.

Breathe Roger, breathe—suck in—blow out—'atta boy. Humans need air to live. I'm gonna kill Simone for that one.

He was feeling much better now. Oxygen in one's lungs tends to do that for a person. And so does water. Hopping down once again from his pylon *(Shouldn't I be wearing a parachute at this height?)* Roger made his way off of the stage and over to the water cooler. Grabbing one of the large paper cups, he filled it about halfway and began to slowly drink the invigoratingly cold water.

"Dr. Hand, is there anything you would like to say before we do the wrap-up?" a familiar female voice asked as she strode up alongside him at the cooler, one hand holding her own personal cup full of water while she delicately ran the ring finger of her other hand around the rim of the cup.

"No, not really. I think that everything's being handled quite nicely by the crew." *I'm still going to kill Simone, even though I love how she handled you, lady.* Then he added, "Don't you think so, Ms. Vandale?"

With a distant look in her eyes, she absently retorted, practically under her breath, "Almost too nicely, Dr. Hand."

25

Roger completely ignored her answer and said, "Oh, by the way, Ms. Vandale ..."

"Yes, Doctor?"

"Do you live here on the set, or do you ever go out into the real world and do things real people do, like oh, eat?" *I can't believe you said that, Roger!*

"Why, Dr. Roger Hand, are you asking me out on a dinner date?"

"In three thousand six hundred fifty two words or less; Yes, I guess I am."

"Well then, in a hundred words or less, I'd love to. And by the way, my name is Jessica."

"One minute, everyone, let's do it!"

Once again, the set was a flurry of activity. But somehow, it didn't seem so hostile to Roger anymore; even the stupid chair was no longer any match for him.

"On in ten." There was a brief silence, and then, "Five, four, three—"

I always did wonder why they don't count down all the way; that would drive an astronaut batty. He smiled to himself as he looked over at Ralph Marlowe, who was over behind one of the video control consoles.

Someday he has got to tell me how he managed to land a shuttle in the ocean. And with that last thought, he turned his attention to Jessica Vandale, who was about to speak and looked somehow somewhat friendlier.

"We are back and we have a real treat for our audience. Commander Moore is about to take us on a short tour of spaceship *Magellan*." Smiling once again for the camera, she continued, "So, all you space cadets, it's time to look into the future of space travel." She dramatically spun herself around in her chair so she could face the monitor behind her and said, "Commander Moore, are you ready?"

"Yes, ma'am, *Magellan* is at your disposal."

"Well then, Commander Matt Moore, for the next five minutes, you have full control of World News One and the undivided attention of planet Earth."

"Thank you, Jessica, and once again hello to all you good people back on planet Earth." The commander was on the move, walking past a few of the crew members toward a door. "So far, the interior shots you have seen have been here, in what we call the 'situation room.' It's kind of a control center for *Magellan*. From this room, every system, every person, every movement—inside or outside—of this spacecraft can be monitored.

However," Moore continued, speaking as he made his way out the room's door and into a corridor, "what I would like to show you now is the real control room of the ship."

It was as if on cue the doors immediately ahead of him silently slid open to reveal the command bridge of *Magellan*. Moore turned to face the camera that was following him and made a sweeping gesture with his hand as he once again continued his monologue. "This is where we plan on spending much of our time for the next week or so. As you can see," the commander walked over to the nearest hull section then continued, "there are no windows." He paused just long enough for the camera operator to quickly pan the room then added, "Or are there?"

Without hesitating, Moore tapped a control button on a console next to him and the entire hull of the bridge seemed to melt away, revealing a spectacular 180-degree view of space that was breathtaking even on the monitors on Earth. He continued, "Throughout *Magellan* are entire outer hull plating sections, designed by the Crysteel Corporation, which can instantly be altered from the typical space ship steel interior wall into breathtaking views of space." He continued speaking as a command officer, but his face was gleaming like a child on Christmas morn. "This ship has all the latest technological wizardry mankind has to offer."

Back on Earth, Roger Hand was beginning to sense a spirit of pride in his top commander, and a sense of showmanship.

"You may notice" the commander continued, "very few readouts or computer screens on the bridge. That is because," once again a quick, almost imperceptible movement of his hand upon a control panel and the entire hull changed from its pictorial view of space into one of the largest sets of computer readout screens, "all of our ship's information goes up on LGDs. Most of you know that stands for 'Laser Generated Displays' so we see it in a three-dimensional laser-generated view. Not altogether a new technology but it's never been done on such an enormously comprehensive scale before." Once more he tapped a control, and the array disappeared and the dull blue hull reappeared. Commander Moore looked at the camera and said, "So you see, *Magellan* is ready to go."

"Commander Moore, may I ask a peculiar question?" came the voice of Jessica Vandale.

"Of course you can, Ms. Vandale."

"As we look at the exterior shot of *Magellan* we see no windows or light shining out from any sections of the space craft—how is that done?"

"Ah, that is the glory and wonder of technology, ma'am! One of the design parameters of the Crysteel hull is that we can see out but, none of the space invaders can see in!"

Roger Hand was wondering how much they should charge Crysteel, Inc., for all the wonderful publicity they were getting. There's nothing like getting free airtime and covering the entire world with a plug for your latest product.

"Very good, Commander Moore, thank you." Jessica said, and then with that incredible smile of hers she added, "We'll be right back."

—

In the darkened room, the wall monitor went black then turned to bluescreen just before a still picture of Roger Hand appeared.

"I want to know everything you can find out on the American Roger Hand. There seems to be a veil around him. He appears to me to be more than what the media, or public, sees." The man at the end of the table was speaking to one man sitting to his right. "Use whatever approach you need to use."

"It is as good as done, my old friend," an older man in his sixties said as he arose from the table. Immediately, a younger man bolted to his feet to follow the older one out the door.

—

"Twenty seconds, people. Looking good so far, let's keep it up."

Jessica now turned to her left as another camera silently came in closer on stage. "Our coverage of the *Magellan* test flight using the IGS system will continue tomorrow on World News One. I'm Jessica Vandale, and I would like to thank everyone for joining us tonight for this very special show. Goodnight, *Magellan,* and goodnight planet Earth."

All the lights on the cameras went out at once, and Roger Hand felt an incredible sense of relief—relief and hunger.

Jessica was already twenty feet away, heading toward a hallway exit marked "Dressing Rooms" when she yelled, "You still buying this girl dinner?"

Same voice, different attitude. *Hey, this might work!* Roger thought as he answered the question.

"Of course. I'm ready when you are."

"Good! Be right back," she said as she trotted off to the dressing rooms.

"Hey, buddy," Ralph said as he eyed the newscaster leaving the set. "You be careful with that one. She's really good at getting what she wants."

"I'm a big boy, Ralph." Roger was smiling at his old friend.

"Yeah, I know. Just be careful what you start talking about. She's a pro at getting information." Ralph saw her coming and made his way over to the other side of the stage.

"Are you ready, Doctor?" she said.

"Let's go," he answered her as he offered her his arm the way any gentleman suitor would do.

CHAPTER 6

PREPARATIONS

Although Martin Sherfy had set his alarm for four a.m., he was awake long before the annoying buzzer came to life, shattering the peaceful solitude of the pre-dawn hours. Jumping up from the overly large and painfully empty king-size bed, the professor slowly made his way to the kitchen and began his usual regimen of coffee making and mind waking.

"Thank You, God, for caffeine," Martin chuckled as he lifted his coffee mug up in a toast of sorts to his Savior.

He started to reminisce of days gone by when his lovely wife, Sharon, would be making the coffee while he dressed, but he made the choice to put those thoughts aside. Instead, he reached out to grab his Bible and opened it up to the book of Psalms. Martin had made it a habit to start his day in the hymnbook of the Bible and today he opened it to Psalm 139 and read aloud as if to all of creation itself, "Search me, O God, and know my heart—"

—

Roger Hand loved to awaken early in the morning and get out of the house as quickly as possible, jump in his old Jeep, and drive. It never mattered where, just "man and machine." *Me and Houston, no traffic, no hassles,* Roger thought as he got on the interstate. It was during these early-morning drive times that he would often imagine himself being the sole survivor of some terrible holocaust and the whole planet belonged to him. He laughed out loud as he realized he was a little old for those kinds of thoughts. Nevertheless, Roger Hand loved to drive. He made enough money to have literally any car in the world, but he was quite content with his "Sadie," an old eighties-style four-wheel drive Jeep. Even had her painted army tank green.

This morning's drive was not an aimless one, however. He wasn't speeding out of downtown Houston so that he could watch the sunrise over the plains of Texas; no, this morning's drive was quite different. This morning Dr. Roger Hand was speeding along I-45 south toward Johnson Space Center listening to an old song he had dug up on the Internet. The excitement of the day was beginning to mount as he sang along, "Ground control to Major Tom ..."

—

Martin Sherfy would usually spend some quiet time in prayer with his Savior every morning. This morning was a little different as he quickly read the Psalms and headed out the door. In an instant, he was out the door and in his pickup heading down old US 40 toward the Cahokia Mounds Historic Site. Reaching the site area and then passing the big mound on his right, Martin continued heading west another quarter mile or so till he reached his destination; Woodhenge.

"Five-thirty, and all is well with the world," Martin said aloud as he parked in the gravel parking lot and stepped out of his truck. The air was unusually warm and humid for this time of year, and he even saw a low-clinging shroud of fog across the highway on the south side in one of the many prairie restoration areas of the site. It was still quite dark, with plenty of stars visible in the early morning sky. The dimly faint aura of St. Louis to the west and the lights of nearby Collinsville to the east added an ethereal flair to the entire scene. Looking at his watch, then looking heavenward, Martin said aloud, "Good morning, my Lord, and what a beautiful morning You have given me ..."

—

On *Magellan*, Simone Sytte had tossed and turned all night. The previous evening's interview seemed to go well enough, but yet, there was something gnawing at her from deep inside her spirit. Surely the entire planet wasn't as absurdly paranoid with nuclear-powered spacecraft as Jessica Vandale seemed to be. Yet, there felt like there was something more, something much more, and she couldn't put her finger on it. With still a full hour to go before her alarm would sound, Simone decided to get up and get a head start on the day. She wisely abandoned the idea of jumping from her bed onto the floor as she remembered the rather awkward experience she had had just a couple weeks ago during *Magellan's* first trial run to the moon.

Artificial gravity onboard *Magellan* was limited to a light negative magnetic charge embedded in the crew's clothing material, while the whole interior flooring of the ship had an equally miniscule positive magnetic charge (*A rather ingenious use of a magnetic field,* Simone mused). However, one could easily enough "break orbit" by, oh let's say, jumping out of one's bed with a little too much zeal. It is so embarrassing to spend twenty minutes hovering near the ceiling trying to "swim" to the nearest wall so you can walk your way down to the floor. But alas, that is exactly what had happened to Simone. *At least,* she thought to herself, *I didn't have to call for help.*

Nevertheless, Simone was acclimatizing well enough to space travel. She had loved the trip up on the *Yangtze,* especially the "fancy maneuvers," as Dr. Armone called them, en route to *Magellan.* Truth is, Simone simply loved to fly, and she loved flights that were especially turbulent, much to the chagrin of fellow passengers, who would be holding on to anything for dear life while Simone would sit and smile and let out the occasional, "Whee!" when the airliner would suddenly lose altitude. Yes indeed, Uganda's unofficial princess was a tough girl, fearless and bright. However, this morning she cautiously, gingerly slipped out of her bunk and said quietly to her Hummingbyrd computer, "Little Shepherd."

"Chirp."

"Run worship scenario P-Twenty Three on LGD, full exterior view please."

"Chirp."

Even as she spoke, all of her exterior walls, ceiling, and even a small section of flooring changed from the light metallic blue to transparent, revealing a breathtaking view not only of Earth, but also, to her leftmost view, she could see the moon in a crescent phase and in the distance Mars was shining, almost beckoning to whomever would come. *Magellan* was cruising up from Antarctica and would soon pass over the equator in the Indian Ocean. In just over three hours, they would be on the other side of the planet. *Magellan* would be cruising silently over North America, preparing to embark on mankind's newest space adventure.

The IGS system, Simone thought (and hoped), would do for space travel what jet (and now hyper-jet) engines did for earthbound aircraft. Realizing the importance of the day before her, as well as the busyness that would soon envelop her and the other crewmembers, Simone began to read the words aloud that were emblazoned in the very air before her in eight inch white letters: "The LORD is my Shepherd; I shall not be in want—"

—

As Roger Hand pulled up to the main gates at the parking lot entrance to Johnson Space Center, someone was running over to his Jeep, obviously attempting to gain his attention.

"You NASA boys really do start early, don't you?"

The voice, the hair, the smile, the persona: Jessica Vandale.

"And good morning to you, Jess." Roger was quite surprised to see his newfound friend here at the Center.

"You look wide-eyed and bushy-tailed, rarin' to go, Mister."

"I didn't know you had this assignment today. You, ah, didn't mention anything about it last night," he said.

"That's because I didn't come here as a reporter." She brushed the hair away from her face and then continued, "I was kind of hoping to be able to hang out with you. You know—see the real stuff that goes on behind the scenes."

"Not here for a story, huh?" He was eyeing her closely.

"Nope, not at all."

Even though these two lonely people did seem to have a nice dinner together the night before, Roger still had his doubts about the motives involved in this particular conversation, it all seemed a little too planned.

"Well—" he said, fumbling with the stick-shift with one hand and grabbing the steering wheel with the other. "Protocol dictates that since I didn't clear you beforehand, you will have to either go in the public entrance or I could ..." his voice trailed off as he weighed the pros and cons of bringing in a potential liability, "pull some strings and get you in the hot seats."

Jessica didn't even ask what the hot seats were. She knew they were a small group of seats that were situated above and behind the newly designed command center floor, aka mission control. They were enclosed in glass and somewhat secluded, but still very close to the action.

"Oh, could you, Roger? That would be great! I would really love that!"

She almost seemed like a schoolgirl all excited to see her favorite rock star up close and personal. In fact, she seemed a little too excited.

"You sure you're not on assignment, lady?"

Holding her hand up as if in a solemn pledge, she said, "Honest Injun." She smiled that smile of hers. It could probably gain her entrance into Ft. Knox.

"All right, wait here. After I get in, I'll send for you."

Pulling away and up to the gate's security terminal, Dr. Hand took his security ID and slid it through the scanner. The gates came to life with a jolt and rolled away to the side. Driving into the complex, Roger felt like a high school kid himself, grinning ear to ear.

—

Onboard *Magellan,* a voice began to speak: "OK, everyone knows their jobs today. The world is watching, all our investors are nervous, and several dozen high-tech companies are ready to make a killing on the sale of new stock. Let's see, did I forget anything?" Dr. Jon Armone was speaking like a true motivational speaker on the bridge of *Magellan,* standing before the crew.

"Yeah, we could all die today," the com officer said with a snort.

"Or become quite famous," Mike Beck retorted.

"Or both. Wouldn't that would put a damper on any book deals we might have?" Dr. Armone replied to both remarks with a touch of mock cynicism. Slapping his hands then rubbing them together in a "let's get going" action, Armone added, "Time to get some breakfast and then get this show on the road."

CHAPTER 7

INTO THE NIGHT

Soon everyone was gathered in the ship's galley. Everyone had their mouths full, and everyone somehow had a horseshoe of some kind.

"All right, people," Commander Moore began, "one hour till we do the IGS burn. Any questions?"

"Nope."

"Nuh-uh."

"No sir," was the reply from Simone and Dr. Armone practically in stereo.

Looking at his crew, standing with both hands behind him, a perfect picture of iconic leadership, Commander Matt Moore continued, "As you all are quite aware, we really don't know what is going to happen when we engage IGS. We don't know if it will work or how far it will propel us." He stole a glance over to the two designers of the system in an almost-apologetic gesture. "Dr. Armone, would you like to add anything?"

"Yes I would, thanks, Matt," he said as he slapped the commander on the shoulder and positioned himself in front of the crew. Smiling, he again rubbed his hands together as he said, "Today is a big day. For the most part, the test will all be automated. When we engage the system, IGS will engage and burn for five seconds, and then braking jets will fire till we stop. Then we simply look around to see where we are. It will be up to you people to record data, and hopefully, enjoy the ride. Sounds simple enough. Let's just hope and pray it stays that way." The doctor gave a command to the computer, and a map of near space appeared floating before them. "As you know, NASA has been sending up provisional platforms for the last eighteen months to be at various distances from Earth in our projected trajectory, uh, just in case." He was pointing to three different points on the 3D map in front of him and then pointed to an area just past the last platform position. "I personally hope to be at least halfway to Mars by the time we stop." He paused, looked around, and shrugging his shoulders, added "It never hurts to be a little overly optimistic. IGS works: in theory. Truth is, we just don't know how well it will work in real life."

"It sounds a little too much like Los Alamos and the Manhattan Project to me, Doc," Captain Williamson said with a laugh.

"Oh, great, there you go talking nuclear." Armone was having his own bit of fun now. "You're starting to sound like the blasted media, Tom."

Everyone seemed to get a chuckle out of that one—everyone, that is, but Simone.

"Perhaps it would be well for us to realize the importance of today," she responded in all seriousness.

Jon Armone went over to her and took her hand in his as he looked deeply into the eyes of the young Ugandan. After a slight pause, he smiled and spoke.

"We do realize the importance of this day, my friend, but," he said with a quiet, commanding sense of wisdom, "we cannot afford to let the weight of the hour become a burden."

Then a familiar twinkle sparkled in his eye as he added, "I think, when we are once again earthbound, I need to spend some more time with you explaining the intricacies of American humor." Simone smiled knowingly at her friend as he turned and asked, "So, any more questions?"

Not getting any further response, he excitedly proclaimed, "So, let's rock and roll!"

"All right, let's get to our stations on the bridge everyone," the commander announced. Then, looking over at the beautiful Ugandan, he added, "Let's take that next giant leap for mankind."

The Twilight

The sun was at high point, and several dozen canoes filled with warriors were lined up on the banks of the great river ready to embark on the adventure of a lifetime, while the remainder of the tribe stood silently along the edge of the cliffs high above the river. A few of the women let out small whimpers of disconsolation when Kobi-nana took his wife and son to his canoe and placed them in it.

"It is time to go, my brave ones," his voice roared. As the chain of canoes began their trek, Kobi-nana thought of the ones left behind. He looked up to those on the bluffs high above and spoke softly as if to himself, "I find no fault in you, my brothers, for not coming along—after all, someone must protect our homes and women. Someone must plant this year's crop and tend to our mighty temple while I am gone." He then saw his young brother standing on the river's edge, the water splashing playfully at his knees as he stood there silently watching the procession pass on by.

"Be strong, my brother, and lead our people till I return!" he triumphantly (if not a bit prematurely) proclaimed. Kobi-nana then sat down and began to steer toward the great rock that marked the entrance to the underground river. He set the pace and entered the chasm in the bluff just beneath the silent stone sentinel that had been placed there by the ancient ones.

Kobi-nana and his family, along with some of his bravest warriors, were on their way to enter a place unlike anything a man could ever imagine or would ever want to imagine. And they would never be heard from, nor would they ever step foot on Earth, again.

The Dawn

Jessica felt as if she had waited hours to gain entrance into Johnson Space Center when she heard, "Ms. Vandale, I have been sent to escort you into the command center." The vocal inflections were as highly polished as the young woman was in her MP uniform.

"Follow me, please," she added as she made her way to an exterior civilian gate entrance. Walking through the gate that opened as the young guard placed her hand, palm down, on a laser-grid screen, the M.P. stopped just outside an interior entrance to the center and spoke again.

"Ma'am, I need to have you walk through that scanner please." She pointed and Jessica started to walk over to the scanner. "And ma'am, I need to check your purse as well please."

"Wow, it's not like I'm a terrorist or anything," Jessica said as she thought to herself, *Doesn't she know who I am?*

"Yes ma'am, your purse please."

Jessica thought about raising a slight protest but decided that, as long as she was this close to getting in, the distraction would not be beneficial to her at all. So, handing over the purse, she walked through the scanner and got the green light to proceed. The MP was waiting at the other side of the walkway, and as Jessica received back her purse, both women proceeded through the security area and into Johnson Space Center.

Walking briskly down a rather long but well-lit hallway, Jessica Vandale felt as if she was on top of her game. She smiled inwardly as she thought, *Nothing can stop me from getting what I came here for. Nothing at all.*

—

"Houston, this is *Magellan*, do you copy?"

"Loud and clear, *Magellan*. How did you all sleep?" answered the com manager.

It was the face of Commander Moore that filled the main screen, but the peripheral screens showed the various crewmembers in a variety of poses. "We slept like babies, and we are ready to get this little baby bumper cart a rollin'."

"All right, *Magellan*." Roger Hand was speaking on com now. "We want to look good for our audiences around the world." He stole a glance over his shoulder to the hot seat area to make sure his guest was there watching. "Are all systems go on your end?"

"Roger that, Houston, we are green across the board. Any greener and we'd be a Christmas tree."

"OK, *Magellan*, you are looking good down here as well." There was a slight pause as Dr. Hand was looking over a hard copy of some information, and then he spoke again.

"*Magellan*, we have a slight course alteration for you to make. We need you to make a twelve-point-five percent lateral shift to the east. It seems that there is too much cloud cover over the Kansas station, so we're gonna watch you guys from the St. Louis station instead. Hope you all don't mind."

"So you got cameras up on the St. Louis arch now, Roger?" came a chuckle-laden remark from Jon Armone.

"Course correction is being initiated Houston," was the response from *Magellan's* pilot as he was obviously trying not to laugh at Armone's little quip.

"Hey, Jon," Roger continued, "you just never know where our cameras are hiding. Oh, and by the way, don't forget, the whole planet is going to be listening in live here shortly, so watch yourselves and make sure language is as flowery as granny's garden."

More laughs from space, "Roger that, control. Course correction is complete in five, four, three, two, and we're on it, Houston. We'll be coming up on St. Louis in about fifteen minutes."

"Roger that, *Magellan.*"

"Hey, Roger Hand," came the playful voice of Jon Armone once again.

"I'm right here, Jon."

"Loved your little TV show last night. So who was the sidekick with all the nuclear paranoia?"

"Jessica's right here in the hot seats, Jon, would you like to talk to her?"

"Oh, hello Ms. Vandale-ah, and how are you, my dear?"

"Jon, your monitor shows elevated heart rate and, from here, your face seems a little blushed; you feeling OK?"

Now it was Roger Hand's turn to have some fun.

"OK, you got me. Now if you'll excuse me, I have some calibrations to make." Jon Armone definitely knew when to make a hasty retreat. Now, for a moment, there was laughter on the Earth below and in the heavens above.

—

At the Woodhenge site, Professor Martin Sherfy was deeply involved in a silent conversation with his Creator when the first car parked alongside his vehicle on the gravel parking lot. Five very sleepy young adults unfolded themselves from the 2002 version of the classic VW Beetle. His, "Ah, good morning, my young friends!" was met with simple waves and a few yawns. Undaunted, he poured out his enthusiasm upon the students like a waterfall flowing down into the river below. "What a glorious morning we have before us! Smell the air! Feel the crisp spring breeze!" Then, lifting both hands, he concluded his greeting in triumph, "Listen to the symphonic majesty of the dawn!"

Still, there was very little response even as two more dangerously overcrowded cars pulled up and parked. Woodhenge was beginning to awaken as the sound of slamming car doors and now, laughter began to unite and interlace with the birdsong of the first day of spring. The scene was now awash in the colors of pre-sunrise dawn, sunrise now only a few moments away.

"All right, people," Professor Sherfy said aloud even as, silently, he was taking roll call. "Let's all go over to this side." Martin began to lead the flock of young adults toward the western edge of the site; the morning's dew was so heavy that they could see their footprints in the grass.

"Hey, look!" one of the female students excitedly exclaimed as she pointed to a small grass-covered mound of earth that lay thirty yards away. A doe and two small fawns had been stirring just on the other side of the mound and had wandered to the southern side where they could be seen. Upon hearing the shrill activity of the girls, the deer simply jaunted off across the highway and were soon lost in the distant fog of the morning. "They're so cuuute!" another young lady squealed.

The professor was smiling as he spoke. "It really is pretty cool to see the wildlife here in the park. Last count, there was just about a thousand head of deer right here in the park." The professor continued almost as if to himself, "OK, most of us are here, so where is—oh, there they are." Even as he spoke, the candy-apple red Ford Mustang belonging to his favorite student was pulling off of old US 40 and stealthily slipping into a parking place.

Without a word of warning, the opening note of *"Also Sprach Zarathustra"* was emanating from the vehicle at about 120 decibels. Martin was smiling to himself as he remembered some of his college pranks, many of which, if not all, were to "never be mentioned again," as his dean had told him on more than one occasion. Knowing it would be useless to try and speak over the symphonic attack of subwoofers and compression drivers, he simply waved the young men to get out of the car and join them. Deep down in his heart of hearts, he knew these young people needed to learn so much more than archaeology and the sciences. They needed to know the God who wrote the framework of the archaeological story beforehand and made the science work in the first place.

All things considered, with everyone now present and in place, they were about to watch a glorious sunrise, and it would be the single event in their lives that they would never forget.

—

"Control, we are reading a red on number one IGS stabilizer; do you confirm?"

"Negative, *Magellan*, check pressurization and balance of ionization particles.

"Roger." There was a slight pause, and then, "Got it. All green now." Matt Moore's voice was now heard. "Three minutes, everyone; I need systems go."

The first to chime in was Simone. "Reactor is powered down to twenty-five point eight-three percent. Core is in default mode and stable, cooling systems fully operational."

"Everything seems to be secure in the ship." Mike Beck was next to speak, and then looking over at the ship's pilot, he added, "Even the horseshoes."

"Miss Dean, are all co-ordinates entered and updated since course modification?"

"Affirmative, sir, navigation is go."

Jon Armone then added, "IGS is activated and powering up. Induction modules are at thirty-eight percent, now forty-seven percent and climbing. We will begin sequencing in ninety-three seconds." On the giant screen at mission control, Dr. Armone was seen looking into the readout grid seemingly hypnotized by what he saw. He said questioningly, "Hello, what in the name of—"

It was at that very instant all screens went blank at mission control with the unnerving message centered on screen in an ominous red font: "NO SIGNAL."

In the main control room at Johnson Space Center, every conceivable bell, warning siren, and whistle erupted to life simultaneously as Jessica Vandale leaned forward in the hot seats to get a better view. Then she jumped back, startled, as the "windows" before her immediately turned from transparent to a pastel green. "Crysteel!" she hissed aloud, none too happily at the inability to observe the situation unfolding before her.

On the floor, Roger Hand was frantically checking system readouts, trying to decipher what the problem was.

"*Magellan*, respond please—control to *Magellan*, please respond." The communications manager's concentration was intense, pushing the handheld receiver so hard against his ear that the tips of his fingers were turning white.

"Speak to me, people!" Dr. Hand was anxiously pleading with his command crew. "What's going on, folks?"

A single, almost-hushed voice came from the satellite imaging station, speaking words that no one wanted to hear: "She's gone, sir."

"Say again, Mister!" Hand angrily barked.

"*Magellan*—she's, she's gone, sir."

"Find her!" Roger growled.

As the professor and his class stood on the westernmost perimeter of Woodhenge, the sun was slowly, gloriously making its ascent above the horizon. At the southern foot of the largest mound, as the sun began to peek out from its lair, the professor was busy showing the class how the sun lined up directly with the center and eastern posts of the Woodhenge site; it was truly a spectacular site to behold.

Professor Martin Sherfy began his narrative, "As you can see, even ancient people were exacting in their astronomical studies. Note how, from this vantage point, it almost seems as if Monks Mound was built directly under the sun's equinoctial path." Standing in front of the small huddled group with the sun behind him, he effectively made his main point, "It is actually the precise positioning of Woodhenge that completes the Delta Circuit. Pretty cool, huh?"

A few of the students were nodding assent to the professor's final question when the first wave hit. It was if someone had pulled the ground from right underneath their feet.

Instinctively, Martin checked his watch and was looking at it when the second, third, fourth, and fifth ground wave hit. Five ground wave pulses and each one on the second he noticed. Five seconds. The ground seemed to simply drop, heave, and roll by about a full foot beneath them. It seemed to Martin to have the motion of a waterbed when someone jumps on it.

"Earthquake!" someone yelled as others started to scream in terror. It was almost amusing to see these young adults frantically seeking safety and almost instantaneously realizing that they were in the safest place they could be during an earthquake, the wide open outdoors.

Waiting and then not sensing anything else, the professor held up a hand and spoke loudly above all the other voices, "No, that was no earthquake. But I gotta tell you that I've never felt anything like that be—"

"Here it comes again! Listen!" came a frightened voice, and the professor silently listened. Then he heard it. A faint rumbling noise in the distance seemed to be gaining volume and was headed their way.

"Look!" The young Mr. Jones spoke up as he pointed to the south across the old highway into the prairie area. Out of the haze and fog of the morning came a sight into focus that none of the witnesses had ever seen. At first there were only a few, then just seconds later came what must have been the entire herd of deer, at least a thousand strong—all running away. But away from what?

"They're running away from the mounds!" Martin quickly realized as he watched the unprecedented event unfolding before him and his troop.

"Turn those blasted alarms off, please!" an exasperated Roger Hand was pleading with the ground crew. One by one they were silenced, and the cacophony of noise faded into the sound of a busy mission control.

"I need information, folks, talk to me," Hand was saying as he scanned the room.

"Communication, what d'ya got?" he continued.

"Nothing, sir," the man said as he still held the receiver to his ear, shaking his head in disbelief, "Nothing at all."

Roger turned to his left and barked, "Radar—satellite imaging?"

"All clear, sir. No debris, no visible sign of explosion or collision."

"Well, at least that's something positive. So, where in the blazes are they? Logistics!"

"Sir!"

"I want hard copies of all instrument readouts, stat!"

"We're on it, sir!"

It was at that moment that a very unsettling thought wormed its way into the mind of Roger Hand—

"What about thermal imaging—" He was almost afraid to continue. "Any radiation spikes in *Magellan's* proximity?"

"None, sir. All thermal imaging is showing normal bandwidth radiation."

Now the floor manager chimed in, "It seems that they must have somehow engaged the drive system prematurely. At least that's how it looks right now." Then looking up at Dr. Hand, she added, "We have absolutely nothing to indicate any kind of failure or accident, sir."

"That's a nice, comforting thought; however, I don't want nice, comforting thoughts. I want facts, people, *facts!* Now, where are those hard copies?"

"Almost got 'em, sir."

Looking over to the com manager, Roger said, "Run the tapes of the last transmission."

"Comin' up on main screen, sir."

There was a deafening silence as every soul stared up at the giant screen centered on the wall before them. All along the edge of the main screen were smaller ones that showed the various stations on the bridge as well. The sequence showed Jon Armone as he was monitoring and calibrating the propulsion drive system. Over his shoulders could be seen the systems readouts.

"Freeze image!" Dr. Hand shouted just as Dr. Armone said, "Hello, what in—" freezing Jon Armone's face in an interesting contortion. It was almost a look of total confusion; but it wasn't Jon's face that interested Roger Hand. It was the LGD readouts over his shoulders that held his attention.

"Holy cow!" someone on the floor said, probably louder than he meant to, while someone else let out a long, low whistle.

At that instant, on screen, the mission control team saw all of *Magellan's* LGD bar graphs showing the current IGS systems readouts 'buried' well past 100 percent. Definitely not what anyone would expect or want to see.

—

Back at Woodhenge the students, as well as their teacher, were gingerly regaining their footing on terra firma.

"Look at that!" one of the students said as she regained her footing and was staring skyward. "What is that?"

Martin Sherfy had seen a lot of strange sights in his life as he had been around the world on various archaeological expeditions, but nothing could remotely come close to this; even though the sun was well above the horizon, straight up overhead at the twelve o'clock position in the sky, was a perfectly circular black dot the size of a full moon.

Then, as quickly as it had appeared, it seemed to shrink into itself. And then it was gone.

CHAPTER 8

AT WITS' END

Jessica Vandale was furious with a capital F. Here she was, sitting in a viewing room with no view, no sound, and no information! What was going on? She was running various scenarios in her mind of *the Magellan Incident,* as she would probably be calling it. Did the ship explode? Did it hit something? Did something hit it? She resisted the impulse to call up network and do a live feed over the phone until she had more (or at least some) information. And although she had rejected the thought of calling the network, she couldn't help but speculate about other reporters in this complex who might be getting the scoop of their lives. Or were they? If any information was getting out, it would be going to the pool room where all the reporters would be gathered, and that would include Ralph Marlowe! He would be there watching the monitors as well and would have the access to information from mission control. Normally, she would simply go and find the pool room (actually, it is called the press pool room, but that sounded too much like cesspool to her), but she didn't dare leave her current berth—just in case.

"The phone, the phone, dummy," she mumbled to herself as she fumbled through her purse trying to snatch the ever-elusive piece of hardware. Finally she found it and hit the direct link to Ralph's phone.

"Answer, buddy, *answer!*" She was practically pleading to the lifeless piece of plastic and aluminum in her hand. Then, "Marlowe."

"Hey, Ralph, what's going on?"

"Jessica! Where in the world are you?"

"I'm here, Ralph. Here in the center."

"Where?" he asked as he scoped out the pool-room looking for her.

"I'm in the hot seats."

"My, my, I guess your little dinner date went well."

"Oh, stop it, please. Just tell me what's going on. Here I am watching the show and all of a sudden—*bam!* They shut me completely out. No sight, no sound, nothing!"

"Actually sweetie, we don't know anything more than you do. Evidently something went wrong, but we have no clue as to what it could have been."

Ralph sounds as ticked as I am, Jessica was thinking to herself.

"Well, they can't keep us in the dark forever."

—

A young lieutenant briskly walked over to Dr. Hand and gave him several dozen sheets of computer printout paper. Hurriedly racing through the pages while at the same time glancing at the screens before and above him in disbelief, Roger finally found what he was looking for: IGS SYSTEMS ANALYSIS.

"What is this all about?" he was asking no one in particular, so no one in particular tried to answer.

"The whole blasted IGS system lit up like Fourth of July fireworks." In subtle apprehension, he continued in a more somber tone, "Every single reading is buried well past one hundred percent."

It was at that very moment he realized how quiet it had become in the control room.

"Communications—all com links up and running?"

"Yes sir, all links are up and running. There's nothing coming down the pike."

Roger was calculating in his head how long it would take for a signal from *Magellan* to reach mission control. He looked at his watch and sighed slightly; time was long past for communication.

Roger began to walk slowly, somewhat aimlessly around the room, as he spoke his thoughts aloud to everyone, and yet to no one in particular.

"Our primary objective was, at best, to reach the halfway mark between Earth and Mars. Now, if *Magellan* reached that goal, she should be in contact by now. But after fifteen minutes, she is still silent, and I want to know; where are they?"

He continued, "OK, people, no one leaves their station unmonitored for a single second. If there is so much as a chirp on subspace channels or a blip on anyone's screen, *I want to know! Is that absolutely clear to everyone?*"

Everyone at Houston Control was either silently nodding or offering an answer verbally to their commander. Even under these uncertain circumstances, Roger Hand felt very comfortable, even confident, with the people he was working with. These were all seasoned, handpicked (he smiled at the unintentional pun) professionals he was working with. Two of these people even went as far back as the Columbia disaster of '03, he reminded himself.

"Dr. Hand?

Roger was almost startled out of his wits by the young man that had silently walked up behind him.

"Yes, what is it, Ensign?" he asked as he spun around.

The ensign was visibly uncertain as to how he should word his message.

"Sir, there's—um, there's a woman up in the hot seats and she seems to be, uh, well she seems to be quite furious at you, sir." The ensign's face turning slightly red, he continued. "She is demanding to see you, sir."

Roger actually felt sorry for the young man and smiled inwardly as he said, "Go tell her I'm on my way, son."

"Yes sir," was the simple reply as the ensign quickly made a 180 degree turn and headed for the stairs at the rear of the room.

Roger, Roger, Roger. When are you ever going to stop mixing business and pleasure? he was asking himself. One thing was for sure; he certainly wasn't looking forward to this particular conversation with Little Ms. Nuclear.

She's probably already told the whole world that "The sky is falling" or that there was some kind of terrible nuclear accident onboard Magellan, he surmised with a shudder and turned floor control over to the com manager. He then began to make his way back to the hot seats, wondering on the way who was in greater danger—himself or the crew of *Magellan*.

—

"Braking jets have fired, Commander," said *Magellan's* Texan pilot. "All shipboard engine systems seem to be operational."

Matt Moore looked around at all his colleagues and asked,

"Is everyone all right?"

Affirmations came from all.

"OK, everyone, report; Communications?"

"Communications are—" Carl Lewis was frantically pushing buttons as he spoke. "Inoperative, sir. I don't understand. Transmitters, receivers all check out and the dish is pointed home but …" He held his hands up in the "I don't have a clue" position and then added, "I'm not hearing a peep. Nothing. Anyway, I'm working on it."

"All right, keep on it. Navigation, report."

Deborah Dean seemed unusually quiet. For a moment, Moore thought she hadn't heard him, and then almost sheepishly, she began to speak.

"Sir, navigation must be down as well."

"What is it, Deb?" Moore suspected a problem was about to rear its ugly head by the way she was hesitating. He had worked with her before, and her current demeanor was not setting right with him at all.

"I don't, I mean I'm not—" A dark cloud was rapidly forming over this woman's countenance as her commander listened intently.

She looked up at Moore and said, "I don't know where we are. I mean, I don't believe the data I am looking at, sir! It must be wrong somehow. A glitch of some kind."

Matt Moore laid his hand on Dean's shoulder as he said, "OK, people, I guess we need to have a look and see for ourselves." Tapping the console before him, the hull around them instantly began to melt into a one-way view of space. It was a view of space as well as a view that they were all quite unprepared to see—the planet Saturn up close and very personal.

—

Professor Sherfy was checking to see that all his students were all right, taking the time to speak to each one of them individually, and he was thankful that no one had been injured. In fact, not only were they fine, they were all ready to leave the mounds site ASAP.

"Wow! Spooky place ya got here, Professor." One student smiled as she walked past him. "Bet'cha don't read about anything like this in that old Bible of yours."

He wanted to respond to that one, but after a quick second thought, he spoke to everyone instead. "Listen, I'm not sure what happened here, but I want you all to go on about your daily affairs and I'll let you know what I find out as soon as I can."

"Gee, Professor, it was just a little earthquake. We don't live too far from the New Madrid fault, ya know."

Martin Sherfy was still taking in all the sights and sounds around him as he spoke. "Yes, I do know that, Mr. Colasse, and that was no faultal movement of any kind, my young friend."

"Hey, Professor, what about that black dot up in the sky? What was that all about?"

"I haven't got the slightest idea, but I'm going to find out as soon as I can." He was making a shooing motion with his hands as he said, "Come on now, let's clear out and get going. I know that most of you have early classes." Slowly, one by one, the students left in their cars and headed back to campus. Now Martin was alone and could do some investigating, and he knew where he was going to start. Thinking about the phrase "Black dot in the sky" sent an unexpected shiver down his spine and almost into his very soul. What was that indeed! He had never seen anything like that before—anywhere. Climbing into his pickup and starting the engine, he reached over and turned on the radio. He loved St. Louis talk radio, and today he wasn't disappointed as he sat spellbound staring at the digital readout on the unit's faceplate listening to the chatter of the day.

"For the last twenty minutes, and nothing has been heard from *Magellan*. Repeating once again, the spacecraft *Magellan* has either disappeared or been somehow disabled, we honestly don't know at this point. She was only seconds away from a five-second engine trial of the IGS system when all communication was lost and *Magellan* is nowhere to be found."

"Five seconds—hmmm," Martin said aloud as he was already sensing a connection.

"Their orbit was taking them over the midsection of the country; uh, right over St. Louis, in fact, when the malfunction occurred," the announcer said.

Martin found himself staring out his window into the morning sky. Knowing his God and the fact that nothing ever just happens, Professor Martin Sherfy could taste a new adventure, could sense a new mystery unfolding around him, enveloping him, intriguing him. And this time, he promised himself, he would be ready for anything.

—

"Jessica," Roger said as disarmingly as he possibly could, "I really am sorry about—"

"Don't you give me that convoluted crap about how sorry you are! I want to know what's going on. I mean, you bring me here." She practically did a pirouette in the middle of the room as she pointed out her surroundings. "You shut me in here all alone and then, then you shut me out of everything!"

She started to walk (actually, it was more like a missile launching) toward Roger and really tear into him when her cell rang.

Whew! Roger thought as he watched her fumble through her purse for the phone. "Timing is everything," he managed to mumble to himself unheard by the two-legged hurricane that had been temporarily sidetracked by, of all things, a telephone.

"Not now!" was all she said as she activated the cell. Then she slapped it shut and turned her attention back to him.

This doesn't look good, Roger was thinking as Hurricane Jessica began her assault.

—

"It seems that our female counterpart has something else on her mind at the moment," the man said as he hung up the phone and then folded his hands on the table before him. He looked over to his right and spoke to the two men closest to him. "Go. Find out what our little newsfly is up to."

Immediately the men rose silently to their feet to leave the room. As they opened the door, light flooded in like a laser, causing one man to squint harshly as he cursed something Arabic under his breath and then turned his head to look once more at the head of the table.

"Whatever trickery these infidels are attempting shall not hamper our operations. We shall have that which we seek soon enough. May Allah be praised!"

—

"How did we get *here?*" was the question of the hour being asked by just about everyone on *Magellan*'s bridge. It was Jon Armone that first walked up to the 'window' (if you can call an entire hull section a 'window') and triumphantly proclaimed; "It works, *it works!* IGS is a success!" His excitement was building into a massive crescendo. "Look at this! Far beyond what we ever expected or even hoped for. Earth to Saturn in five seconds flat!"

Looking over at the mission clock, Commander Moore spoke up.

"It's been twenty minutes or so since we arrived here." He paused and looked around at every member of the crew and then continued, "I think it's time to let Earth know where we are; how 'bout you guys?"

"Oh yeah, you betcha!" came the overzealous response from the com officer as he turned his attention away from the ringed orb before him.

"So, tell me, Carl—can we reach Earth from here?"

"Piece of cake." Carl was beaming. "One little bitty thing though—"

"And that would be?" the commander asked with eyebrows raised.

"Time lag. In fact, that would explain why I thought something was wrong with communications." Carl got up and walked over to the incredible view before him and then continued. "Our signal, traveling at the speed of light, is gonna take just about eighty or ninety minutes to reach mission control."

"So, as of right now, it's going to be the better part of two hours from the time that control lost our signal and then hears from us again. Am I right?" Matt said.

"That pretty well sums it up sir."

"Get on it, Carl. We don't want our home world thinking we nuked ourselves now, do we?"

"Oh, I dunno boss, if we let the media go crazy with their imagination just a little while longer, we could help them look really, *really* stupid. Not that it would be that hard to do—"

"Make the call, Mr. Lewis."

"Yes sir. I'm on it."

Simone couldn't help but notice the disappointment in the com officer's voice. American humor; she could do without it at a time like this. And even as she listened and formed that opinion, another part of her mind was trying to piece together what had transpired in five seconds.

"It may, as you say, be fun to watch and see the media spin a story around *Magellan*'s apparent disappearance, Mr. Lewis, but," Simone paused as she beheld the Saturnian system before them and then continued, "we really *do* need to contact Earth ASAP. We need to find out what happened." She then turned to her mentor/friend. "Something *somehow* triggered IGS, and we need to know what that something is, Jon."

Letting out a sigh, Dr. Armone conceded, "You're right. I guess I just got caught up in the moment." Once again, it seemed the scientist was blushing.

"Hey, Commander, would you like to send a video feed to our earthbound partners?"

Commander Moore smiled as he looked out once again at the massive orb before them and said, "You bet I would."

It was still fairly early, at least too early for the Interpretive Center at the Cahokia Mounds State Historic Site to be open. However, Martin knew the site manager as well as most of the park rangers who were stationed there, so he didn't see any problems getting in to have a chat with someone to get information. *This is one strange morning, Lord,* Martin was thinking as he turned east onto Highway 40 and began the quarter-mile jaunt to the center's entrance. He had barely gotten on the road when he saw three police cars turning into the center from the other direction with their lights on. *Now **that's** interesting,* he thought just as an Illinois State Trooper came up silently from behind him without any siren and flew past with only his lights flashing red and blue, practically giving him cardiac arrest.

"Well, well, well, there must be something going on after all." He said aloud, "Maybe I can get some answers to all this."

—

"I want some answers and I want them *now!*" Jessica Vandale was practically screaming at Roger by this point. "It's like you planned all along to shut me out of the loop. That's it, isn't it? Shut me in here and shut me up."

Roger was trying to placate this newfound friend of his, but he couldn't get a word in edgewise as this world-renowned anchorwoman was morphing into the fiercest of combatants right before his very eyes. Looking at his watch, he saw that he had already wasted four full minutes listening to this raging fireball.

"I demand that you tell me what in the (expletives galore, not a pretty sight) world is going on with *Magellan!* What happened? Where are they? Roger, *what is going on?*"

Dr. Roger Hand had had enough of this game. He waited patiently for the tirade to run its course, and then he spoke.

"First of all, I brought you in as a guest—*remember?*"

"Next, this is not, and I repeat, not your show. This is my territory, girl, and you have way overstepped your boundaries. I've got more important things to deal with than your blasted ego!" Opening the door halfway, he yelled, "Security!" and instantly two rather hefty, well-armed men appeared in the room looking as if they were ready for anything. "Take Miss Vandale and show her the way out, please."

"Oh, no you don't Roger Hand, you owe me an—"

It was Roger's turn to be colorfully explosive now. "I don't owe you anything, young lady! You will not speak to me as a dog." Roger began to walk out the door when he heard Jessica speak from behind him.

"OK, I'm, I'm really sorry. It was just the excitement of the moment. I just want to know what happened to *Magellan* and—"

Roger spun around and was in extreme proximity to Jessica's face as he spoke one last time eyeball to eyeball, "Miss Vandale, what has happened is unknown at the moment, and quite frankly, when I do find out, you won't be here for me to tell you that information!"

"Aw, c'mon, Roger, at least let me go to the press pool," she pleaded unsuccessfully.

Roger looked deep into her eyes once again and practically growled, "I'm not in the mood to have you anywhere in this complex at the moment." Then, looking at the guards, he said, "This conversation is finished." Without another word, the security personnel escorted a fuming Jessica Vandale out into the morning sun.

I'm not done with you yet, Roger Hand! Jessica screamed inside of her mind where no one could hear.

CHAPTER 9

CONTACT

Commander Moore had just finished his video message to mission control and was headed over to Simone's station to gather any more current scientific data that she may have uncovered. He could easily tell that she was deeply engrossed in her endless lists of readouts and computations, so he walked slowly, watching for an opening to present itself, and before he had the chance to say a word, Simone sat straight up and proclaimed, "Dr. Armone, you have to see this."

Dr. Armone was standing, hands clasped behind his back, gazing out at the gas giant before him. He turned, and as he proceeded over to Simone, he stopped at the navigation console, and leaning over Deborah Dean's shoulder, spoke almost in a whisper to her. "One point two million miles away, and look how big she is!" He heard a ripping sound from Simone's station and looked over to see her standing up, and making eye contact with her, she gave him the old "follow me" body language that only close friends can sense of each other. She began to make her way toward the door, and turning her head to confirm that her colleague had responded, she stepped out into the corridor.

Simone was waiting for him when he came through the doorway and looked both directions before she began to speak. There was a sense of urgency as well as excitement in her voice as she spoke. "What do you think, Doctor?" she asked.

"Uh-oh, every time you ask me that question, you have something up your sleeve."

"Doctor," she almost seemed as if she was about to explode with excitement now, "you *do* realize that we have shattered the illusion of light speed travel, don't you?"

The doctor was eyeing up his friend as he answered, "Yes I do. We were hoping to break it just getting halfway to Mars, but not by breaking it a thousand times over." He paused for the briefest of seconds and then continued, "But that's not what you're being so secretive about, is it? Really, Simone, everyone on board has already figured that one out."

"No, you're right. There is something else. I've been going over the grav data, and well, I want you to look at this." She was handing him a hard copy of what she had been so diligently working on since their arrival some forty-five minutes ago. It was a comparison chart. On one side was the digital printout of the Earth's gravitational wave that they had supposedly tapped into, and on the other side was the G-wave that was actually locked onto.

"Whoa, this can't be right, Simone."

"I know, Jon, but I have checked and rechecked the data, the systems, and the IGS memory buffer." Simone looked deeper into her friend's eyes as she spoke again. "We didn't lock onto the Earth's G-wave at all. Something else locked onto us. Something big. Something *very* big."

Simone paused, letting the weight of that statement settle upon him, and then continued, "The G-wave that carried us here was at least one thousand to the twenty-third power times more powerful than the Earth's entire gravitational field. Jon, that's about a billion times more powerful than the sun!"

"It's a good thing we only had a five-second burn programmed or it's hard telling where we would have ended up." The doctor was thinking out loud now, his eyes squinting as he did some abstract equations in his mind.

"There's something else, Jon. The G-wave that propelled us here was not a wide-band wave. It was more like a beam, a, oh—" She was obviously searching for an analogy or example to use, and then it came to her. "It was like a laser beam of amplified G's, if you will."

Jon Armone was as white as a sheet now. Facts and data do not lie. "What in the world could we have stumbled upon? It almost seems like— no, that would be too ridiculous to even think."

"A black hole?" Simone was standing fully erect now, staring down at the six-foot-tall doctor with an intensity that was almost overbearing as she continued. "Right now, that is the only thing that fits. I guess the real question is, where was it? All the gear and the drive system were focused on Earth-wave emanations. The only place it could have been was …" Her voice now trailed off as her human reasoning began to catch up with her faster than light train of thought.

"On Earth?" Jon Armone was helping her now.

"On Earth," she responded.

—

Roger Hand entered the control room as quietly as he could. Looking up at the mission clock, he saw that they were coming up on the one-hour mark. *This has **got** to change,* he angrily thought to himself.

"OK, people, who's got some answers for me?"

"Sir, I might have something—but I don't know what it means," came a voice from behind the satellite imaging station console.

"What is it, uh," he said, looking at the security tag and then the man, "Brookfield?"

"Look up on screen, sir."

Looking up, Hand saw nothing but stars, lots and lots of stars, and his patience was wearing thin. "What exactly am I looking for?" he asked in a tone that was less than cordial.

"Watch, sir—*there!* Did you see that? Five seconds exactly."

"What? See what, man?" Mount Hand was about to blow.

"The stars, sir, a whole patch of stars—I guess I should say sector of stars—*disappear*. Then five seconds later, there they are back and pretty as you please. Almost like someone turned them off, then back on again."

Roger was intrigued. "Play it again, Brookfield. In fact, loop it."

Everyone on the command floor was watching the twenty-second loop of computer imaging with unsettled interest. Sure enough: stars on, stars off, and stars on again.

Roger didn't take his eyes from the screen as he said, "Give me a time comparison between our missing stars and the IGS firing sequence."

"Time codes concur with one another; they match!"

"All right, people, it's not much—in fact, it's kinda weird—but it is a start. Good work, Brookfield. All right, let's get to work people, get on it!"

—

Ralph Marlowe had a mouthful of chocolate doughnut when his cell phone rang. He managed to get out a muffled, "Marlowe," and then his ear began to melt as an enraged, crazed Jessica Vandale exploded into his ear gate.

"—even had me escorted out of the building! *Me!* Jessica Vandale! Taken out of the story! The nerve of that man! He wouldn't even listen to reason. I can't believe he's doing this to me. He even—"

"Hey, hey, hey, hold on there, girl." He at least had the time to swallow the doughnut and some coffee while Jessica unloaded her first round. Now he could talk. "Who had you escorted out?"

"Hand," came the simple answer. Way too simple.

"Why did he do that, Jess?"

"I was kind of, well you know how I am; I got mad when he shut down the view I had of the control room, and I let him know it!"

"Jess, Jess, Jess. Those screens in the hot seats are automatic, just like our monitors here in the pool room. The second there's a problem, they shut down for security reasons. You of all people should know that, girl."

"Spare me the parental chastisement, will you? she snarled. It's not right, Ralph! We have the right to know what's going on with *Magellan.*"

Ralph was almost feeling sorry for his comrade, so he said, "It's all right. Tell you what; let me see if I can sneak you in to the pool room."

Outside in the warm Texas sunshine, Jessica Vandale was grinning ear to ear. "Thanks, Ralph. I'm out by the Senior Ops gate."

—

As he pulled into the parking lot of the Mounds Interpretive Center, Martin could hear the burglar alarms clamoring in the morning air drowning out the birdsong. One by one, they were being silenced as he made his way from his truck to the main entrance of the center. At the door, one lone policeman was standing guard. "Can I help you, sir?" came the less-than-friendly greeting from the sentry.

"Actually, I might be of assistance to you, sir. My name is Professor Martin Sherfy." Martin offered his hand as a gesture of professional courtesy and promptly saw that he was getting no response, so he simply continued his intro. "I'm the archaeology professor at Edwardsville University and was over at the Woodhenge site with a class when the tremors," he couldn't think of what else to call them, "hit." Martin paused just long enough to look around the greeting area behind the policeman before he continued. "So, is that what set off the alarms?"

The policeman eyed him with what seemed to be petty annoyance and then spoke matter-of-factly. "We've had no reports of any tremors, sir. And what we have here is probably just the work of some bored juveniles that had nothing better to do."

It was clear that the usual pleasantries were not going to gain Martin any information, let alone entrance, so he decided to try the oldest trick in the book: name dropping.

"I'm also a personal friend of Bob Mengersi, the site manager here. I was stopping by to see him for a moment and—"

He held both hands out from his side, indicating the unsaid, "All this is going on."

"I'm sure Ranger Mengersi would love to see you, but at the moment he's probably pretty busy checking for damage or thefts."

Martin just smiled at the officer and said, "That's OK, I'll wait." Then he made his way back out the same way he came in.

It's gonna be a long day. He was hoping that he only thought that and didn't say it out loud.

CHAPTER 10

TALKING WITH THE STARS

"OK, people, talk to me. We're comin' up on the two-hour mark, and we still don't know one blessed thing!" Roger was once again stalking the floor, ready to divert any and all his attention to anyone who so much as even coughed. "How 'bout some ideas, people? Even stupid ones are viable right now." He raised his voice a few decibels and began to recite the past few moments. "The media is going nuts, the president has called twice, and I don't even have a tidbit, a morsel to give him."

It was right at that moment that the main screen began to come to life. First some static and white noise, then some snowy shapes attempting to coalesce, then some hazy double images.

"Amplify, augment, *draw in that signal!*" Hand's adrenaline was pumping at one thousand PSI now as he looked to the screen and saw a smiling Matt Moore.

"Houston control, this is *Magellan*, do you copy? Oh, I'm sorry we are on a bit of a time delay here. Everything and everyone on board is, and are, fine. Sorry it has taken so long to contact you guys but, as I said, we are experiencing somewhat of a time lag here."

Roger took his eyes off the screen long enough to look at the com manager and see him hold up one finger and state simply, "One-way com."

"At the time we are recording this message, it has been thirty minutes since IGS malfunctioned and prematurely engaged—"

Thirty minutes, Hand thought to himself. *That would have been an hour and a half ago.*

60

"—but as I'm about to show you, IGS works." He was grinning ear to ear as he continued, "Oh, by the way, you might want to sit down for this one, Roger." As he spoke, the bulkhead right behind him melted from ship diagnostic displays into a window—a window that was showing a spectacular view of deep space and the massive crescent phase of the planet Saturn. From off-screen, Moore continued, "We are sending a nice little package of data along with this transmission to give you guys something to work on—uh, like how we got all the way out here."

It was clear by his smile and demeanor that Commander Matt Moore was having the time of his life. This was truly *his* moment, and he was playing it to the hilt. "All IGS-related data, ship's data, even personnel data is included. I repeat—*Magellan* is secure. No damage and no problems, uh, at least not yet. We just happened to go a tad bit further than we had originally planned.

"You now have our coordinates, so we shall look forward to hearing from you real soon, or at least as soon as possible. For now, I have some things to take care of—you know, gotta earn my pay. *Magellan* out."

At first, the room was silent. It was a stunned silence, in fact. One could hear the spider over in the corner of the ceiling spinning her web as all eyes were fixed on the freeze-framed image of Matt Moore standing on *Magellan's* deck with Saturn peeking over his shoulder. Then, "That's it? That's all he's got to say? How in the world did they get *there?*" Once again came the oft-repeated, "All right, people, let's get to work—let's go! We've got a lot of work to do, and now we have the data to do it! Let's get busy, folks!"

—

Bob Mengersi lived on site in a small two-story house that had been renovated to accommodate the park superintendent as he ran the day-to-day business at the mounds site. He was headed out the southwest door of the center that led to his home when he saw an all-too-familiar truck parked in the parking lot. He began to smile as he made his way counterclockwise around the building to the place where he knew he would find Martin. Sure enough, there was Martin Sherfy sitting more like a college student than a professor, on one of the low brick and mortar walls that guided guests toward the two massive main entry doors of the center. As he continued to make his way up behind his friend, the main doors opened and the policemen were being let out by one of the park volunteers. As the officers were approaching their cars, they saw Mengersi and waved as they got into the cruisers and drove off down the quarter-mile drive toward the highway. By now, Bob Mengersi was standing right behind his colleague completely unnoticed. "All these police and they still let the local riffraff in," Bob said in a much louder than normal voice that launched Martin straight up from his perch.

"Man, don't *do that!*" Martin huffed.

"Here you are, a leading top-notch archaeologist, a trained observer, and you didn't even notice an old man sneak up behind you." Bob was laughing, but he could sense something in his friend that told him he wasn't here to just visit.

Martin was standing watching the police enter the highway and muttered, "I saw those guys wave; I just thought that they were waving to me. That did seem a little odd." Then turning to Mengersi, he continued, "Speaking of odd, did you feel anything this morning at about sunrise?"

"Feel anything? Buddy, let me tell you, I took some sneezy snotty so I could sleep stuff, and I didn't even hear the alarm go off. At least, not 'till Mark there," he said, pointing to the volunteer, "came pounding on my door. Just about gave me a heart-astroke!"

Martin was studying the young man coming up to them and asked him, "So, did you feel anything this morning?"

"The earthquake?"

"No, well yeah, I guess. The earthquake." What else could he call it? At least for now.

"Kinda weird, if you ask me." The man was brushing his hand across his head as if he was trying to generate some static electricity. "It almost felt like giant footsteps."

Now that was an interesting concept; footsteps.

So now Mengersi got back into the conversation. "What in the world are you guys talking about?"

The two men looked at each other, and then Martin spoke up. "Listen, I had my entire class out at Woodhenge for the equinoctial sunrise, and just after the event, the earth shook five times."

It was clear that Martin was not satisfied with his choice of words, and he abruptly added, "Pulsated, that's better, pulsated five times." At the moment, Martin Sherfy had that distant look about him—a look that spoke of hypothetical reasoning and formulations coming into his mind.

Mengersi knew his friend well enough to know that he probably would like to carry on this conversation in a more private manner, so he asked

Mark if he would take care of the paperwork for the police reports and then turned to his friend.

"Let's walk," was all he had to say, and the two of them headed out for one of the trails that meandered around the mounds site.

The further they got from the center, the more certain Mengersi was that something was definitely up. Finally, he could take no more of the silence, so he asked, "You gonna tell me what's going on in that grave-diggin' mind of yours, or are we gonna play twenty questions?"

Martin broke into a slight chuckle and answered, "I'm sorry, Bob, but I gotta say, something really strange happened here today, and I can't quite make the connections."

"Connections?" queried Bob as the two men made their way 'round the back stretch of the park. However, once again the park ranger was met with nothing but silence, silence and a whole lot of fallen trees. Some of the oldest trees in the park were lying along the ground as if someone (or something) had simply slapped them down. It was now clear that a mystery was unfolding right before them, enveloping them with its lure as Martin seemed to be in his own little world muttering, "The ground heaves, the deer leave, a hole in the sky, and trees lying down in a blast pattern."

"Would you like to let me in on your private little discourse that you seem to be enjoying with yourself?" Bob said, and then it hit him; he hadn't seen a single deer the whole time they had been away from the center. *Now that* is *strange, in fact, downright eerie,* he thought. There were countless herds of deer on the site, yet not one to be seen. Now his interest was piqued. "So, what's up?" he asked as he steeled himself for some kind of theorem on plate tectonics or even that the big mound was sinking into the Illinois countryside. The answer he got wasn't anywhere near the expected response.

"Magellan."

"Magellan. Um, like the spacecraft *Magellan?"*

"The one and same; she's disappeared or something."

"Boy, I have been sleeping too much! All this happened this morning, huh?"

"Listen, I don't know how this fits together, but bear with me a moment. When we felt the ground pulse or quake or whatever it was that it did, *Magellan* was right over St. Louis. Right over us! We looked up into the sky and saw this black dot or something that—I'm, I'm tellin' ya, it just seemed to inhale the morning light. I know it sounds weird, but I think it's all tied together somehow. *Magellan* was supposed to have a five-second test firing of those experimental engines of hers. Now listen, Bob, those quakes or tremors or whatever they were, they were on the second. Five of them, five seconds."

Both men let the conversation hang as they contemplated the ramifications of the coincidence. Where they stood, there was two of the smaller mounds, one on each side of them some thirty feet high and sixty to eighty feet in diameter, and directly north of their position less than a quarter mile away was Monks Mound sitting silently, just as it had for the last one thousand years, yet now seemingly taunting them, beckoning them, whispering, "I've got a secret."

CHAPTER 11

DEBRIEFING

To say the pressroom was full of reporters would have to be one of the biggest understatements of the last hundred years. In fact, the pool room was more like a three-ring circus that needed a forth, even a fifth, ring. Over in one corner, Jessica Vandale was trying to remain unnoticed as she sat underneath a mural of the shuttles *Challenger* and *Columbia* that had been painted as a memorial to the crewmembers and the two ships that had been lost. As she sat there, she turned to look at the mural and saw something she hadn't noticed before; the painting depicted the two orbiters leaving their launch pads with the combined plume from their rocket engines, creating a shadow image of an old Apollo spacecraft. *"Apollo One,"* she said to no one as she remembered just how dangerous spaceflight really was.

"Well now, here's the lady of the day! Hello, Jess."

"Hi, Ron. Do we know anything yet?" Ron White— this was the last person she wanted to talk to right now. He was part of the reason she left CNN—a real creep of a man. He thought he could have any woman he wanted. Jessica showed him the big picture, even did it in front of a national audience during a live broadcast. The network execs didn't think it was very funny, but Jessica found herself smiling at the distant memory.

"No, and if you ask me, it's been too quiet too long," he answered and was just about to say something else that was prefaced with, "Listen, Jess—" when the main door opened and Roger Hand strutted into the room and made a very short announcement;

"Ladies and gentlemen, we have heard from the crew of *Magellan,* and everything is fine. We will have a press conference in one hour. Thank you all for your patience." He then turned around and walked out just as quickly as he walked in.

Because Jessica wanted an inside angle to this story, she found herself wishing that she had conducted herself a little more pleasant toward Roger Hand. She was already conniving a way to start over with the man, but for now, she was as happy as a little girl at Disneyworld to simply be inside of Johnson Space Center.

The entire crew of *Magellan* was now gathered in the mess hall. Simone had chosen wisely to program the interior hull section to remain slate blue instead of transparent so that all attention would focus on her and Dr. Armone as they spoke. The room had been designed to easily accommodate fifteen to twenty people, so there was plenty of room for everyone to make themselves comfortable. Unfortunately, comfortable was everything but what Simone was feeling at the moment. There seemed to be an uneasiness, a tenseness inside her that she couldn't quite put her finger on.

Surely the fact of being ten astronomical units away from her home world couldn't be the reason, or the fact that she had hardly slept (due to the stress of the mission as well as having to end a long-lived relationship) for the last week or so. *Absolutely not,* she reasoned.

*I'll be fine. Nothing is wrong. The **Lord** loves me. He is in control,* she kept telling herself as she made her way from the side of the gathering up to the front. One thing was certain, Simone was very uneasy about the stark reality of the subject matter they needed to discuss. It was all starting to eat away at this young woman, and she hoped it wasn't beginning to show.

"We need to talk," she began rather sheepishly. Jon Armone was watching closely as he was seeing a side of his young friend he had not seen, or at least noticed, before. Simone continued.

"Upon arrival, I immediately started monitoring all data flow from *Magellan*'s IGS burn. The good news is that the IGS drive system appears to be in perfect shape. There doesn't seem to be any damage done to the system at all. Our reactor is now up to ninety percent capacity as we orbit—" She almost let down her guard as she spit out, "um, Saturn. Life support is nominal and all the other systems are well within acceptable parameters. The bad news is—"

Simone was interrupted by a short chuckle, followed by the voice of Matt Moore commenting, "Finally! Finally the great Simone Sytte is getting into the finer points of American humor! Good news, bad news, I must say I'm impressed." Simone could see that *Magellan's* commander was genuine in his exultation, but she did not see the look that Jon Armone gave him.

Quickly recovering her faculties, Simone continued this time with a smile, "Yes commander, the bad news. Actually, not bad, just ..." There was a short pause as Simone searched for the correct idiom that would not be lost on her American counterparts. "Odd."

That got their attention.

"As you all are aware, IGS prematurely engaged and brought us here. What we don't know is the how or why. That is why Dr. Armone and I have called this meeting to let you in on some pretty intriguing data. Data that doesn't, how do you say, *fit*."

"What data is that, Simone?" came the voice of the ship's navigator.

"Well," Simone let that word hang a little too long, causing even more uneasiness among the crew. The tension in the room unintentionally being turned up a notch. "As you all are well aware of, we easily beat the light-speed ceiling, and we are further out than any human has ever been—"

"Where no man has gone before—" came the overly melodramatic tone from Charlie Hodson. Then in a normal, albeit deliriously restless, voice, he added, "and I can't wait to EVA out here!" He was looking dead on at his commander with that one.

"Don't you be getting in too big a hurry there, space cowboy. We still need you to hang around. Don't want any accidents way out here, now do we?" Matt responded.

"Aw, Dad, I'll be careful. I'll even have the jetpack back in the hanger by midnight."

That short discourse seemed to break up some of the tension that was building, but everyone knew there was more to the story.

"Please continue, Simone," came the doctor's soft prodding from across the room. He thought he had detected a slight tremor in her voice, and he was watching the young scientist for any other warning signs of trouble.

Simone's hands were clasped together almost as if in prayer, and she held them against her chest as she cautiously continued.

"As you know, focusing on Earth's broadband G-wave, we were hoping to get close to Mars. We certainly did not expect to come nine hundred million miles. Not in five seconds."

"Hey, Doc, think there are any Dairy Queens out here? Sure could use a banana split right about now."

Jon Armone shot the resident Texan a look that would have sent a longhorn steer scampering away with its tail between its legs.

"Sorry."

Clearing her throat, Simone continued, "According to the data, IGS did not lock onto Earth's G-wave at all. Something else locked onto us."

Now there was a lot of noise as one word blurbs like, "what," "huh," and "who" filled the mess hall.

Simone let the clamor die down before she continued. "It seems that a gravity wave of one thousand to the twenty-third power triggered the drive system and flung us halfway out of our solar system. Dr. Armone and I have gone over the data time and time again…" She paused to look into every set of eyes that was locked onto hers and then continued. "We think we have found ourselves a black hole. Now, that's not the biggest part of the mystery. The location of this black hole is the biggest part. It seems to be located on, or in, the Earth itself, somewhere in North America. The Midwestern United States, to be exact." Just getting this far, just sharing this much information, was doing a world of good for Simone. Slowly the weight was lifting. "We have encrypted the data and sent it to Dr. Hand at mission control in hopes that the Houston techies can extrapolate an exact location. But for now, all we can do is wait. And pray."

"Will we be able to go home?" came a sob-filled voice from the ship's navigator; Deborah Dean's face was streaked with tears, sheer terror in her eyes.

Jon Armone walked across the room and knelt down in front of the ship's navigator. "It's OK, Deb. We're going to be fine. We will go home." Then with a somewhat crooked smile he added, "We just don't know when." It was at this moment Dr. Jon Armone took over the proceedings. He raised himself up, walked over to the room control console, and started to key in a command but abruptly aborted the attempt and chose rather to speak the command to the computer.

"Igor."

"Chirp," came the voice recognition response.

Jon shook his head and mumbled, "What a name for a mess hall worker." Then he continued, "Starboard one-quarter exterior view please."

"Chirp." The acknowledgment of the order was proclaimed.

Instantly, the side of the mess hall facing away from Saturn began to melt away (Armone loved to watch the magic of metal turning to clear glass) in degrees until it seemed as if one could reach out and touch the stars—or at least one star in particular, the biggest and brightest one, Sol. That beautiful hydrogen reactor had shone over Earth for untold millennia, watching mankind crawl from the Middle East to the moon; the star at the very center of this solar system around which all humanity huddled. And just a few degrees away from that center was a much smaller dot of bluish light; Earth. All eyes were fixed on that tiny point of light as Dr. Armone continued.

"Commander Moore, what is *Magellan*'s top speed using her own engines?"

"Somewhere in the neighborhood of one hundred twenty to one hundred twenty-five thousand miles per hour—we think." He was grinning like a sixteen-year-old who just got his license and his first hot rod when he added, "We haven't gotten to open her up yet."

After doing some quick mental arithmetic, Armone then began to set forth a hypothesis for the crew. "If worst came to worst, using her own engines and getting that one twenty-five K speed, *Magellan* could conceivably be parked nice and comfy in Earth orbit in just about three hundred days. Just about ten months."

It was clear that Jon Armone was looking for input from the crew. He wanted to know their feelings of being in space that long. He didn't have to wait long to find an answer.

"Life-support and food production is fine for that, Doc, but what about using IGS?" Moore responded.

" Aha, that, my friend, is what we need to find out." Armone said as he sat down next to the window and looked longingly out at his home world.

"What we need at the moment is real-time communications with Houston," the commander said to no one in particular.

"I'm working on that one," came the unprompted response from Simone. Then turning her attention to the communications officer, she spoke almost knowingly. "If we can move an object that has physical mass properties like *Magellan* faster than light, there has to be a way of moving a purely electronic signal, which has no physical mass, faster than light as well."

Carl Lewis was up to the challenge. "Let's do it! We gonna use IGS for that one too?"

"It seems logical to me."

Jumping to his feet, he said, "Well, all righty then; let's rock!"

CHAPTER 12

SECRETS

"Sir!" exclaimed an excited com officer. "We're getting a secondary feed from *Magellan*. Wait—" Then with a look of complete surprise, he added, "It's, it's encoded, sir; for your eyes only."

Everyone on the floor seemed to look at everyone else then simultaneously looked at Roger Hand. He was almost amused; it actually seemed as if someone had choreographed the moment.

Knowing that the hot seats were now vacant as well as soundproofed, he said, "Feed it to the personal monitors in the hot seats."

"Yes sir."

Roger Hand was more excited than he had been in years as he climbed the stairs in the rear of the room two steps at a time and then entered his own private interplanetary communications room.

It was uncanny how the com officer timed the decrypt prompt to come on screen just as Roger sat down. Quickly typing in his private decrypt code, he was immediately looking into the face of his longtime friend Jon Armone. His face was showing signs of what, intrigue, fascination? Behind Dr. Armone, the banded bulk of Saturn was in view, and Hand was transfixed as he peered past Armone and gazed upon the Saturnian system. About one-quarter of the planet's ring system was in view jutting out from beneath the screen as if *Magellan* were sitting on some kind of magical highway. The Cassini Division was so clear that Roger could count stars through it as his eyes adjusted to the light.

"Roger we have a, um—" Obviously searching for words the doctor unceremoniously continued, "A situation that we need you and your

70

people," leaning into the screen he added, "your specialized team, that is, to look into. It seems that we may have accidentally found something on Earth. I'm probably gonna sound a little off on this one, but bear with me, old buddy. We think that IGS has found a black hole in a very unlikely place. Yeah, I know that sounds insane. After all, you boys have been trying to find one and prove their existence for years but—" Jon's face began to grow even more serious now; much more serious. "It might be possible that we have been sitting right on top of one all these years, and I mean that literally. Look, Simone is using the Pentagon's encrypt on the data to send to you as we speak." He sat back in his chair as he gave a sigh and then added, "This is some pretty compelling stuff, buddy. You're going to need the White House on this one. What we need to know is where or what were we over when IGS was activated. Oh, by the way, whatever we are looking for prematurely activated IGS, we didn't." Armone paused for a second to let that one register and then continued, "We need all the technology you can muster on this one—pull strings at the Pentagon, State Department, whatever you have to do, but we need some answers, and we need them fast."

Roger found himself still transfixed by the visual as his friend continued. "Anyway, for right now, Simone is going to work on a way to communicate in real-time—this three- or four-hour time lag in two-way conversation doesn't help at all." Once again, Dr. Armone leaned closer in to the screen and added, "I don't need to tell you this is big, Roger. Keep a lid on it! Last thing we need is a media blitz or some moron proclaiming Armageddon. Well, I gotta go for now. Don't let me down." Then smiling, he added, "I know I can count on you. *Magellan* out."

Roger Hand was stunned momentarily by what he had just heard. Then, gathering his wits about him, he copied all the material onto a handheld device and cleaned the system in the hot seats so that no one would ever be able to read any of the data that he had received. Unfortunately, Roger had never noticed the peculiar, albeit unsuspicious-looking, flat piece of metal that was hanging on the side of the vid monitor.

—

Jessica Vandale was still sitting underneath the mural as she played back the message on her phone. She was so glad to have had the additional memory chip installed in her unit; this would have been a cruel twist of fate moment to run out of recording time.

"What're you grinning about, young lady?" Ralph asked as he handed her a fresh cup of coffee.

Not wanting to let the cat out of the bag, Jess simply looked up at Ralph, smiled that knockout smile of hers, and said, "I'm going to give him another chance."

"S'cuse me?"

"Roger, ah, Dr. Hand. I think I'll give him another chance."

"OK. Look, I know you too well, girl. What are you up to?"

Jessica gave the famous faraway look in her eyes as she practically whispered, "I think I like him, Ralph."

Ralph's face was pointed down toward his cup of coffee, but his eyes were raised attentively toward the face of the anchorwoman as he simply said, "Uh-huh."

"Seriously! He's mature; he doesn't take any bull from anyone—"

"Including you," Ralph interjected.

Jessica ignored the comment and continued, "He's smart. He's a straight-shooter; you know right where you stand with him."

"OK," he said, with a long emphasis on the K part. "So what are you *really* up to, Ms. Vandale?"

"Ralph, come on! I've never met anyone like him." Then she got that wistful look again. "I need to apologize to the man."

Ralph slowly exhaled and said, "Now I know you're up to something, but hey, it's your life. Off the record, Jess, listen to me." Ralph got into her personal space so he could speak nice and softly as he looked deeply into her eyes. He looked around to make sure no one was close by as he said simply and succinctly, "Roger Hand is not someone you want to mess with."

"How so?" Jessica said a little too quickly.

"The man knows his stuff, and listen to me girl, if you're playing games, he has plenty of ways to find out."

"He's connected?"

Ralph actually chuckled as he said, "Connected? Like a neuro-chip." Ralph glanced around again then added, "Look, Jessica, the man can do anything he wants to with or without the blessings of the White House or the Pentagon." He secretly wished he had not gone that far; had he divulged too much?

"Good." Jessica just let that word hang in the air and pretended to drift off into a blissfully blank expression of fascination, hoping her friend would leave and simply forget the entire conversation. After only a few seconds, he did just that, and Jessica Vandale began to plot a course of action that would not only change her life forever but could alter the entire world's future as well.

—

Carl and Simone were just about to leave the mess hall when Jon Armone pulled Simone aside.

"Are you all right?" came the doctor's concerned inquiry.

"I'm fine; I'm just a little tired. That's all. Really."

Raising his eyebrows, questioning her sincerity, he asked, "So when was the last time you had any real downtime?"

Simone had to stop and think a moment on this one. She was truly surprised at herself when she realized it had been at least forty hours since she had had any real rest. Three hours of tossing and turning last night before the flight did not help her physical or mental capacities much at all. "It's been awhile," she finally said as she sighed. Then she added, "I'll get the com situation worked out, and then I'll get some rest."

"People make mistakes when they're tired, my young friend. Even you can't go on at this pace without any real rest. I've been watching you, Simone." Jon continued now in more of a fatherly tone, "Your edges are getting a tad bit frayed."

Simone looked inquisitively at the doctor, and he realized that she didn't understand the metaphor. He smiled at this young, beautiful scientist and said, "You're tired and it shows, girl. Tell you what, work out the theory and the algorithms, and then let Carl and I deal with the communication problem for a few hours. We can't hurt anything trying." He then looked directly, deeply into her eyes and spoke with the full-vested authority that he had. "I want you to get at least a good five hours of rest before you continue with any serious work. Do you understand me, young lady?"

Simone smiled a tired smile and said, "Yes, Doctor."

"Good! Let's get to engineering and get all the data together that we need, and then it's 'Good night, Simone.'"

Jon was about to turn to walk out the mess hall door when Simone reached out her hand and placed it gently upon his shoulder. "Jon," she said, almost in a whisper. "Thank you."

Jon smiled, took her hand in his, patted it with his other hand softly, and said, "You're quite welcome, my dear."

CHAPTER 13

NOTHING'S EVER EASY

The mission clock chimed softly at the four-hour mark of *Magellan*'s unexpected adventure. Roger Hand had just put down the secure-phone on its cradle and walked out onto the main floor of control and realized that he had made a promise—a promise he needed to keep. Smiling inwardly, he looked at his second-in-command and announced, "It's show time. You have control; let me know immediately if anything comes up." Looking at his watch, he then added, "It's time for my little press conference so you know where I'll be if you need me, and hopefully I won't be too long."

"Yes sir," came the reply, and then, "ah, Dr. Hand."

"Yes, Commander."

"Sir, how do you suppose they got all the way to Saturn?"

Roger Hand slapped the commander on the shoulder and said, "That is what we are going to find out."

Roger then quickly turned and headed out of mission control and strolled down the long hallway until he got to the pool room. For some odd reason, he was debating whether jumping into a swimming pool filled with hungry piranhas would be more desirable than entering this room filled with reporters. Nevertheless, as he approached the double doors, they were opened for him by two security officers, and Roger Hand walked into a room full of hungry sharks. "Piranhas are so much cuter," he muttered to himself as he thought of the New York Stock Exchange on a late afternoon rally. One by one, however, the voices quieted as reporters recognized the newest member in the room. As he made his way to the podium, the group of sharks orchestrated themselves into a semblance of order. Almost immediately, one could have heard a pin drop in the room as all eyes were fixed on Dr. Roger Hand. Tapping on the mic to see if it was on, Roger began.

"Good morning once again, everyone." Roger was smiling; he really was quite good at this kind of thing. "We do have good news to report. All is well with *Magellan*. Crew and ship are fine." Roger was surprised to see how quickly the applause died down and the room's attention turned to focus on every word that came from his lips.

"The IGS system performed flawlessly. In fact, it works much better than we had ever dreamed it would." He looked around to see expressions and then continued, "As you know, our goal was to be at least halfway to Mars right now. But thanks to Jon Armone, *Magellan* is quite a bit farther out than that."

"So, where are they?" came a voice from way in the back of the room.

"Magellan is currently in orbit around the planet Saturn."

Nothing but stunned silence ensued as the news people did what they seldom were best at doing; they listened.

Roger continued, "About two hours ago, we received a message from *Magellan,* and we have since replied with instructions for their ongoing, albeit somewhat varied, mission. At this point, we are awaiting their reply. You see, we are restrained by an eighty- to ninety-minute delay each way. Instantaneous communication is impossible at the moment, as we are separated by more than eight hundred million miles of interplanetary space."

Posturing himself with both hands up in the "I surrender" mode, Dr. Hand added, "I really don't have much else to give you right now, but I do have a few moments for Q and A."

—

Even with a cloak of secrecy already darkening the room, it got even darker as the live feed from Houston was cut and the screen before them went black. A heavily Middle-Eastern accent pierced through the darkness, "An interesting turn of events, my brothers; I am sure that we can see clearly the American's duplicity. As I have stated before, *Magellan* is simply an American hoax, a ploy to position nuclear weapons in space." Tapping out his Cuban cigar, the man added, "Nuclear weapons that will soon belong to us and our cause."

—

Martin hopped into his pickup and was headed back to campus when his cell rang. Looking at the ID, he saw it was the dean's number shining in luminescent blue. "Huh!" was all he grunted as he hit the answer button. "Hello?"

"Martin, this is Dean Albl. Are you anywhere near the campus, by chance?"

"Actually, Dean, I'm on my way in right now and should be there in about fifteen minutes or so."

"Good, good." Then he said, "I'd like to talk to you about some issues that have been brought to my attention. Please come straight to my office as soon as you get here."

At the same time that Martin was hearing in his head, *That's odd,* he was hearing his voice say, "Sure, no problem."

"Very good, then, see you in a little bit."

Martin was about to say good-bye as he heard the line go dead.

Doesn't anybody say good-bye anymore? he thought cynically as he drove down the highway that ran on the westernmost edge of Collinsville and headed northward toward the ISU campus. He found himself looking out to his left at the rich fertile farmland soil of the Mississippi River Valley wondering what else this day could possibly have in store for him. It was still early enough in the morning that the mist of dawn lingered, covering the lowest parts of the lowlands, and he thought to himself that he really didn't want any more surprises. This day had already proved eventful enough, but still, the dean's call had him wondering what was next.

—

Back on *Magellan,* everyone had a job to do. A massive amount of information was coming in on the great gas giant they were orbiting. More had been learned about Saturn since they arrived than in the centuries since Galileo made his first telescope. Now the eyes of the adventurers were fixed on the path that would soon take them to the backside of the planet, into the lonely darkness of the solar system. No one spoke the obvious, but all on board *Magellan* knew that as they entered the shadow of the ringed giant, they would be more alone than any human in history had ever been.

Dr. Armone, Simone, and Carl Lewis were huddled together before a giant computer LGD that hung magically in midair when they heard the voice of Mission Specialist Mike Beck announce that in seven minutes they would be entering the penumbral shadow of Saturn. He continued his announcement by adding in twenty minutes, they would be totally cut off from mankind's constant companion, the sun.

"Once we are in the umbral plane, we should be able to see stars and constellations that no human eye has ever seen," Mike said as *Magellan* swept silently, majestically past two more moons on her way to the darkest of darkness.

"You guys gotta admit this is a really cool ride!" Carl said through a rather toothy ear-to-ear Cheshire grin as he entered in a typed command to the room's Hummingbyrd. Instantly the room's right wall began to melt away into a large window, and they all watched in wistful awe as the light of their sun slowly began to wane behind the dense atmosphere of Saturn.

"A cool ride, as you say, yes it is. However, Mr. Lewis, we have work to do," Simone said as she turned her full attention to the algorithms on the LGD before her. Then she added, "I would like to have this communication dilemma worked out before we round out from this planet's shadow."

"Can I ask you something, Simone, something somewhat personal?"

"One can always ask, Mr. Lewis," Simone said with a half-crooked smile, her eyes gleaming playfully through the LGD.

"Where do you get all this from—I mean," Lewis was obviously searching for the right words. "What is it that drives you?"

"Drives me, Carl?" Simone was lost once again in American euphemisms.

Dr. Armone was watching the interplay between these two from the other side of the room where he was working on some time/space algorithms of his own when he offered, "He wants to know why you are constantly, incessantly pushing yourself so hard to discover new things, Simone."

"Oh, I see," Simone said almost embarrassed. She seemed to be weighing her response when she hesitantly said, "God has challenged me."

"God has challenged you? What, to a game of interplanetary chess or something?"

"No, seriously, I believe that the Bible is God's Word, His message to mankind, and there are things in there to be discovered. In fact, here, look."

She pulled a small leather-bound Bible from her leg pocket, leafed through some pages, and then laid the book down on the desk and showed Carl what she was looking for.

"Deuteronomy 29:29 says, 'The secret things belong to the Lord our God, but those things that are revealed belong to us and to our children forever, that we may do all the words of this Law.' That is what drives me, Carl—to find out the things of this great creation," she swept her hands to the window, encompassing the beauty that was before them, "that God is allowing me, or us, to discover. I truly believe we have a long way to go before we learn all that God will allow us to learn."

It was obvious that Carl Lewis was not a man given to much spiritual fancy.

"That's just great. The Bible. In space. Behind Saturn. Nine hundred million miles from Earth. With all due respect, Simone, I thought you were a scientist, not a fanatic."

Dr. Armone was watching his friend to see how she would react to Carl's rebuff. Once again, his young protégé proved her worth. "Carl," she said ever so softly in her heavily accented English, "one can be a scientist and a believer in the God of the Bible. There are so many scientific evidences in God's Word that proves it to be reliable."

"Like what?" now Carl seemed to be warming up to the subject or at least mildly intrigued as he sat cross-legged Indian style on top of the reactor chamber.

"Are you aware that seven centuries B.C. a man by the name of Isaiah declared the earth to be round?"

"No, but I heard that other ancient civilizations believed that," came Carl's reply.

"OK, but only the Bible has it in writing." She continued, "In one of the oldest books known to mankind, there are references to giant animals that don't even worry about rivers at flood stage. Got any ideas on that one?"

"Dinosaurs?"

"Yes, dinosaurs, Carl, those incredible prehistoric animals that weren't even known about by the scientific community until around the early 1800s, but nonetheless might be alluded to in Hebrew Scripture." Simone paused and caught herself yawning as a soft beep came from the Hummingbyrd console behind her.

"All the data's here. All we need to do is put it together so we can talk to earth," Simone said tiredly.

"No, my young friend, all Carl and I need to do is put it together; you," he looked straight into her eyes now and spoke with that fatherly authority that comes with age and wisdom, "are going to say good night and get some rest. I want you down for at least five hours. Got it?"

Simone started once again to object then simply looked at Carl and said, "We can talk biblical science later, OK?"

"Sure, Simone," came an almost interested reply. Simone turned and walked to the door, said good night, and disappeared down the corridor.

"That is one complex lady, my young friend."

"I'm beginning to think she's just plain weird."

"Aren't we all?" the doctor replied and then started working on a way to talk to earth.

CHAPTER 14

CONCEPTIONS OF THE DAY

"So what you are telling us, Dr. Hand, is that for America to once again take the lead in the world's scientific and economic circles, we have to go to the other planets?"

"What are you holding in your hand, sir?"

"What?"

"Your hand, your hand, what is in it?"

"It's a palm pad to record data and audio."

"Yes, a palm pad, and quite a neat little piece of engineering at that." Roger smiled and then said, "Would you hold it up please."

"What?"

"Hold it up for everyone to see."

The reporter looked rather incensed as he held the small unit up for everyone to see. "No real news here since most of you have had one of these for the last five years," the reporter said.

"Exactly, sir!" came the practically explosive remark from Dr. Hand as he stood before them. "Some seventy years ago, the Gemini spacecraft had that kind of technical hardware on board. Of course her systems were substantially larger than what you are holding in your hand. In fact, a system like that would have been the size of, oh several large suitcases. Then came the Apollo lunar missions and processing systems got even smaller. All of that technology continually shrank in size until we had small handheld calculators, at about one hundred dollars a pop. Then came the PC craze, and technology got more powerful, even smaller, and *cheaper*; and that, ladies and gentlemen was all because of space."

Now Roger had them eating out of his hand, he knew it, and he wasn't about to stop now.

"Six years ago, a company by the name of Pfalzford Crystal had a net worth around twenty million dollars. The company's CEO took all of their liquid assets and invested in the nanotech futures, developing a new type of steel, and now we have the Crysteel Corporation with a net worth of two hundred billion and growing daily. All of this in six years, people. And remember, *Magellan* is one of Crysteel's investments. Space, people; space! We need to go there, we need to invest in our future there, and we need to grow there. Humanity is ready for the stars."

Feeling quite proud of himself right about now, Roger saw a shadow of a man by the door, and he knew he had an appointment to keep, so he said one last bit of quirky wisdom to the news media that he borrowed and modified from an old outer space alien movie.

"People, in space, no one can steal your dreams."

Then with an all-too-polite smile, he bid good-bye and a thank you to all in the room. That's when he saw her. He noticed she was trying to remain unnoticed, yet he couldn't help but detect a hint of reticence about her. Quickly weighing his options, he decided to simply ignore her—that is, if one can indeed ignore Jessica Vandale.

—

"You're fired."

They were two simple words that Martin Sherfy had never dreamed he would hear. Indeed, how could one be fired from an academic institution when the aforementioned has tenure?

An entire board of his peers had all turned against him. He was accused by one of "reading his Bible and preaching his God to the students." Martin felt sick. He never tried to proselytize while acting as a professor of Archeology. But he also never failed to point people to the God of the Bible when the correct opportunity availed itself.

He knew in his heart that the snob of the school must have had her part in this, her dad being one of the corporate sponsors of many programs at ISU: Kathy Kulner. He remembered spending time with her last semester after the tragic death of her brother, telling her of the hope in the Jesus of the Bible that he had found.

"So, this is what it feels like, huh, Lord?" He spoke to the midday sky as he drove away from campus. "I mean, to have your friends turn against you, or at least, to leave you all alone to die." Martin Sherfy was tired of people that he loved and cared about running away from him. A hot, salty tear ran down his cheek as he pulled into the driveway of his home.

Part II: Mound Thirty-Eight

CHAPTER 15

SATURN'S LURE

Simone tried to pray as she knelt by her bunk, but she kept drifting off to sleep, only to jolt herself awake when she felt her chin dropping to her chest.

"I'm so sorry, Father," she would say and then once again, attempt to talk to the One she loved more than life itself. Finally, after several failed attempts to commune with her Lord, Simone said, "Good night, Lord Jesus," and climbed into her bed and was fast asleep. And she dreamed the dreams of childhood innocence in places far, far away.

—

"This is Jessica; I need a Lear to be ready at any moment. No, no I don't know where to yet, just—will you shut up and listen to me! I'm on to something really big. I need full clearance. Pull whatever strings you have to; just *do it!* I gotta go; I'll call back soon as I can." She quickly closed her phone as Ralph Marlow walked up to her.

"Now what are you up to, girl?" Ralph was seriously eyeing his friend, trying to square up some answers.

"Hey, Ralph," she was speaking as she was trying to walk away rather hurriedly. "I really gotta go. I'll catch up with you tomorrow."

"Yeah, sure, Jess." Ralph had a reporter's nose, one that could smell. He knew something was up with little Ms. Vandale. And he was going to find out what that was if it killed him.

—

Roger Hand stepped into one of the secure rooms at Johnson Space Center and keyed in a number he never thought he would use again. He waited rather intolerantly as the necessary protocol of security systems engaged to ensure both the one he called, as well as himself, complete privacy.

"Mr. President, I need a satellite and a tech team. It's *Magellan*, sir. She's found something here on Earth, and I need the resources to get to it before anyone else does." There was a pause as the expected question came, and then he answered, "A black hole sir."

There were another few seconds of silence on Roger's end of the phone, and then he concluded the conversation by politely saying, "Thank you, sir, I'll get right on it."

—

"This is it!" Dr Armone proclaimed triumphantly. "The missing piece; look." The doctor was showing the com officer what he had found when the intercom came to life. Using the voice recognition system for the Hummingbyrd, he opened the com channel. "Yes, this is Jon."

"Hey, Doc, you've got to see this." Matt Moore seemed almost sophomorically ecstatic in his delightful demeanor. "The whole blessed planet glows, Doc, it *glows!*"

While he and Carl had been working on communications, they had wisely chosen to close the window to space. One gets very little work done when staring at the stars, dreaming the same dreams, wondering the same wonders as our ancient ancestors did in millennia past.

"Samson."

"Chirp."

"Full view of Saturn, please."

"Chirp." Then there was the usual sliding type of sound as the tiny molecules of robotic steel changed their sub-atomic substruction, making themselves invisible.

The doctor and the communication officer stood in a dazed bewilderment as their minds attempted to explain to themselves what exactly they were seeing.

"Wow."

"That's the understatement of the hour." The professor replied, "And we're not even completely behind the planet yet." Jon did not want to get into a discussion about the fact that this glowing of Saturn was something that was new. The Cassini probe had orbited Saturn for over a decade and never saw anything like this; this was a new and possibly dangerous sign.

If Carl Lewis had his mouth open any wider, his chin would have been resting on the floor. The two men stood speechless for what seemed like an eternity as the gas giant beckoned their limitless imagination to run wild.

"As intoxicating as the song of the Sirens," Dr. Armone was wistfully saying to no one in particular.

"Say what?"

"Greek mythology, my friend; on an island in the straits between Sicily and Italy, ancient mariners were lured by the inescapable and indescribable song of the maidens attempting to attract them to their island."

"That doesn't sound so bad," Carl replied without taking his eyes off the dazzling light before them.

"On its own, no it's not. The complication was the fact of a dangerous reef system around the island that no ship could safely maneuver around."

"Must have made for many a short romance, huh?"

"Indeed," the doctor replied as he was wondering how long Carl could keep his mouth wide open without swallowing the entire universe. Then his compatriot snapped to and asked, "Is there any way *Magellan* could land?"

"Aha, Carl, there it is; the song of the Sirens, luring a man to certain death in search of untold beauty and majesty. Do you realize, only a few thousand miles closer and we would be sucked right into the planet by its massive gravitational force? We are truly living on the edge, my friend."

"Oh yeah." He looked around rather sheepishly. "I know that. So, Doc, what-dya think makes it glow like that?"

"I'm sure the fact that the planet is just one big gas ball has plenty to do with it. But the color and the patterns ..." His voice trailed off in thought as he instinctively did what all scientists do. He started to rub his chin. "Electrical impulses, plasma, magnetic fields." He wanted to add black holes but wisely chose not to. "All I can really say is that it is absolutely *beautiful!*"

"Your lady friend is gonna be really ticked-off at you for not waking her up to see this," Carl said.

Neither man took his eyes off of the majestic dark-side beauty of Saturn for any length of time; they silently stood there almost as if each were weighing his own mortality.

"What a little witch! How could you be so stupid?" Kevin Jones was practically screaming at the top of his lungs so he would be heard above the crowd of students walking up and down the stairs around him.

"All I did was tell the truth," Kathy retorted to her adversary. "He's supposed to be a teacher, not some kind of church-boy preacher. If I wanted to hear about his stupid God, I'd go to church, not college. My dad doesn't pay good money to this school so some idiot can talk fantasy."

Kathy Kulner was standing her ground. She never did like the campus prankster that was now approaching her from the top of the stairs. As she stood at the bottom platform of the stairwell, one could see the fires of hatred burning in her eyes.

Kevin Jones wasn't about to back down. He reached the bottom platform, and standing face to face with his opponent, spit out, "So, you ruin a man's life 'cause he's religious or something? If ya ask me, the wrong person committed suicide in your family."

Jones pushed past the young woman, and storming down the hallway and then out the doors, never saw the fire in her eyes turn to pain and tears.

CHAPTER 16

MORE SECRETS

Jessica Vandale was doing her best to be at the right place at the right time. Standing in the hallway, she could see past a myriad of doors all the way to the control room. What she didn't expect was the door next to her opening up and Roger Hand stepping out and looking directly into her deep green eyes.

"Do I need to get security again?"

"Roger, hey, I'm sorry. I know that you have a lot on your plate. I, I just went stupid for a moment. I really am sorry. I can leave if you want—"

"Forget it, Jessica. Just stay out of my way, all right?"

"Sure." She couldn't believe how easy that was. She stood there and watched as Roger Hand walked down the hall and disappeared back into the control room.

Roger sat down at a computer console and started to work. He had a lot to do, and he had to be very careful not to draw any attention to himself. Typing furiously (he really did envy those on board *Magellan* with their voice activated Hummingbyrds), he tapped into top-secret areas of the Pentagon's website. After going past all of the necessary clearances, he finally achieved his goal. The satellite that didn't exist—Orion 1.

Uploading all the pertinent data from the mainframe took more time than he liked, but there wasn't a whole lot he could do about that. Now all he could do was wait.

It would take the satellite a little more than an hour to reposition itself from its current position over Easter Island (don't those guys at the pentagon have anything better to look at?) and geosync over the St. Louis region. Once there, it would zero-in on the exact triangulation and start its scanning of the area. He wasn't really sure of the capabilities of the newest spy toy, but he knew it was his best bet, and it was at his disposal. Having one of the highest security clearances in the country does have its perks. Hopefully, four or five hours from now, Roger Hand would have information that no human eyes had ever seen before.

Roger was about to relax a bit when the big screen came to life once again.

"Johnson Space Center, this is *Magellan*, we are about to enter the dark side of Saturn, so I guess it's good-bye for now. All systems are optimal, and we should be comin' 'round the mountain in about four hours. So, unless our good Dr. Armone devises a new com link, you won't be hearing from us for about five and a half to six hours from now. Don't worry; we'll take plenty of pictures." Roger was watching Commander Matt Moore as he gave his recitation and wondered if the commander had any idea just how big this mission had become.

"So, for now, *Magellan* out."

Hand instantly checked his watch. *It has now been seven hours since Magellan had left her parking orbit around earth. What else could possibly happen today to top this?* he mused to himself.

Some thoughts are better left unthunk.

—

Martin Sherfy had only been at his house for a few moments. He quickly went in, got what he wanted, and then left without checking his messages. As he was headed for the door, he paused for just a few seconds at the picture of his wife and himself taken two years ago when they were on vacation in the Dells area of Wisconsin. He remembered the sunset dinner cruise, the soft music, the cool evening air of Wisconsin. Now she was gone. No good-bye, just a venomous note telling him where she wished he would go and what he could do with his God. He turned, walked out the door, and never looked back.

—

Jessica was still meandering at the less-than-secure areas of the center, wondering how she could glean more information. She was careful to never be more than a two- or three-minute walk from control at any given time should her, "expertise" be needed. This was a busy place, and many of those who purposefully walked these halls would take a mental note of the reporter as they passed her by without even acknowledging her presence. For once, she was enjoying the anonymity of the moment, factitious as it was. Small groups of armed men also roamed the halls of the famous space center always on guard against anyone with hostile intent. *If they only knew,* Jessica mused to herself. That's when her investigative senses were aroused. She heard steps coming toward her from around a corner some thirty feet away. They sounded different. Purposeful. She quickly took out her phone so she could look busy and waited. Then she saw them. Being escorted by two security personnel and three lab assistants who were toting some pretty impressive electronic gear, two men and a woman were making their way up to her, then past, without even a glance her way. Using her patent skill at following without detection, she managed to see where this small party was headed for. She almost laughed out loud when she saw their destination. The hot seats. Jessica Vandale was about to get a lot more information than she ever could have hoped for.

Turning her attention back to her phone, hitting the scramble mechanism, she dialed up her contact. "Got that Lear ready yet? Good. I might need it any moment. Keep her warm." Closing the phone, and then opening it up again to listen to the conversation in the closed room, she realized that she was wide open to observation by anyone in the area. Since she had been roaming the halls for the last hour or so, she remembered seeing a visitors' lounge not far away and headed in that direction.

It wasn't very large, but it was cozy and most important of all, empty. Jessica grabbed one of the science magazines and found a nice, quiet corner. She could glance over the magazine and look directly into the hall since the hallway wall was one large glass window. *Or is it that stupid Crysteel?* she wondered. Once she felt secure, she stealthily opened her phone, and along with the record function, formatted the audio into print on the small screen. Jessica Vandale was soon to get the scoop of a lifetime: But she had no intention of this scoop going to print. She was involved in other plans. Much *bigger* plans.

CHAPTER 17

COMMUNICATIONS

"Commander Moore, could you meet with us here in engineering please?" Armone was anxious to show his captain their new toy.

"Be there in ten minutes, Doctor," was the immediate reply. "I can't wait to try this out." Carl's voice sounded excited.

"According to the numbers, it should work."

"Well, we'll see soon enough. We should be coming out of the umbral plane in about thirty-five minutes or so. I can't get over this view, Doc. It's incredible!"

"Yes it is. You know," Armone paused and weighed his words carefully, "I don't buy into the God thing like Simone does, but I just don't believe all of this just happened either."

"I know what you mean. It's too perfect or exact."

Once again, both men found themselves quietly staring into the vastness, the austere grandeur of the Saturnian's opacity.

"You know, Carl, another name for Saturn is Kronos."

"More mythology, Doc?"

"Yep. The god who ate his own children"

"Real nice, Doc. Hope he doesn't like spaceships."

"Me too, Carl," he said, then laughing. "Me too!"

The entry hatch opened behind them then, and the commander stepped into engineering.

"So, what kind of toys have we got today, boys?"

—

Roger Hand sat at the computer terminal in mission control and was selecting a team of people to look into this enigma that was beginning to unnerve him. For just a moment, he let his mind wander (he really did know better than this, but under the circumstances …). *What if there really was a black hole right under our noses? Where did it come from, how did it get here, and why didn't it swallow the planet like those blasted physicists swore one could do? And more notable at the moment, where is it?* The computer gave a soft chime announcing that it had performed the assigned task of contacting the list of people Roger had summoned to create a quick response team.

These people knew the protocol. They would ask no questions, and they would give no explanation of their immediate departure. The one thing they could say is that they had been called to active duty. Each one of these individuals had the highest security clearances one could have in the United States of America, or in fact, the entire world.

I never thought I would be a part of a covert operation within the States, let alone organize one! Roger was thinking. He knew the QRT had to be brought to the St. Louis area, so he set up airline tickets for Mid-America Airport, just outside of Scott AFB in Illinois some twenty minutes outside of St. Louis proper, actually placing them closer to the investigation site. Then realizing just how small of an airport that was and wanting to be as discreet as possible, he redirected their tickets for St. Louis International.

The more the merrier, he thought as he realized he had done all he could until Orion 1 started spitting out the info of their dark little secret's locale—if it even existed at all.

—

Jessica Vandale began to sense the directional flow of the secret investigation that was unfolding before her, and wanting to get a head start on the event, she programmed the transmitter in the hot seat room to send all information her home PC (encoded, of course) so she could be in constant communication with the events transpiring with no direct link to her cell phone that could be detected or discovered. All that being done, she decided it was time to head to St. Louis.

"Ah good, a little bitty airport outside the city, no one will even know I'm there," she said to herself smugly as she quickly researched St. Louis-area airports, purchased her ticket online, and then closed her phone and walked out of the room and headed to the nearest exit that led out of

Johnson Space Center. It seemed that Ms. Jessica Vandale had a date with a black hole, and it would be a date she would never forget.

Once outside the center and in her car, she once again hit speed dial and was speaking to the pilot of her Lear jet. A man with a very heavy Arabic accent was on the other end.

"Yes, that's right. The St. Louis, Missouri, area. Actually, across the river to the east is where we are going, it's called Mid-America Airport. That's right. I'll be there in twenty minutes or so."

Closing her cell phone, she quickly got onto Space Center Parkway and was headed as quickly as possible to the Houston Airport.

—

"We'll be coming around from the dark side in about fifteen minutes, folks," the nav engineer announced over the com system. Then she said, "Last chance for any photo ops of this big old gas ball."

It was amazing just how much at ease the crew of *Magellan* really was. They didn't even know for sure just how they would get home yet; one thing everyone on board was certain of was the fact that they would be going home. The nonsensical idea of a five-second flight taking them more than halfway out of their planetary system only ignited their imaginations and their dreams of real space flight. No one said it specifically, and no one had to, for on board *Magellan*, the crown of human scientific engineering, her crew was already dreaming of the stars. But first, they had to get home. The one thing they knew for certain was that IGS worked and they would all go down in history as explorers, furthering the footprint of mankind's dominion.

The two EVA specialists were in the airlocks checking and re-checking all the gear just in case they needed to go outside to play. One never knew what to expect in space—or in life, for that matter.

Back in engineering, Matt Moore was completely engrossed in the explanation of *Magellan's* newest toy.

"And you guys did this without the help of our star pitcher?" Matt said.

Carl and Jon were absolutely beaming with pride acknowledging the fact that they had indeed discovered a faster-than-light communication system, at least on paper.

"Well, we don't really know if it will work." Dr. Armone let the last word hang in midair. Carl quickly chimed in, "But it looks good on paper."

"Yeah, it does at that. But, um, what grav wave are you gonna ride the signal on? Saturn's?"

"No, the sun—it is the strongest wave in the system." Then Armone paused for a moment as he remembered how *Magellan* had gotten to this world in the first place and then added, "At least, the most stable one we can lock on to."

Matt really was intrigued. "So how do you get the signal to go to earth if it's using a different focal point to draw from?"

Smiling ear to ear, Carl responded, "Ride the wave, baby."

Matt was not amused but still waited patiently as Dr. Armone picked up the baton that his young colleague had so ineloquently dropped.

"Think of a nice, still pond. Now, drop a rock right in the middle of it. From where the rock enters the water, that's the sun; now impact waves ripple out from the center in concentric rings. Tap onto a ring, jump to the next, so on, and so on. Now on any given ring, you can travel the orb of that ring as well."

"We're bending light," Carl once again chimed in.

"Wow!" Matt couldn't get enough of this new technology, and he began to ask another question when *Magellan*'s com came to life.

"Commander Moore," came the obviously tense voice of *Magellan*'s captain.

"Yeah, Tom, what's up?"

"I need you on the bridge, sir."

Matt waited for more, but the com light went off, indicating that the conversation had run its course.

"Guess I gotta go. Hey, good work, guys. Guess we'll see soon enough if it works," he said as he made his way past the reactor core and then out the door into the hallway.

CHAPTER 18

CHANGING SCENERY

Back in his pickup, Martin got on the interstate and headed north. In no time at all, he was on a state highway passing the Clarke Bridge in Alton, an absolutely stunning piece of engineering spanning the Mississippi River. Martin laughed as he remembered the old bridge that this modern piece of art had replaced. He quickly passed through the western edge of Alton, and now opening up before him was the Great River Road. *One of the best-kept secrets of mid-America,* Martin thought. This scenic four-lane highway stretched for miles, connecting the cities of Alton and Grafton. On the eastern side of the highway were ancient bluffs, some as high as eight hundred feet; on the western side was the mighty Mississippi. Martin would often reminisce seeing the old Ice Breakers that used to keep the channel clear for large traffic. How many years ago? He didn't even want to think about that. All he wanted to concern himself with at the moment was his destination, now less than twenty minutes away.

—

Jessica's brakes squealed as she pulled up to the hanger at Houston Airport. The afternoon was turning warm as she jumped out of her car and went into the hanger. One man with sunglasses on looked at her as she entered the bay, and she spoke one simple word in Arabic and proceeded calmly, purposely, past the silent sentinel. Her heart was pounding inside her breast as she neared the sleek, streamlined Lear Jet. *This is what they used to train F-15 pilots on,* she mused to herself as she walked toward the stairway from the tail of the plane. Almost sensuously, she ran her hand along the fuselage of the jet as she got closer to the door. Skipping half of the stairs as she excitedly entered the craft, she entered the ship's cabin and went immediately toward the cockpit.

Realizing that the captain was speaking to the flight tower, she tapped him on the shoulder and then gave him a thumbs-up. He returned the gesture, and then, pointing at his watch, held up five fingers. She turned and went back to the hatch and pulled the door to the craft closed. Sitting down, she prepared to remotely get into her home PC when she realized she had one very important call she needed to make. Opening up her phone, she hit one button and waited patiently.

"Ralph, hey, it's Jessica. Listen, I have an emergency that I need to take care of. I know, I know, the *Magellan* thing is still in the air, but this won't wait. No, listen this is a personal matter. Look—" She started to get angry but didn't want to give any wrong impressions and began to sob. "I can't tell you, I've just got to go, Ralph. It's, it's, um, a family thing. Take care of the office, OK? I'll call in a couple days." Just then the engines came to life. "Hey, I gotta go." She whined as sorrowful as she knew how. "I'll call." Then she ended the call, quite pleased with her performance.

The Lear began to move slowly out of the hangar. The late afternoon sun that reflected off of the wings lit the entire cabin. Coasting out to the nearest runway, the jet paused for about three or four more minutes and then came to life again. The engines whined, and the small but mighty aircraft began to lurch forward. Quickly gaining speed, the craft seemed to jump off the ground into the air for which it was made.

Closing her eyes and lifting her hands into the air, Jessica Vandale softly said to her god, "Allah, please let your servant be successful this day."

—

"So you're telling me our fuel is dying?"

"I don't know if that's how I would put it, Matt. It's, it's more like its fading—"

"Is there a difference?"

"Yeah." The pilot of *Magellan* was obviously searching for the words to convey the thought to his commander. "It's like putting a candle under a bucket—yeah that's it! The candle is still burning, but the bucket is stopping the light from shining through."

"Could IGS be causing it?"

"Maybe, I just dunno. I still have some diagnostics to run. I just wanted to give you a head's up on the situation."

"OK, keep on it and keep me posted." Then he had a thought. "Do you want our princess to come give you a hand?"

"Naw, this is preliminary stuff. I'll get all the data together then let her see it all in one lump. Sure is strange stuff though..." His voice trailed off.

"Hey, Tom, none of this is normal if you ask me. I mean, just look at where we are! Five seconds!"

"Good thing we didn't go ten!" Tom said as he spun around and began working at his console.

"Guess I better go tell Armone the news," the commander said as he once again headed back to engineering.

CHAPTER 19

UNCERTAINTIES

I can't believe I've slept seven hours straight, Simone was thinking as she looked at the mission clock by her bunk. Tapping the com, she called for Armone and waited patiently for him to answer.

"Well good morning, young lady, I trust you rested well?"

"Actually," Simone thought about what or how she wanted to say this, "I haven't felt this refreshed in a long time."

"Good! You needed to have some good old-fashioned down time. Listen, when you get ready, head straight down to engineering, OK?"

"Be there in a little bit." Simone switched off the com. She was feeling absolutely giddy, like a child without a care in the world.

—

Roger was looking over the first of the data from the top secret spy satellite. Orion 1 really was more of a piece of art than a piece of technology. The entire skin of the craft was a solar collector, gathering the sun's rays and turning it into a usable energy source. Designed to look as if it were simply a piece of rock orbiting the earth, this three-meter-wide eye in the sky was the pinnacle of scientific information gathering systems. And now Roger Hand was beginning to realize why this piece of machinery had a one hundred billion–dollar price tag.

Roger was just about to look at some of the pictures from space when the intercom on the wall of the hot seat room sparked to life.

"Dr. Hand?"

"Yes."

"Sir, we are receiving a transmission from *Magellan*. Um, sir."

"Yes?"

"It's in real time."

"Understood, I'm on my way"

Roger felt like jumping down from the platform that served as the entry way to the twenty-step stairway down to the control room floor but thought otherwise as he (pensively) realized his age. *I'm not as young as I want to be sometimes,* he mused as he did manage going down two steps at a time while holding on to both handrails.

His eyes were fixed on the big screen as he descended and he found himself smiling at his old friend on the screen. Jon Armone was already in the middle of his technical monologue explaining faster than light communications.

"So get those fellas at JPL on this right away, Roger. We need two-way in real-time. It's still no good talking to you and then waiting eighty-five or ninety minutes for an answer." Then smiling like the cat that ate the canary, he added, "I don't know 'bout you folks on earth, but we are having the time of our lives up here. Wait till you see the file on the dark side of the planet. It is incredible! We're also sending all data current on IGS Systems and a glitch we are seeing in the, um, reactor. See if you guys can spot any false imaging or redundancy errors. Hey, I would love to talk longer, but I need to go and do more exploring if you don't mind, so get back to us as soon as you can; *Magellan* out."

Roger sat and just soaked it all in. In less than fifteen hours, speed of light spaceflight had (he hoped) became a reality and for icing on the cake, faster than light com links were about to become two-way. What a day!

"Make triple backups of all data, folks; let's do this right the first time."

"Dr. Hand?"

"Yes, Lieutenant?"

"JPL has all pertinent files, sir."

"Thank you," he answered and then stood up and walked to the front of the room. Roger continued, "We've got a whole boatload of data people. Needless to say, this is all top-of-the-line security stuff. Then, almost as an afterthought, he added, "How's it feel to be part of history?"

—

Martin Sherfy had always enjoyed camping at Pierre Marquette State park along the edge of the river. Getting his campsite set up, he jumped in his truck and headed up the bluff access road to where the lookout points were. It was the time of year when the eagles would be building their nests, so he hoped to see one of the nest builders in action. Reaching the highest point of the park and pulling to a stop in the small parking lot that could accommodate perhaps twenty vehicles, Martin got out and walked the thirty yards or so to the lookout area. Breathing in the fresh, crisp March air, in deep, purposeful breaths, Martin looked out upon the vast Illinois valley beneath him. He wondered just how far he could see from this vantage point. The Illinois River was just a mile or so away and maybe a quarter mile beneath him, and even further away, in a place hidden by hills and trees, the mighty Mississippi rolled on carelessly in her stride. As beautiful as this scene was, Martin found himself continually scanning the sky, searching for the mysterious black dot that had only momentarily shown itself just hours before. Hours—it already seemed a lifetime removed. Everything now is gone. When his lovely wife Shannon left him, at least he still had his research, his work. Now even that was gone; all gone.

"Why are You doing this to me, God?"

—

The heavy Middle-Eastern accent shattered the silence of the cabin.

"We are on final approach, Miss Vandale."

"Thank you." She didn't feel like chastising the ingrate for demeaning her by calling her "Miss." Instead, she busied herself by checking and rechecking the data flow that she had been receiving from the cleverly placed "ear" she left behind in the hot seat area. *Not much on conversation,* she mused as she listened into the last twenty-minute segment of audio stream. Thankful that she now had her laptop before her, she deftly assimilated all the data (encrypted, of course) into the sleek, powerful computer and started to plot her next course of action. She was deep in thought when the Leer touched down with a subtle thump. "So this is the heartland of America," she said aloud to the cabin air as she peered out to see the small (tiny compared to what she was used to) airport complex that would serve as a temporary haven for her mode of escape. The jet taxied up to the disembarkment area, and the door automatically hissed to life, exposing the interior cabin to the outside air of Illinois. Taking a deep breath to smell the unfamiliar smells of unfamiliar territory, much like a predator, Jessica Vandale walked, no, strutted out of the jet after a few words of instruction to her pilot.

"First things first," she said aloud. "I need a car; a nice car."

—

Martin put another log on the campfire, the sparks sputtering heavenward. Above him was God's great canopy of stars stretching across the entire sky—horizon to horizon. He remembered the Bible story of Abraham, how God told him that his offspring would be as the stars of heaven, countless, innumerable. He thought of a young shepherd boy named David, and he wondered what David was thinking at night in the fields of Bethlehem staring up into the night sky. "What an awesome God!" Martin was speaking up to the heavens, "You have created all this, this beautiful canopy of lights. You made the stars, planets, moons. You made earth. You made man in Your image. Yet, forgive me, Lord, but this is how I feel; You won't help me." His job now gone and his wife long gone, carrying with her the child in her womb that was his own flesh and blood, Martin Sherfy sat Indian style on the cold, hard river bank, staring now into the fire before him. His eyes and face were soaked with tears that he had for so long denied shedding. Yet, in the back of his mind, the events of this past day were haunting him, taunting him, whispering to him in the night.

—

Roger Hand slid his key through the laser reader, and the now-secure door of the hot seat area of Johnson Space Center came to life with a loud *click.*

Walking into the room, he didn't even get a word out before the specialists, as they were called, were surrounding him with all kinds of data from Orion 1.

"We think we have found something here," the first one said. The woman of the group, affectionately dubbed "Mom," was an attractive redhead of perhaps forty-five years. Her highly polished demeanor underscored her authority in the room populated by pages and pages of data from Orion 1.

"Look at this. The coordinate triangulate is right over this Indian mound in Midwestern Illinois. That is where the event emanated from. Cahokia Mounds is what the area is called. I'm getting more info on that area now."

"So what do we know so far?" Roger asked.

"We know that the G-wave burst came from directly beneath that particular mound right *there,*" the oldest man said as he held up a picture from Orion 1 showing the entire Cahokia Mounds site and pointing to the largest mound that seemed to dominated the picture.

Now the younger man began to speak. "We started simple with thermal imaging, and then we went to magnetic and then wideband UV, infrared HD, and came up with very little until we used the proton collector core." As soon as he said that, he stopped, obviously realizing he may have said too much.

The other two specialists both looked at the man and then each other in a shared panic.

Roger knew all about those looks. "You know I've got the highest clearance possible."

"We know, sir. It's just that, well quite honestly, we're not supposed to have this technology yet," answered the woman.

"At least not up there, sir," came an expanded explanation from the young man.

This conversation's implication was not lost on Roger Hand. He asked one simple question, using one simple word as he looked at each of the people standing before him: "Nuclear?"

"Nuclear," was the simple reply.

"OK, what else?"

"Our mound has a root."

"Say again?" Roger was taken off guard by that one.

"A root; a solid core of copper just about a meter in diameter goes from inside the mound to just about one mile beneath it."

"One mile?" Roger was afraid that he had spoken a little more incredulously than he meant.

"And that's not all."

"Please." Roger made the famous sweeping motion with his hand inviting the one speaking to continue.

"Just north of the mound, an underground river breaks off from the Mississippi and flows," now the older man was speaking and using his finger as a pointer on a satellite imaging map, "all along this path straight to the mound"

"And then?"

"No, that's it. It's like it just disappears"

"It's the same with the copper core. It goes down and well, it just fades away. From the point where it starts to disappear, we can still detect the signature atoms are present two and a half inches past demarcation."

"Wait a minute," Roger said. "Orion 1 is what, a thousand miles up, and you can detect in inches? I know she's a real piece of work, but c'mon two and a half inches from a thousand miles?"

"Sir, we live in a very dangerous age. We need the kind of precise spying capability that two years ago didn't even exist. It's the nanotech age, sir. We are developing technology that even those blasted sci-fi writers haven't even thought of."

"So, just how accurate, or rather, um, let me put it this way; can we truly trust the data we are getting from our little secret rock?"

All three of the specialists looked at one another in that, "Should we tell him?" kind of way. Then it was Mom who spoke up.

"There was an incident six months ago that has never been reported to the general public, sir. It involved Orion 1 and an oil tanker licensed to a whole trail of people. It seemed that the tanker was heading to the New Orleans port area when suspicions were aroused for several reasons. Anyway, Orion 1 was positioned over the gulf area. Using some very sensitive probing methods, Orion 1 detected a hint of weapons-grade plutonium. Now, that on its own is impressive. However," she said, letting the "however" stretch out, "the plutonium was encased in a six-foot by six-foot room made with six-inch thick lead."

"Wow," was all Roger could get out.

"But that's not all. Our little plutonium blurp was nestled into a rather nasty chain reaction instigator."

"A bomb?"

"Just about seventy megatons worth of blast. I'm surprised you didn't hear of the incident, especially with the security clearance you obviously have."

Now all Roger could get out was a long, low whistle, and then, "I guess we can count on Orion 1. I'll let you guys in on a little secret, sometimes I'm busy in other areas and not necessarily in the immediate loop. Still, I have to admit I'm surprised that I missed that one" and he left it at that.

CHAPTER 20

CLOSE ENCOUNTERS OF THE JESUS KIND

Simone had not felt this good in years. Now she realized just how much she needed the downtime. In fact, she actually felt like Little Red Riding Hood skipping her way through the forest on her way to Grandma's house. She smiled at that thought and then spoke aloud.

"Little Shepherd."

"Chirp."

"Run worship program P-twenty-three please."

"Chirp."

"Full exterior view. Red, no pink letters on LGD, please."

"Chirp."

She smiled as she realized she just had said please to a piece of electronic gear.

As the walls of her room transitioned from blue to transparent, Simone said again, "Little Shepherd."

"Chirp."

"Hold worship program for two minutes and then implement, please." She stood at first a meter or so away from the windows of her room and then walked up and put her hands and then her forehead against the wall. The view was incredible. She could see a rather large crescent of Saturn before her and the ring systems stretched before and behind her.

It was at this moment Simone realized the intensely precarious situation she and her shipmates were in. The weight was beginning to drag her spirits down like a spacecraft attempting to escape a planet's gravitational pull and not having quite enough thrust to do the job. The giddiness was suddenly gone, and terror began to siege the young woman. She had held up in her own strength as long as she could, and now as she realized the mortal danger they all were in, she knew only God could help, even protect them. What if they couldn't get IGS to work again? What if Saturn's gravity started to pull them in, and as an afterthought, did *Magellan's* own engines even have the thrust to take them out of orbit, let alone get them home? Her whole body began to tremble, and tears were welling up in her dark eyes.

Suddenly the large pink letters faded into view. As Simone looked at the Scripture before her, she was slightly consoled by the fact that her left hand was on the word Lord and her right hand was on the word Shepherd. Suddenly, softly the piano sounds began to emanate around her. Crysteel's Invisisteel was indeed an ingenious use of nano/hybridized-technology. Not only was every ship's readout at her immediate disposal upon the hull around her, but even the loudspeakers were a part of the wall itself, and sound seemed to come from everywhere.

As the twenty-third Psalm was displayed on her entire wall/window, her favorite worship song had already begun. Three piano chords, then the same three chords a step down then, "My Jesus—"

Simone suddenly could stand no longer.

"My Savior."

She knelt on her knees with her face to the room's floor.

"Lord, there is none like You."

She lifted her hands high and began to sing along.

"All of my days."

Those were the only words she could utter, for she had to let go of her regal demeanor and melt into uncontrolled sobs on the floor of her room. The fearless, brilliantly talented Simone Sytte was at this moment nothing but a very frightened little girl.

"Oh God, what are we going to do?" she said with her face to the floor, her tears already forming a small pool before her.

"I am so scared, my Lord. Please help us."

At this moment, Simone was wide open before her God, with no false pretenses and certainly no pride. She just knelt, trembling and afraid for her life and the lives of those who were with her. It was at that instant, she saw it. In her mind's eye, she saw what the Bible calls Calvary, Golgotha, the place of the skull where her Savior died. It wasn't so much the visual aspect;

no, it was far more intense in nature than one can see with human eyes. It was the darkness that engulfed the scene. It wasn't so much seeing crosses as sensing that darkness. Her whole body, no, her very soul could feel the dark. The heaviness of that darkness was what Simone was engulfed in. The whole incident only lasted a mere second, but it was a second Simone would never forget, no matter how long she would live.

She cried out, "Lord, I'm so sorry!" and it was gone. She remained on the floor crying and sobbing loudly, uncontrollably. It was then that she realized a presence. —His presence—and He was right there in the room with her. Her mind and physical body sensed the presence of God but not with the usual goose pimples and tears as at a church service. No, this was different. Much different.

Simone felt as if she was completely engulfed by the presence of the Ancient of Days. If she was frightened by her predicament at Saturn, she now knelt frozen in absolute terror, for the One who was visiting her was holy. For the first time in her life, Simone understood what "Holy is the Lord" truly meant! She could almost taste His holiness. To make matters even worse, for the first time Simone realized just how dirty she was—a good Christian girl absolutely filthy and degenerate, kneeling before her Creator and Lord. If it wasn't for Calvary, she could not have survived being in His presence. Her mind was flooded with every instance in the Bible of people coming into the presence of the King. Total fear was the common denominator among the people. Someone once said that if you are ever in the presence of God and not absolutely terrified, you haven't been in the presence of the God of the Bible.

Jehovah; the Lord God Almighty.

YHWH; Jesus Christ.

—

Jessica was nestled quite nicely in the Humvee she had acquired. She was surprised to discover that an independent manufacturer still produced yearly models for a select group of clients. "Lots of space for anything I need and all the muscle I could ask for," she said aloud as she entered onto Interstate 64 heading west toward St. Louis. Three minutes down the road she saw the sign for Scott AFB and remembered an old contact she used to have in the military. She smiled again as she remembered the last time she saw him, pleading with her not to use his name on a report she was giving in a primetime spot. She then recalled reading of his suicide and felt a twinge of sadness for a second. But that was short lived.

Jessica Vandale was a real piece of work. She cared for no one, especially in America. "The day will come," she said aloud, "that you will have your way with this despicable country, my lord and my god." Tears of self-pride were streaming down her cheeks, as she continued, "Too long they have shunned you, great and mighty Allah. They will pay the price. I swear it to you, my god." Her last line of prayer to her god was through gritted teeth and was as venomous as any viper could ever be. "Ah, Illinois 157 North. Here I come, Collinsville. Let's find your dark little secret."

—

Sitting around a table at the Starbucks in St. Louis International Airport, three men were inauspiciously sipping coffee telling old, used-up jokes when a fourth man approached.

"Hey, guess they'll let anyone in these airports these days," came the rather obnoxiously chipper greeting from a debonair-looking black man who appeared to be in his mid-sixties.

"Yeah, long as we keep paying cash for everything, they don't mind us too much," came the reply.

"Have a seat, Commander."

"Just Mr. for now if you don't mind." Then he gave a shy glance around. "Are we ready to rock?"

"What, no coffee?"

"Oh, no thanks, I had plenty on the plane. In fact, you boys finish up while I go over to the men's room. When I get back, we can get to work."

"Sounds good to me," came the voice of the youngest of the men still wearing his sunglasses sitting in the farthest corner.

—

Roger Hand just finished talking to his friend at the coast guard. In less than eight hours, he was hoping to have a small two-man exploratory sub going into the underground river. No sense in leaving any rock unturned. Anyway, that was in the able hands of the US Coast Guard who, by the way, would be answering only to him in this matter. Roger wondered if all this power would go to his head. He mused at the idea of the power he was currently wielding. Yes, mused at it, for Roger Hand never took anything for granted, nor did he ever take himself too seriously. That usually got people into trouble. Speaking of which, where was Little Miss Nuclear? He realized he hadn't seen Jessica Vandale for quite some time now. He decided to take a stroll down to the pool room when his pager buzzed him. He was needed in control. So, putting Ms. Vandale out of his mind (at least for now), he headed for the control room, hoping that the folks at JPL had conquered light speed for him. As he started to descend the stairs to control, the intensity of the day started to pronounce itself to Roger, who knew the feeling of fatigue all too well, so he promised himself he would soon get some shut eye.

Standing at his computer, a young man was waving one hand in the air, motioning for Roger to head over to him. Heading over toward him, he spoke first to the man.

"Watcha got?"

"JPL, sir, they think they've got the communications ready to go."

Roger was beginning to get edgy, and he knew it. Holding back any hint of annoyance, Roger asked, "Didn't they try it out?"

"No sir, they said they thought that you should be the first to speak to *Magellan* if ..."

"If it works, son?"

"Um, yes sir, if it works." The man was embarrassed, it seemed.

"Young man," Roger said, looking the fellow in the eyes and holding his gaze, "this is new to all of us. Don't feel embarrassed about any doubts you have. Just don't ever let your doubts get in the way of your progress or your dreams." Then almost as an afterthought, he added, "Dream big and hope bigger."

The young man clearly didn't know what to say or do, so Roger simply said, "Thank you, sir. Which line is JPL?"

"Line 4, sir." Then the man quickly made an exit and headed over to another section to give Roger Hand his space.

Roger knew JPL's protocol. He should; he helped draft it. He waited for the proper tone then punched in a private code known only to him and JPL's monitoring computers. Soon he was greeted with a hearty, "Hello, Dr. Hand, it is truly an honor to speak with you. I'm Jeff Campbell. I trust that you've gotten your message?"

"Yes I have, sir, and I must say I'm quite impressed with you guys getting this done so quickly."

"Actually, it practically worked itself out. The download was incredible!"

"Yep, we're making history, all right." That bed was calling his name, and he really wasn't feeling like small talk. "So, is it gonna work?"

"Should. You guys at Houston should be good to go."

"Thank you, Dr. Campbell. Guess I've got a call to make"

"Yes sir you do. Um, sir, tell Dr. Armone that we're all pulling for him and everyone, I mean," he paused and then said, "on *Magellan.*"

It was clear to Roger Hand that the person on the other end of the phone was about as green as they come.

"I'll do that, and again, thank you." Then, almost abruptly, he said, "Good-bye."

"OK, people, are we ready to talk faster than light?"

"Let's make Ma Bell proud," came a voice from off to his left. Then, "We're ready, sir," came the young man who had returned to his spot at his console next to where Roger was standing.

"Let's do the Saturnian two-way," came a voice from up front. That one was followed by a few chuckles and claps.

Roger engaged the com mic and said boldly, *"Magellan*, this is Houston control, do you copy?" Then he waited for what seemed like a lifetime. Then finally came the voice and face of an old, old friend.

"It's about time you guys bought a color TV. Ain't it great?"

Roger was feeling about as good as he ever had right about now. *If I only had a cigar,* was the only thing he could think as he stood there smiling.

CHAPTER 21

CLOSING IN

Jessica smiled a half-crooked smile as she saw the sign for the Illinois State Police station on the road just beyond the entrance to the Holiday Inn. *Interesting neighbors,* she thought as she pulled into the Holiday Inn. "If they only knew," she said half aloud as she parked the Humvee and gathered her belongings together. Then she walked confidently to the lobby.

The hotel clerk greeted her warmly as she walked toward him.

"Good evening, ma'am, may I help you?"

"I certainly hope so. My name is Jessica Smith, and I believe you have a reservation for me."

Quickly and efficiently, the young man was entering her name on the keyboard.

"Smith, Smith, Jessica Smith, here it is; the presidential suite. We have it ready, and you can go right up. I'll get a porter to carry your bags, ma'am."

"Thank you." This was going to be a lot easier than she thought. He didn't even recognize her. It's amazing what a little hair color can do for a girl. As he was handing her the key to her suite, a younger man was walking up, and grabbing her bags from the floor, he smiled and spoke up.

"My name is Erik, and I'd be glad to show you to your room, ma'am."

"That would be excellent, Erik, lead on."

Walking to the elevator, Jessica heard the sound of man chatter behind her. Entering the elevator and then turning around to face the door, she saw four men making idle chitchat as they entered the motel lobby. Innocent enough. However, as the door silently closed on her temporary ride, she was certain she recognized one of the men. Under her breath, Jessica Vandale muttered, "There goes the neighborhood."

—

Simone had no idea how much time had elapsed when her mind began to focus once again on her surroundings. She was trying to understand what had happened to her and why, when she heard it; the soft chirp of her Hummingbyrd computer as if it were acknowledging a command. Then there was another chirp. Simone began to speak aloud to her helper.

"Little Shepherd," she said as she began to look up, "I have not given any orders for you to acknowledge."

That's when she saw it. The LGD display had been changed and now had a very different message displayed before her. The oddest thing was the fact that the message was in her native tongue.

Simone had been raised in a small village on the North shore of Lake Kwania in Central Uganda about twenty miles south of Lira. There in her village the almost-forgotten language of her people was a mix of Swahili and Luganda, but here and now, that language was staring her in the face.

"Those illegitimate sons of dogs and their cursed American humor," were the first words that she spit out of her mouth. Simone had reasoned (rather quickly and carelessly) that her compatriots were playing a joke on her. After spending time in the presence of her God, it really was amazing to see how quickly she went from "in the Spirit" to "in the flesh." She hastily readied herself for the confrontation by washing her tear-stained face and then she stormed toward her door ready for battle. As she reached for the open button, she heard a sound she could not quite make out coming from behind her—a type of scratching sound that instantly froze her in terror.

Slowly, hesitantly she began to force herself to turn to investigate this anomaly by first turning only her eyes, then her face and head, followed by her shoulders and torso. Finally her whole body had turned and was facing the wall that just moments before had been invisible but now was once more metallic blue. She couldn't move. She wanted to scream but was unable to make a sound, let alone breathe. Ten feet away from her was a hand, no body, just a hand scratching a message into the Crysteel hull of her room. Small metallic shavings wafted carelessly to the floor as the hand crafted its message. It was almost the same message that was just on LGD in her native tongue, but now, it was in everyday English and etched into the hull for all aboard *Magellan* to see. And this time, instead of being only the first line of a single verse from the Psalms, it was the entire verse;

"Be still, and know that I am God; I will be exalted among the nations. I will be exalted in all the earth!"

Chapter 22

ENIGMA'S DOORPOSTS

On the LGD screen and all over the bridge, lights were flashing and alarms were sounding. Mike Beck and Captain Williamson were both scrambling to find out what was going on. After flicking through a few screen readouts, they both saw the announcement from the control Hummingbyrd flashing before them;

Hull degradation; level two, room one.

"That's Simone's room," Williamson said as they simultaneously jumped from the console and headed down the hallway to the pole well. (There were no stairs on *Magellan*, just a series of fireman's poles to get to different levels. Much faster in a lower G environment and a lot more fun). Finally reaching Simone's room and using a command override, they unlocked and opened the door to see the Ugandan kneeling on the floor scooping up metallic shavings and letting them fall once again to the floor.

The mission specialist reached out to Simone and softly questioned if she was all right.

"I, I think so, yes, I am." She spoke as if in a dream state or even a drug-induced state of mind. Mike started to ask something else when the captain's hand grabbed his shoulder tightly enough to instantly garnish his attention away from the young, beautiful scientist. He looked up at *Magellan*'s captain and saw that his face was as pale as any notepad he had ever seen. Following his line of sight, he looked just above Simone's head and saw the message that was written into *Magellan*'s hull. Then looking back down at Simone, he saw her gently rocking, swaying back and forth saying something softly in a language he had never heard before.

"Come out here," he heard from just behind him, so he arose and followed Williamson out to the hall.

"Go get Armone. I don't want to mess with that girl without her friend. I'll keep watch and make sure she doesn't try to take out any more of the hull while you're gone."

"You think she did that?" Beck asked almost incredulously.

"Who do you think? The Boogie Man? ET? Of course she did it. She's been losing it for the past ten hours or so, and she finally snapped."

Mike couldn't believe that the Ugandan was capable of doing what he saw on her wall, but without any further contesting, he headed down the hall to engineering. For the first time since they had arrived in orbit around Saturn, Mike Beck was beginning to get more than just a little nervous.

—

"Ladies and gentlemen, it has been a long day, and your commander is going to get some shut eye. I want to know immediately if anything happens on *Magellan*. If a piece of space dust scrapes the outer hull, *I want to know*. Is that understood? I want you all to go on down shifts starting with those who were here with me in pre-launch. I need sharp minds, people. I'll be back at," he paused, looking up to the mission clock on the wall and seeing it was already twenty-three hundred hours, "o-five hundred. Any questions?"

None were voiced, so JPL's chief executive officer said something that helped to take the edge off of the situation;

"Nighty-night, folks."

Roger went up the stairs and went into the hot seat area, and after checking in with his "secret pals" headed down several exceedingly long hallways (*Could I be suffering from sleep deprivation already? I must be getting too old for this kind of stuff.*) to the living area of the center.

Getting to his room and disrobing for some downtime, Roger quickly ran through the events of the past day.

"*Magellan*.

"Saturn.

"Black hole.

"Jessica Vandale.

"Orion 1.

"Those computer geeks from Orion 1.

"Faster-than-light travel.

"The media.

"Cahokia Mounds Historic Site.

"Underground river.

"Rapid response team.

"Faster-than-light communications.

"Jessica Vandale—wait, didn't I already say that one?" Somewhere in the back recesses of Roger Hand's mind, that same tiny red flag was once again raising itself up, trying to be noticed. At the time, he paid it no attention; he simply attributed it to fatigue.

"What else? Oh yeah—

"Coast Guard.

"Submarine.

"That's pretty good for one day's work."

Roger Hand stretched himself out on the ridiculously hard bed at Johnson Space Center and quickly nodded off to a blissful sleep.

CHAPTER 23

SECRETS AND PUZZLES

A lone helicopter flew over the St. Louis skyline in the darkness. Twenty feet beneath the belly of the copter was a metal crate large enough to be a railroad car. After circling the coast guard station once waiting for instructions for the cargo drop, the helicopter finally hovered over a rather old-looking, decrepit barge parked on the Mississippi River just a few miles north of the city. Once the drop was made, the helicopter disappeared back into the darkness from which it came. As the sound of hydraulic motors began, massive steel doors slid over the hold of the simple barge. Three men were down in the hold with the package inspecting the crate for any damage.

"Looks fine on the outside."

"Yeah, I can't wait to open her up."

One man walked over to a computer console in the hold then said, "Watch out; here she comes." Then, after tapping in a command on the computer, he turned to watch the box open itself.

"Wow, now that's cool!" the first one said as the box, which wasn't even metal as it seemed, began to fold into itself and slide down to the floor, tucking itself neatly into the bottom panel.

"Yeah, just like the *Jetsons*," came the laughing voice of the second man.

"Ain't technology something!"

"Gentleman," came the voice of the computer operator, "I would feel a whole lot better if you would inspect the cargo instead of admiring the box it came in."

"All right," came a feigned disappointed response from the first man. "Let's look at this baby."

"She's a Dart 201, brand spanking new too. All the newest sensors, radar, sonar, and weaponry you would need in just about any covert op."

"James Bond would be proud." This time it was the second man speaking. "All this just to take a little ride underground, huh? Hey, what's this?" he asked, pointing to a small box on the belly of the sub about the size of a cigarette pack. "Looks like it's made of lead."

"It is," came the operator's voice.

The two men simply looked at their commander with a "Well are you gonna tell us what it's for?" look.

"It's a seed pod. There's a radioactive seed in there for tracking purposes."

"You afraid we're gonna steal your new toy, Captain?"

"After all we've done for Washington, those guys still don't trust us." The other man stood with arms folded, shaking his head.

"Knock it off. We need to track every inch of your path. It might get tricky."

"Hey, that's why we make the big bucks."

"OK, c'mon. Let's get her fired up and make sure all systems are online and get going."

Without another word, the two men opened the hatch of the small craft and went in. Almost immediately, the machine seemed to come to life.

In the outer perimeter of the hold, the other man started the remote engines on the tug to begin the short journey to their destination some fifteen or twenty miles away.

—

Jessica tipped the bus boy and laid her bags on the floor. "Nice room," she said aloud as she eyed her home away from home. Over by the bed was a copy of the *Wall Street Journal* as well as a copy of the local newspaper. She loved to read herself to sleep, so she made herself comfortable on the king-sized bed and picked up the local newspaper. There must be some indigenous trait in the human DNA that makes people of all nationalities flick a newspaper to life in both hands before them. After she performed the perfunctory ritual, Jessica's eyes were immediately drawn to the lower corner of the front page, where a small headline read, "Vandalism at Cahokia Mound Interpretive Center." As she read the single-paragraph description of what is commonly called a mess, Jessica once again found herself smiling a crooked smile, thinking to herself of her odd interest in this place. After turning two more pages, her eye caught a story about an earthquake at Woodhenge that morning. It seemed some college kids and their professor had some strange experience at sunrise. "Hmm," she said aloud, making a mental note of the professor's name. *Oddly coincidental that this earthquake happened at the very same time the* Magellan *incident happened. This is getting good,* she thought. Unfortunately, if she was putting together two plus two, those men she spotted in the lobby would be doing the exact same thing.

—

Simone was lost in worship. The Living God of the Bible had not only visited her but had left a message as well. Another song came to her mind, and she quietly sang a solemn whisper of praise to her Lord.

"Who am I, that the Lord of all the Earth would care to know my name, would care to feel my hurt—"

"Simone." She heard the voice speak, ever so gently then, "Simone," a little louder. She recognized the voice of her dear friend Jon Armone. Then, without turning to acknowledge him, she softly said in reply, "Oh, Jon, Jesus was here."

—

"Looks like we are going to have a real bona fide adventure, boys," the commander said as he tossed the newspaper on the coffee table of their suite. In his early sixties, Daniel Blackstone was the "crème de la crème" of covert investigational operations. He helped design Orion 1 and was one of those people who "doesn't exist." He had been handpicked for this job by Roger Hand and wasn't about to let anything or anybody get in the way of this operation.

"Check it out: a break-in at the museum, an earthquake, and then deer stampeding out on the interstate, causing a massive chain reaction. We need to watch ourselves on this one, boys. Smack dab in the middle of the country, these are the kind of news stories to expect, not stories about people looking for a black hole! No one needs to know we're here, and no one needs to know that we were here once we leave; understood?"

They were all gathered around a laptop now looking the situation over.

"We'll cover all the angles from here. Smithton, you go to the mounds museum and find out what you can."

"That's Cahokia Mounds Interpretive Center," came the sharp reply.

"Very good, Smithton, and all these years I thought all you knew about was Middle Eastern politics," Blackstone replied with his patent half-smile.

"Conrad, I want you to look around at the local media and see what you can find out about our stampede."

This drew a long, drawn-out "OK" from the man known as Stalker. Then he said, "What, so we want to know about some stupid deer running out on the highway?"

"Hey, says here there were, and I quote, 'as many as a hundred head of deer involved in the melee.'"

"So is that deer or deers?" another jumped in.

"I think it's oh dear. Maybe even yes dear—"

The two men having fun with the Stalker were silenced quickly enough simply with one look from their commander.

Again his infamous half-smile emerged when he finally spoke. "Are you two done yet?"

The men just looked at each other and shrugged. "Yeah, I guess."

Then he said, "How 'bout it, Smitty?"

"Oh, I'm fine, dear."

"Good enough. Look," he said, turning to Conrad, "the deer, the quake, and the vandalism, if that's what it was, are probably all tied together and somehow, it's all tied to our little *Magellan* incident. We just need to know how it all fits together."

Blackstone was pacing around the room now. "Harry, I want you here to monitor all the situations got it?"

"Got it, boss-dude."

"I want to be updated on any developments with *Magellan* or anything happening here locally that even smells funny."

"No problem, sir."

"Good. As for me, I'm going to college tomorrow to find this professor ..." His voice trailed off as he scanned the article about the quake. "Sherfy."

Commander Moore was on the bridge of *Magellan* talking with his two EVA people about checking the structural integrity of the hull in Simone's room.

"I know you two have been dying to go out and play. I guess now you get your wish."

"Yeah, what's up with our princess, commander? Most of us graduate from graffiti by the time we're twenty."

The voice of Cathy Parker echoed across the bridge, "She always did give me the creeps."

"Hold on now, Kat; Simone is tops in her field. I really don't think she's anything to worry about."

"So what about her wall?" she asked incredulously.

"I really don't know," he answered.

Now the other EVA specialist chimed in, "You both realize the hardness of Crysteel, don't you? From what I've seen, she would've needed a cutting laser to do what is on her wall." Then, almost as an afterthought, he added, "And there is only one of those on board, and we have it." He spoke as he looked over to his partner.

She looked him in the eyes and asked, "Is it where it's supposed to be?"

"Under lock and key; still only has one hour of use on its register." Then turning to Moore, he asked, "What do you think happened, Matt?"

"She claims God did it."

"Boy, that makes me feel better."

"Hey, Cathy, she could've said the devil made her do it."

"Same thing if you ask me. I'm telling ya, she's one of those religious weirdo's," she said, looking her commander square in the eyes, "and you better keep that woman away from me!"

Commander Moore knew he had a serious situation on his hands. When you're some nine hundred million miles from home, you need to be able to trust your crew. Now for all he knew, he had a possible lunatic to contend with, and he had no idea yet how the rest of the crew was reacting to the situation.

"You two need to go out and check hull viability. I really don't think there's any problem, but just to be safe."

"Sure, we'll go outside and play with our toys."

"Be careful," he sternly said.

"Yes, Mommy," came the reply from Charlie as he grinned from ear to ear.

—

After dialing the phone, Jessica was relieved to hear an answering service at the other end pick up the call. "Hello, you've reached the office of Bob Samuels, CEO of Fox World Net. Please leave a brief message."

Beep.

"Hi, Bob, it's Jess Vandale. Hey, I didn't mean to let you hang in midair, I just had a family emergency pop up. I'm not on any particular assignment, and I'm sure Ralph Marlowe can handle the *Magellan* thing, so I'm going to take a leave of absence for a couple weeks. If there's any problem, call my answering service, and I'll get back to you soon as I can." Then with as much goo and goop she could muster, she said "Thank you," sob, "so," sniffle, "much for understanding; you," sob again louder, "have always been so," sob, "good to me."

"Bye for," sob, "now."

Click. Jessica was once again smiling her famous devious smile as she hung up the telephone.

"That should do quite nicely," she said, obviously quite pleased with herself. She got ready for bed and then tapped once again into her home PC. "Orion 1. Hmmm. That's how they stopped our little surprise."

CHAPTER 24

THE MUDDY GHOST

It was going to be a four-hour wait to get through the Melvin Price Lock and Dam at Alton. It wasn't so much the river traffic at this hour causing the delay as it was preventive maintenance on the pumps and hydraulic systems for the gates. The coast guard commander wasn't too concerned with having their cover blown by cruising up to the locks without proper navigation plans. Many small companies tend to forget proper river protocol from time to time as they hurriedly get their wares to the proper port for sale. Standing up on the topside deck of the barge truly wasn't a necessity. However, it did do two things simultaneously: it made the barge captain appear genuinely anxious to proceed north (and in fact he truly was), and he had the opportunity to check out their camouflage.

One barge fully loaded with coal (although even that was a ruse) should not have multi-colored lights emanating from beneath her water line—especially an old, rusty barge like the *Muddy Ghost*. So, in the darkness of the night, the commander seized the opportunity to check for leaks of light that could betray the real cargo that the *Muddy Ghost* was carrying.

The night sky was spectacular this particular evening, and the commander loved being on this, the mightiest of rivers. He could hear the love call of an owl off of his port side followed by an answer a few seconds later from his starboard side. A very light breeze carried the scent of an Illinois spring to his nostrils, so he breathed the smell in deeply, savoring the moment.

He looked ahead on past the lock and dam. He could see the lights of Alton in the distance. He knew his destination was just beyond the small city, where the river carelessly played alongside what was known as the great river road.

Walking down the starboard side of the barge, stopping periodically at various hoists and winches and ropes should anyone be watching, the commander turned his sights to the southern sky. The aura of the St. Louis skyline was still visible, and he thought aloud of that city's claim, "The gateway to the west."

The St. Louis Arch, the world-renowned St. Louis Zoo, the Cardinals— all these lay behind. He was safe in those thoughts. What lay ahead of him was what he was worried about.

Overhead, a magnificently brilliant shooting star streaked across the night sky from east to west reflecting on the waters of the mighty Mississippi, giving a surreal edge to the moment.

Yes, it was moments like these that he loved the most, moments like these when he truly felt alive. Unfortunately, his moment was shattered when his walkie came to life.

"Hey, Cap'n."

"Here I am."

"Can you come down for a moment, please?"

"On my way."

After one last deep breath, one last look around, the commander silently headed to the tug boat and went downstairs to where the crew's bunks were located. After entering one bunkroom, he punched a code into an intercom keypad on the wall, and within seconds he had an open doorway to the inner hull of the barge where the Dart II was awash in color and purring like a kitten. With the reality of the task at hand weighing upon him, the commander made his way to the sub and the two men who were busy within her.

At one hundred million dollars, this baby could do anything but fly. In fact, the commander was thinking it was a Dart II that foiled the terrorist nuclear plot just a few months ago. Snuck right up on the tanker and quietly made a precision cut in her belly, then literally stealing their little H-bomb from right under their noses. Funniest thing was that terrorists had to call the coast guard to help them get off a sinking ship. *Isn't it funny how these people hate us, yet we're the first people they call on for help?* he mused. He often wondered how the feds got a line on that one. The blasted bomb was shielded, so no radiation could leak, yet; the authorities knew exactly where the bomb was on board the vessel. Law enforcement just hasn't been the same since that September morning in '01 when all America woke up to the reality of terrorism. *Hijacking airplanes and using them as missiles almost seems tame compared to the terrorist plots of today,* he thought to himself as he began to climb into their little toy.

CHAPTER 25

THE DAWN BEFORE THE DARKNESS

At 5:00 a.m., Bob Mengersi was awakened by his alarm. He had it set loud purposely so that he would hear it. For some reason, he just couldn't get to sleep the night before. His mind seemed to be full of thoughts—the senseless damage at the center, the earthquake thing, all the damage done to the trees, and no deer anywhere to be seen and all of this in one day. It almost seemed like a bad sci-fi story. So many of those stories had surfaced over the years explaining everything from the Bermuda triangle to ancient astronauts to lost civilizations (like Atlantis and even his beloved Mississippians) finding the secret pathway to the stars and then just vanishing off the face of the earth. He never did buy into that sort of nonsense, but as the dawn began to scrape against the darkness of the night, he couldn't help but wonder if all this around him somehow had anything to do with *Magellan*. Bob walked out of the house that sat a hundred yards away from the center to the west and went to sit on his favorite swing. Fighting against sleepiness with his usual ridiculously large coffee mug full of hot liquid caffeine, he sat in the stillness, the quiet of the dawn, gazing at the large earthen mound before him to the north.

"What secrets will you share today, my friend?" Bob said aloud as he cupped both hands onto and around his favorite mug, breathing deeply the coffee aroma as the steam arose and then disappeared into the morning air as a phantom whisked away in the night. This was a question he had asked many times to no one in particular, for only the mounds and the trees and deer had ever heard him ask.

He looked up to the sky. Now only the brightest stars were still visible in the waning, weakening grip of darkness. Shaking his head, he simply said in disbelief, "Saturn."

The birds were now beginning to herald the approaching sunrise, and Bob was fully awake now. His body, mind, and spirit were ready for the challenges of the day. It seemed to him that it was going to be a beautiful day; the birdsong, the clear sky, and the crisp morning air all seemed to indicate that fact. This was a man who loved life and its challenges but had no time for anything other than searching for answers—answers that were buried deep in time, buried deep in the ground almost right under his very nose. He was a man with few friends, lonely and too proud to admit it to anyone. Bob Mengersi was also a man with a dark, empty soul who loved and worshiped only his work. His was a soul so empty and vast that a thousand stars could never warm or light it. He was like countless millions of people who were searching for the wrong things in life.

He was a man who would spend his life alone on earth, alone in eternity and would have no hope, no hope at all.

—

Jessica was busy downloading all the information from her little spy. She had a very busy day ahead of her, and she wanted to make every moment count. She had to pave the way for those who would be coming to secure the "black pearl," as she had dubbed it. She had to act and act fast. She knew she had two main paths open to her. One would be to openly defy American law and forever stay on the side of Islamic Fundamentalism. Money wasn't a problem, so this option did have its romantic appeal. Option two would be to continue under cover in the shadows of terrorism. This was also an appealing flavor to her adventurous appetite, but for now, she simply needed to get information. And that was something she was very, very good at.

She pulled her trusty nine millimeter out of her travel bag, popped out the clip to check and make sure it was fully loaded, and then slipped the clip back into the handle of the semi-automatic weapon. Something in the back of her mind was telling her to call Roger Hand, but she refused the impulse and arose from the sofa. She stuck the loaded weapon in her pants below her back as she had been meticulously trained and headed for the doorway. Looking at her watch, she saw it was a full two hours before the museum at the mounds site would open, so she decided to look for a nice, out-of-the-way restaurant where she could have a leisurely breakfast and not worry about being spotted.

She went out into the thickly carpeted hallway and headed down the elevators. As she punched the down button, the doors immediately opened, and Daniel Blackstone stepped out and around her with a curious, "Excuse me." Jess felt as if her heart was in her throat choking her but feigned as if she were ignoring the man and stepped briskly onto the elevator. The elevator made two stops on the way down to the lobby, so Jessica was not alone on the elevator very long. One couple had gotten on, and ignoring the young woman, were busy groping one another. Jess started to say, "Get a room" and then realized they probably had one since they were, after all, in a hotel in the first place. Then the woman spoke to her.

"I'm sorry, we just got married two days ago and ..." She let her voice trail off in that *you know what I mean* unspoken body language. The man (or was he just a kid?) pulled the woman back to himself and was once again Velcroed to her.

On another floor, the doors opened up, and an elderly couple got on board the "Love Boat." Jessica had just about had enough when the doors opened again, this time to the lobby. She walked purposefully over to the counter and was greeted by the day clerk.

"Good morning, ma'am."

"Good morning," she said with a smile. "I've got to kill a couple hours, and I'm looking for a nice, quiet little restaurant for breakfast. Any suggestions?"

"Oh, yes, ma'am, lots of 'em. Right up the road is hamburger row with the usual compliment of fast food places, but ..." He was teasing her, and she knew it. Actually, she was enjoying the fact that this young man almost seemed to be flirting with her.

"I can tell you're not the run-of-the-mill visitor we get."

Jessica was smiling that incredible smile.

"There is a nice little place up in Maryville called Ruby's Apple. I can give you directions. It really is quite easy to find and probably not ten minutes from here."

"Sounds good to me," Jess replied. "Food's good?"

"Great food and fairly cheap too."

The clerk was busy drawing a map while Jessica was eyeing the headline on the paper lying on the table next to her.

"Magellan Safely In Orbit Around Saturn."

If they only knew the half of it, Jessica thought wryly to herself.

"Here you go. I hope you have a nice, relaxing breakfast, ma'am."

"Oh, I will, thank you," she said, and taking the hand-drawn map, she walked as femininely as she could out the lobby door.

—

"The sub's in place, Commander."

"It's Daniel, please, Smitty. Get used to it, OK?"

"Sorry."

"It's all right. Hard to break protocol; believe me, I know."

"The sub's in place, Daniel."

"Very good. Almost sounded authentic too." He was smiling, holding a fresh cup of coffee. Then, walking over to Harry, he said, "Enter this code. It's an uplink access code to Orion 1. We need to monitor the sub from here and see what we can learn. She's got a seed planted on her belly, so she won't be hard to track."

Harry Armsted was the one person in the group who just seemed to not fit in. He and Daniel had worked together on previous assignments, but he was a stranger to the other two men.

"Code entered." Then almost instantaneously, he said, "Locked into Orion 1 link."

"Good, we should be able to communicate with the sub as well as track it." Blackstone was quite pleased with the Orion 1 project. He designed it, built it, and even named it. Opening his cell phone, he dialed up a number. Then he said, "Good morning, Roger; ya up yet?"

Daniel walked into another room of the suite (*Why didn't we get the presidential suite?* he wondered.) and continued his conversation with Roger Hand in private, only a few minutes later to return to "his boys" with the latest scoop.

"We might be having a problem on board *Magellan*," he began and then told of the hull graffiti in the Ugandan's room.

"It surprises me that highly intelligent people always snap under pressure," came the unbidden response from Stalker Conrad.

"With all that's gone on in the past twenty-four hours, I suggest we don't go jumping to conclusions too quickly. Simone's a pro. She's smart and a very controlled person." That came from a faceless man hidden behind a computer screen.

"And what do you know about Little Miss Uganda?" came the obvious question from Smitty, who was sitting in the corner on a sofa trying to bond with a rather large cheese Danish.

A face appeared from behind a computer screen and said, "I spent a year with her at MIT. She's really quite stable, which is a good thing considering she holds black belts in several of the martial arts."

Daniel was eyeing the conversation with only a scant trace of interest, since he already knew the whole story. Smitty continued, "So just how well are you acquainted with our Miss Brainiac? I mean, just a few classes together or ..." He let his hands continue the sentence in a *I want to know* kind of gesture.

"If you feel you need to know, Smitty," he said, stealing a glimpse at Daniel, who simply raised his eyebrows noncommittally, "we were engaged."

CHAPTER 26

DISCOVERY

All eyes were on Simone as she sat at a table drinking a cup of hot spiced tea, both elbows on the table, both hands cradling the cup, allowing the steam to rise before her. Armone sat directly across from her, not saying a word, just studying his friend. He did notice something different about her. She was quite calm now, not the somewhat semi-frazzled bunch of nerves she was before she had gotten some shut-eye. No, she seemed very much herself, possibly even more so than he had ever seen her before. She seemed to speak to everyone without lifting her eyes from her cup of tea with a peaceful intensity and a sense of focused directivity.

"You think I did that."

It was very simple and not even a question, just a matter of fact statement. Simone raised her eyes, met the steady gaze of her mentor-friend, and then smiled and spoke again

"Jon, there is a God. *And* He's here too!"

She was absolutely beaming, and Jon Armone could not figure out his friend. He had oftentimes spoken with her about her faith. He was careful now to call it faith and not religion after all the times she explained to him that she didn't have a religion so much as a relationship. She loved this God of hers so much that she would talk about Him any chance she could. Jon wondered if she had slipped out of reality somewhere and gone off the deep end.

He honestly didn't think she had, and after everything that had happened the last twenty-four hours, he almost wanted to believe that this Jesus guy really did write on (or into) her wall. After all, what did she hope to gain by such a stunt? Remembering that they were not the only people in the room, Jon asked, "What is the status of our knowledge about our little black hole anomaly?"

It was *Magellan*'s commander who spoke up now. "We have gotten all the information of the location on computer, and we've got it ready for you when you're ready."

Jon and Simone shared a glance at one another, and then Simone said, "Let's see what got us here."

—

Martin loved the early morning smell of camping on the river, but with his campfire now nothing more than cooling embers, he began to pack his gear up and load the truck. Martin had spent most of the night watching the news from around the world, and he just couldn't understand the evil that permeated men's souls. And he was tired of it. Wars, rapes, murders, thefts, you name it. For just a moment, it seemed that space exploration really was mankind's only truly decent endeavor. Now where did that thought come from? Oh yeah, *Magellan* and Cahokia Mounds. He still felt an unsettling gnaw in the pit of his stomach when he replayed the previous day's events over in his mind.

"I'm done with that," he said aloud to no one. Then, checking to make sure the campfire was completely doused, he took one final look at the river, the park, and the ancient bluffs that stood silent in the morning mist and then jumped in his truck and started back toward Collinsville.

—

The three men were standing top side of the barge looking over the situation when one of the sub's pilots spoke to the other.

"Hey, look at that. Alton is giving you the bird!"

"What're you talking 'bout now?"

"Well, look up on the bluffs. There's the painting of the infamous Piasa Bird right there." Trying to mimic a state of fear, he said, "He's watching us!"

"Will you stop it? Hey, Cap'n—"

"Yes?"

"Isn't it a little odd to you that our underground insertion is right under that stupid bird?"

"Well, now that you mention it, yeah, I guess it is."

The main pilot of the sub spoke up again.

"Maybe the little birdie is guarding the entrance to the river."

"You two have a lot more to be worried about than a painting on a cliff. C'mon, let's get some breakfast down in the galley and go over your mission one last time." The captain turned to the doorway of the tug and disappeared inside, followed by the two sub pilots.

"Do you really think we're gonna find a black hole?" one said to the other as they too were heading into the tug.

"Naw, I'm hopin' to find Santa's workshop. I'm still waiting for an electric train set he promised me when I was a kid."

"You're a moron, you know that?"

They both started laughing, and as they entered the tug, the morning sun peeked out from behind the Alton Bluffs bathing the mighty Mississippi in glorious light.

—

Roger Hand put the phone down and picked up his cup of coffee. Taking a healthy sip, he proclaimed, "Yuck! This stuff is terrible!"

Once again picking up the phone, he direct-dialed the mission control room, and speaking to the operator on duty, informed him (or her, he wasn't quite sure by the sound of the voice) that he would be there immediately after he met with a couple other mission people. He then inquired if anything else had happened besides the hull graffiti incident, and pleased with a negative response, he said good-bye. He was concerned about Simone and her little incident, but he knew the crew could handle that, so he started to reach for his coffee cup. Then he thought better of it and began to get dressed.

He had been awakened by the phone call from Daniel Blackstone telling him that a small, high-tech attack sub was in place on the Mississippi River getting ready to launch into the underground branch of the river. Giving the official go ahead to proceed, Roger was already feeling the pressure of command. *This could be dangerous,* he was telling himself, *but how else are they going to find the anomaly, as they are now calling it?*

Blackstone also gave him the plans for the day's inquiries in the Collinsville area as well as the local news rundown. It seemed that something happened in that region, and it sure smelled like it was all connected.

Fully dressed, Roger headed down the corridors that intertwined and then finally led to control and the hot seat area. Getting the green clearance signal, he stepped into his own private control room. It seemed his three Orion 1 friends were well under way for the day.

"Don't you guys ever sleep?"

They all looked up in surprise as Roger spoke; apparently they hadn't ever heard the click and hiss of a secure door opening.

"Of course we sleep. Just not last night," came the woman's voice.

"We have been getting a lot of data from Orion 1 and have been forwarding all of it to *Magellan* as well."

"Very good, anything new?"

"Not really new, just more numbers and parameters of the mounds area and the anomaly itself."

"OK, so tell me what you know about this Cahokia Mounds place."

A three-dimensional model of the mounds historical site popped up on a table in the middle of the makeshift control room, and on the wall was a picture taken from a defense satellite of the area.

Mom took the initiative and began to speak. She spoke authoritatively and succinctly. "Somewhere between one thousand and thirteen hundred AD, the Mississippian culture was at its peak. Upwards of twenty thousand people lived right in this area immediately surrounding the largest mound—"

"Mound thirty-eight," said the younger man.

"Monks Mound," said the eldest.

"The natives built the largest mound," Mom said, looking at her two cohorts over her small silver-toned glasses, "ahem, mound thirty-eight, or more affectionately known to the locals as Monks Mound, by hand carrying twenty-two million cubic feet of dirt in hand-woven baskets.

Roger never took his eyes off of the dot-laser fabricated model before him, his eyes fixed upon the phantom cast before him, his ears and mind focused entirely on Mom.

"The entire mounds culture covered about one hundred twenty-five square miles in the Illinois and Missouri area."

"In fact," she continued almost gleefully, "there are records of twenty-six mounds in the St. Louis City area that were razed as the city grew."

Then she looked at Roger to make sure he was getting all the facts, waiting for him to make eye contact before she continued.

"This city or culture center was huge, second only to Paris in its time era."

"So what happened? Where did the Cahokians—"

"Actually, Dr. Hand, they're referred to as Mississippians," the youngest interjected.

Now it was Roger's turn to be the professional and not let his annoyance show.

"OK, where did the Mississippians go?"

Mom walked over to the display model and took off her glasses. Gazing dreamily at the mound before her, she spoke in a hushed, almost reverent tone.

"No one knows for sure. Some say they migrated to South America. The Incas, the Mayan culture could have taken them in. Maybe they just went westward.

Roger interjected a question, "Are there any written records?"

"No, in fact, we don't even know what language they spoke for certain."

It was clear to Roger that Mom really liked her job. It seemed she was staring right through the mound to another place, another time.

"All we know is that somewhere between thirteen and fifteen hundred, they simply disappeared."

"Like Atlantis?" asked Dr. Hand

"Doctor, Atlantis is a fable. I prefer to stick with the truth, and the truth is, the Mississippians simply, for all practical purposes, vanished off the face of the earth."

CHAPTER 27

HEAVY DARKNESS

Someone turned on the microphone. "Rub a dub dub, two men in a tub—"

The other man grabbed the mic out of his hand.

"Give me that." He actually looked angry. "Hey, Cap'n, Dart II is leaving port."

"Affirmative," came the reply. "Remember, once you get to Alpha section, sensors only, no lights inside or out."

"Got ya, Cap'n. Don't worry; we'll take good care of your baby."

"I just want you two to be careful. This is new territory here. If our little dark anomaly really exists, you've got to be very careful when you get to close proximity."

Just then the captain of the *Muddy Ghost* felt the almost imperceptible vibration of two underwater doors opening.

"We're pullin' out. Gonna stay as deep as we can. No running lights till we need 'em—and baby's away! We're free and clear, Cap'n."

"Roger that, Dart."

"Got a sonar lock on the entry. Big bright blip on screen dead ahead." Just then there was a slight jolt as an underwater current broadsided the small craft.

"Whee, that's fun." Then, speaking to the other sub pilot, he said, "Put engines in standby. Let's see how strong the current is."

"Sure thing, boss"

The sub was being pulled toward the blip by the unseen force of water.

"One hundred yards and closing."

"Got a good clip going. I can see the entry better on screen now; it's pretty good sized. It's a wonder no one has ever seen her before. Course, we are thirty-five feet down in very muddy water."

For a few seconds, the captain onboard the tug began to get apprehensive due to a silent radio. Then he heard, "We're in! Yeehaw! This is better'n any roller coaster! Suction current clocks in at about twenty-seven knots. Plenty of room on screen." The sub's commander started to flick some overhead switches and then continued, "Let there be light. Always nice to see where you're going. This seems to be pretty smooth and still lotsa room. Let's kick in the engines and come to a full stop. I want to take some measurements."

"You got it, boss."

—

Everyone onboard *Magellan* was gathered in engineering. Using the round reactor top as a giant table, they were looking at a dot-laser mockup image of mound thirty-eight. The mound floated about three feet above the reactor, giving the crew an in the round view as it rotated slowly at eye level.

The computer generated the mound in a green matrix. The copper core that ran down from its insides was in an orange matrix, and the water from the underground river was in blue.

The blue matrix stretched out three feet to the side (actually the rear of the mound or the north end), representing the length of the underground feed all the way to Alton, where it began. As they all gazed at the image, suddenly a single white dot appeared at the Alton end of the matrix.

Commander Moore spoke up. "That's an underwater craft just entering into the river. We'll be able to watch its progress from here and," he reached over and ripped off a piece of paper from the main printer in the room, "here's the transcript of all conversion between the sub and her launch vehicle."

Other than those words by the commander, the room was virtually silent as all eyes were fixed on the image before them.

Dr. Armone was completely transfixed by the scene when suddenly Simone's hand squeezed his forearm almost to the point of pain.

He looked over at his young friend and was about to speak when he noticed the look on her face.

Not taking her eyes off the hologram, she spoke. "My Lord and my God, I can't believe what I'm seeing!"

All eyes were on Simone now. Her eyes, however, were now locked onto Jon Armone.

"Jon, don't you see it?"

Clearly at a loss, and still a little bit apprehensive as to Simone's state of mental health, Jon answered, "See what, Simone?"

"The mound, look—it faces south, the two levels are slanted slightly skyward and are always pointing sunward. Then you have the core, collecting the energy and transmitting it downward. The river, Jon, the *river!* Water for cooling."

Then sounding as if she didn't even believe herself, she added, "The whole blessed thing is a containment field."

—

Roger was pacing back and forth in the hot seat area trying to piece this new information into the present puzzle. "Well, it's nice to know all this about ancient civilizations, but uh …" Roger was searching for proper etiquette. "If you don't mind my asking, how does that help us?"

"We're just putting pieces of the puzzle together, Dr. Hand. I truly don't know how this is all connected. The bottom line is that we possibly have a black hole in the middle of our nation, we have a spacecraft halfway out of our solar system, and somehow, *somehow*, it's all connected. Whether the Mississippians played any part in this," she simply raised her hands in question, "is anybody's guess."

"Guess?" Roger was quickly becoming annoyed at the lack of answers, "Guess? Listen, I have a great deal of respect for you people. You're good at what you do, really good, but right now I want answers, not guesses. I need to know how to bring *Magellan* back safely, and I need to know the dangers of that blasted thing, and the worst part of it all is that the two top minds on the planet that could help me right now aren't even on the planet. They're on *Magellan* nine hundred million miles away. It's their rear ends that are in the worst trouble." Roger was beginning to calm down a little; it was always good to let off a little steam before a full blown stupidity eruption. He continued, taking a deep breath, and then said, "OK, so does *Magellan* have all this historical and scientific stuff?"

The oldest man answered Dr. Hand. "Yes sir. We sent it all to them about two hours ago. They also have a link-up with Orion 1, so anything new will be known immediately to them as well."

"Very good." Then a pause, Roger rubbed his weary eyes and continued.

"I really do have complete faith in you and your satellite to get info. On behalf of the president, I want to thank you for your efforts." Then, turning to leave the room, he simply said, "Keep me posted." The door hissed closed behind him, and three scientists looked at each other silently and then went back to work.

—

"Water depth is fifteen feet, temperature is seventy-two degrees. Sensors are detecting oxygen above us, meaning we can surface above water level and have a look."

The sub began to surface and then bounced on the top of the underground river like a fisherman's bobber. Both men were momentarily stunned by the sight of purple amethyst quartz as well as emerald-looking quartz reflecting and refracting the sub's flood lights. The sight was eerily beautiful. A small cavern overhung the craft. Its ceiling was a good fifteen feet high. The cavern appeared to stretch for miles ahead of them, the reflected lights causing a synthesized fog or halo around them.

"Cavern temperature is sixty-seven, and it is absolutely beautiful down here. You getting all this, Captain?"

"Roger that, Dart," came the reply. "If you guys don't mind, you need to get a move on."

"Affirmative."

The sub's main engines came to life and began to propel the craft forward at a slightly faster pace.

"At current speed, we should be nearing alpha quadrant in approximately two and a half hours."

As the second in command uttered the time prediction, the craft lurched a little as if it were being attacked by a down current. A long, low whistle came from the helmsman.

"Look at that! Water depth just went to," there was a slight pause as he doubled checked his readings, "one hundred ten feet and getting deeper."

"Better keep an eye on it."

"You got that right."

"I'm going to charge up the particle canons." Looking at his partner, he added, "Just in case."

"Yeah, good idea, just in case."

"I sure would like to know what's at the bottom of this baby. Maybe on the way out we can take a look."

"I just want to make sure that we do get out," came the helmsman's response.

—

Jessica sat eating breakfast working with her laptop. While she fed her body food, she fed her mind information about Cahokia Mounds (*Thanks to those idiots at Johnson,* she thought to herself). She sipped coffee and checked the time. *Almost nine o'clock; don't want to be the first person through the doors, but don't want to be late either.*

She pulled up information on the site interpreter, as the park ranger was called, and studied the man so she would be able to read him better as she questioned him.

The waitress brought her the check and smiled as she said, "No rush, anytime you're ready. Want more coffee?"

"No thank you," she answered with a reciprocal smile. The waitress walked away, and Jessica finished her coffee.

Might as well get started, she thought and after paying her bill, and leaving a very nice tip, she headed out the door.

—

"Water level is steady at one hundred twenty-five feet. This place is incredible!"

"Getting some nice video feed, Dart. Can you pan the camera more as you go along?"

"Roger, Cap'n"

The two men in the sub continued on their subterranean survey. They were now about halfway to their objective, and both men were beginning to get a little apprehensive about their goal. The sub commander put the mic in mute mode and then spoke to his friend. "You know, we've done some bizarre things for our country, but this one is really out in left field."

"Yeah, I know what you mean. Do you really think we're gonna find a black hole at the end of this ride? What do you think the brass at the top are really up to?"

"You got me on that one," came the reply. Both men were watching out the forward viewing windows. Up ahead they could see that their overhead canopy was slowly disappearing. Soon they would submerge again into the darkest of depths.

"You don't suppose we've got a full-blown terrorist plot going down here in the middle of the country, do ya?"

What, a nuke? Naw, not one mile down. What would that do? Those idiots aren't smart enough to do something just to prove a point. No, they want to kill people. Lots of people. I don't think we're looking for a nuke. I think we're looking for something else—"

"Well, what?"

"Just between you and me, I think we're on a UFO hunt."

A soft chime alerted them that they needed to submerge into the river once again.

"Proximity alert."

"Got it," the navigator said, and after he flipped a single toggle switch, the alarm was silenced.

"Hey, Dart, what's your reading?"

The commander started to answer and then remembered he had muted the mic. Sheepishly, he punched in the open button and then began to speak.

"Looks like we've got about ten miles to go yet. Water level is losing depth now. Looks like sixty feet. Temperature is—wow! Temp has risen to eighty-two degrees. That's wild, course we are deep underground now, and we could be tapping into some hot springs here and there, over."

"Orion 1 puts you at thirty-five hundred feet down. Any problems? I see your prox alert went off."

"No problem, we lost our beautiful overhead scenery, though. We're fully submerged again. Water level has decreased to forty-five feet. Can't see a thing now, too dark and muddy. Now I have an idea about what those Atlantic trenches must look like."

The radio was silent for a few moments as the Dart II made her way along its dark path.

"Still making good time, Captain. Water temp is up another degree. Pitch black and eighty-three degrees outside."

"Roger, Dart. In five miles, you're gonna have to turn off all lights, so you might want to do all your systems checks now."

"Roger, Captain. We'll get right on that and get back to ya when we're done."

"Ten-four, Dart."

Both men were feeling completely shut off from their world, almost like they were out in space and all alone.

"Well, might as well get busy."

"I'll start checking all the sensors," the pilot said as he spun around in his chair and started working at a small computer console.

"Thermal imaging is a go."

"Check."

"Magnetic imaging is a go."

"Check."

"Infrared and ultraviolet sensors are powered up and ready."

"Check."

"And last but not least, the old Geiger counter is on and reading a very scant trace of plutonium. Guess it's working!" he said with a smile.

"Yeah, at least the brass top side know where we are," the commander said cynically and then added, "I've got one more thing to check." He unbuckled himself from his chair and went to the rear of the cabin. Reaching up under a shelf, he pulled out a small handgun and holster.

"What's that for?" came a laughing response from his friend.

"Just in case we run into some little green men with sharp teeth." He was smiling, but you could tell he meant business. He continued, "Look, I really don't know why we're down here, but if we have to leave this vehicle, I want firepower, and every little bit helps."

His friend was laughing out loud now as he unbuttoned the light vest he was wearing, and holding one side of it open, he revealed two small cylinder grenades tucked away.

"I know what you mean, buddy," he said.

—

Roger Hand had a small control desk set up in the rear corner of control so he could oversee all the people and terminals on the floor. At least, that's what everyone was always told. Truth was, he didn't want anyone to see everything that was on his screen. Right now he was watching the Dart II and her two crewmembers advancing toward the black hole. *If that really is what's there,* he thought to himself.

"Some story this will be some day," he muttered half aloud and half to himself.

"Dr. Hand," came an anonymous voice from beyond his view screen, "*Magellan* is on screen, sir."

At that, all screens (save those that were solely for systems monitoring) switched to the incoming video feed from *Magellan*. Jon Armone and Simone Sytte were both on screen, and you could tell something was up.

"Hi, Roger," came the usual greeting from his friend. "Everything is fine here. Nothing to be concerned about for now." *What was that line about?* Roger wondered. "But we do need to talk, ahem," it almost seemed as if the good doctor was embarrassed to continue, "in private, if we may."

"I understand, Jon," Roger responded and continued,

"All these folks we've got here now are the highest level we've got. That *OK?*"

"Yeah." There was a slight pause, almost as if he were playing out different scenarios in his mind. "Yeah, that's fine. We need to talk about our little Indian mound, Roger. I'm going to let Simone explain to you what she thinks it is." Then with a sense of light-hearted banter, he added, "Hold on to your hats, folks. Here's Simone"

CHAPTER 28

LEVIATHAN

The two men were busy reading instrumentation and did not notice the water clearing until it was crystal clear. Both were not only amazed but shocked as well, and then they both jumped when the radio came to life.

"OK, Dart, lights out."

"Ah ... Roger, Captain. Hey, are you still getting video feed?"

"Negative, Dart. Too much interference for a vid feed. You sound fine, though."

"Well, you won't believe this, but our little river has changed from mud to crystal clear on us. Switching lights out now, Captain."

Neither man said a word as a faint blue light filtered through the underground channel and filled the sub with a delicate, almost fragile light.

"Captain, you won't believe this. There's light down here."

"Negative, Dart. Make sure all your exteriors and interiors are out. Copy?"

"Copy. We're running blackout here, but there's a glow filling this place."

No response.

"Hey, Captain, you there?"

Silence.

"Radio's gone. We're on our own."

Both men looked at each other in the faint neon-blue light.

The commander said, "Put on the monitor eyeglasses and check all our readings. In fact, leave 'em on for now."

"All right," came the response as the helmsman took out an odd-looking pair of sunglasses. Tapping on the side of the frames with his right hand, he said, "Water level is only twenty feet now. Temp is—holy cow, temp is ninety-three degrees."

"How far away from target are we?" came the stoically solid voice of the commander. Both men were in top form now. No joking, no pussyfooting around; they were in battle mode and ready for anything.

"'Bout a quarter mile from target, sir."

That's when they heard the first sound of metal cracking. It's the sound you would hear when a submarine is way down deep and under tremendous water pressure. Then came another metallic creaking sound, followed by a soft thump on the hull.

A sense of panic was beginning to unfold.

"Can we surface?"

"Affirmative."

"Do it."

The sub jolted upward for less than a second. They were once again above water level surface, but the compression sounds continued and escalated. That's when they saw it.

"Full stop! Reverse engines *now."*

"No response"

"Oh God! *What is that?"*

On *Magellan*, and at Johnson Space Center, a small white dot on computer screens and matrix imaging fields disappeared, just like someone turned off the light.

Roger Hand jumped up from his half-hidden console on the floor of Johnson Space Center and ran up the stairs in the back of the massive room without making a sound. He entered his ID code on the secure door and bolted into the hot seat area where the techies were busy with their screens adjusting and readjusting various dials and flicking toggle switches. No one said a word as they silently stared at blank screens. Mom was over at the Orion 1 imaging screen and somberly announced, clearly shaken and holding back tears, "We've lost 'em. They're—they're gone"

Roger had enough of hearing those two words together.

"No readout on the seed?"

"Negative, no U-two-thirty-five rad on scope anywhere."

Silence.

"Well, will somebody please tell me something!" Roger said in a hushed but angry-sounding voice that seemed to hiss through gritted teeth.

"You're gonna need to find another way in, sir," came the only reply in the small, now-silent room.

CHAPTER 29

TURNING CORNERS

"Two men gone," Simone said sadly, shaking her head and then lowering it down. "Father God, I hope they knew Jesus. Please, oh God, be with their families." Then she continued, almost as an afterthought, "If they even have any."

It was only her friend and colleague who had closed his eyes as Simone prayed. The rest of the crew was either busy with equipment or looking disdainfully at the Ugandan.

It was Commander Moore's voice that was heard next.

"We've got to go home, people. *Magellan* is a piece of this puzzle, and she's needed back at earth."

He then turned to face two crewmembers and spoke directly to them.

"Parker, Hodson, you both have been dying to go out and play again. Here's your chance for a nice, long EVA. I want every inch of *Magellan*'s outer shell checked out. I don't want to leave here and run into any surprises on the way home. Got it?"

"Got it."

"Good, get your gear and get on it."

"Carl, get Johnson on the phone and tell 'em we're coming home ASAP."

"Check," came the smart military response. Then Moore turned to the ship's captain, who was already bringing up various ship's systems on LGD.

"I want you to check every single system on board, Tom. Triple check the engines if you have to; we might be needing them."

"Are you planning on using IGS, Commander Moore?" Simone asked.

"Yes, unless you or Jon think otherwise."

He paused to watch for any negative reaction, and then seeing none, he continued, "Good. Like I said, we need to get home ASAP."

"Deborah."

"Yes, Commander."

"Plot us a course home. You're gonna need input from Jon and Simone."

"OK, I'm on it." She turned and began to go to her station but stopped in mid-stride and spoke again, somewhat as an afterthought.

"I hope there aren't any more of those power drains down the road."

"Oh yeah, I had forgotten about those," said Moore as he turned to the ship's captain.

"Have there been any more of those anomalies Captain?'

"None. They simply stopped like someone turned them off."

Simone could not contain the anxiety in her voice as she asked, "Anomalies, Commander?"

"Oh," he said slowly, choosing his words carefully. "A few hours ago, there seemed to be some kind of minute power drain from time to time. Nothing serious, we just couldn't put our finger on the cause."

"Probably radiation or magnetic field flux from our Saturnian guardian," chimed in Captain Williamson.

Simone turned to Dr. Armone and asked him if the sled was shielded from such cosmic bombardment.

"Yeah, the whole sled platform that the IGS system is nestled on is completely shielded but, uh ..." Turning to face the giant world just outside their window, Jon shrugged his shoulders and said, "But who knows what that giant ball of gas is throwing our way."

"Commander Moore, please have the EVA team look very carefully at the drive platform and send me the exterior readouts, would you please?"

"Sure, Simone."

—

Daniel Blackstone looked at his watch as he got into the rental sedan. *Nine thirty-seven and nothing is well,* he thought to himself. He pulled out his phone and dialed up Harry back at the hotel. There was not even a half ring, and the youngest one of the group said hello.

"Harry, I need you to get an Omni scan virus loaded into the college's mainframe. Not a parking monitor, I want an in-and-out copier. I think I just got the runaround, and I don't have time to play stupid little games."

"Sure thing, boss. Give me forty minutes or so and I'll be able to tell you anything you want to know."

"Good enough. Any news on *Magellan?*"

Blackstone knew how to read people well enough to sense the hesitant (worried, he wondered) pause from the young digital genius. Then Harry replied, "Last report in says they're getting ready to come home. Checking drive system viability and taking an outside look at the ship as well. Guess they don't like the neighborhood." There was a nervous chuckle in his voice.

"She'll be fine, Harry. They know what they're doing, buddy."

"I know, I know. If you don't hang up, I can't get started."

"OK, I can take a hint. I'm on my way to the mounds area. Let me know as soon as you have anything."

"Roger that one, boss."

—

Bob Mengersi was seated behind his desk looking at files when she walked in.

"You don't look like Jessica Vandale," he said as he stood and offered his hand to the dark-haired woman who had just walked into his office. It was when she offered the smile that the whole world knew he began to suspect that she indeed was who she said she was.

"I sometimes must go undercover, Mr. Mengersi."

"Bob, please."

Smile. Disarmament.

"Sure, Bob. Thank you. This really is a neat place you have here."

"Thank you, Ms. Vandale"

"No, no, Bob, not fair. It's Jessica or," she paused, smiling seductively, "Jess is fine too." This girl was in top form today.

"Oh, all right, you got me. So, what can I do for you, Jessica?"

"I've been researching ancient burial rituals worldwide and looking for any type of connection in them. That's when I stumbled upon the mounds here. Never even knew they existed, to tell you the truth."

"I'm not surprised, Jessica. Most people, even those around here, are oblivious to this place. It's actually quite an area. In nineteen sixty-nine, we were declared a national historical landmark, and in eighty-two, we became a world heritage site. I tell ya, Jessica, lots of history and mystery surround this place."

If you only knew, Jessica was thinking to herself.

"How about a private tour of the facilities?" Mengersi offered up.

"Sure." *Almost too eager there, girl,* she thought to herself. "But can we keep my identity secret? It's a lot easier to work when you're not being asked for autographs."

"Done!"

"Let's go," she said, and they were heading out of the office and into the heart of the interpretive center. She could tell this man loved his work by the way he was telling her all the details of every display. Jessica's ears were attentive, but her thoughts were on Monks Mound itself. She listened patiently and feigned great interest even though she was truly bored to death. *C'mon, man, take me to the mound!* she hoped she didn't say that aloud, realized she didn't, and smiled some more.

It was turning out to be a spectacular spring day. The temp had already climbed into the low sixties, and it wasn't even ten o'clock yet.

—

Martin was feeling almost euphoric as he made his way back toward Collinsville, once again cruising along the Great River Road. Several sailboats were on the river already, giving the scenery an almost coastal feel. One thing seemed slightly out of place, he thought to himself as he drove along. There was an older-looking tug and a single barge parked out in the traffic channel. It was nothing really odd, just something he hadn't seen before. Tugs were usually parked alongside the road, giving the appearance of coming up onto the highway. He approached Alton, and instead of using the bypass around the historic river town, he decided to go through the town's business district one last time. He remembered this city just about as far back in his memory as anything else he remembered. *This is America,* he thought to himself. Then another thought entered his mind, and he could not fathom from where it came. *And to think there are people who want to destroy towns like this, people like this, just because it's American.*

CHAPTER 30

CHASM QUALM

Roger was back on the command floor watching over his mission crew. To the right, technicians were checking and rechecking *Magellan*'s engine stats. In the middle of the room were the EVA monitors watching everything that was happening outside the ship. The two crewmembers had just left their protective shell in space and were making their way from the sleek, rounded bow of *Magellan* back toward the two twin engine canons. The view was spectacular with the colored bands of Saturn lighting up the background of the shot. The rings were visible just to the right of the screen as they arced up from nowhere, only to disappear again on the other side of the banded world.

The camera shot was now panning to the rear of *Magellan*, losing Saturn but gaining three moons in various phase stages and more of the ring. One of the moons was casting its shadow on the ring system, seemingly rippling on the bands' varying depths and widths. Roger could now see the twin-engine canons of *Magellan* as well as the drive sled that stretched across them containing the now-infamous IGS drive system.

Roger was totally mesmerized by the entire scene. No human had ever seen these sights. Even though there would be millions of prints and copies of what they were now witnessing, Roger wanted to play with his own toys and make his own copies to keep. He headed back to his desk in the rear and began to do the necessary finger dance on the keyboard when he noticed it.

Breach.

One simple word flashed almost inconspicuously up in the corner of his personal monitor.

Breach.

In less than half a second, he thought he was going to be ill; he had that heavy, nauseating feeling of apprehension.

Breach.

This could only mean one thing.

Breach.

The cat was out of the bag.

Breach.

As far as he suspected (and he suspected the worst), the whole world now knew about the mounds and the dark little secret that may, or may not, be beneath them.

Breach.

Time to go see Mom and the boys.

Breach.

Although most of the time Roger was envious of the newest computer systems onboard *Magellan*, it was times like these that Roger Hand was very, very glad not to have one of the fancy voice-operated Hummingbyrd computers. He quickly, effortlessly typed some control commands on his console and instantly the breach flag was silenced, and control of the mission floor was discretely channeled to one of the other consoles to be monitored, diagnosed, and appraised from there. Roger silently slid up the stairs once again and was coming up to the hot seat area when he saw the Orion 1 team waiting in the hallway outside the door to the room.

"Let's take a walk," Roger said to them because they all knew that going in to talk in the hot seat area wasn't feasible. Without another word, four people simply started to walk soberly down the halls of Johnson Space Center. For what seemed like an eternity, no one spoke a word. It wasn't that they could not for fear of their conversation being heard by passersby; no, it was the dread of what they were facing. Finally, Roger spoke up among them in an attempt to lighten the dismal reality. "You may not believe this, but this building is easier to get lost in than the pentagon. Hallway after hallway, room after room, soon it all seems like a bad Warhol movie."

"Sir, someone knows."

"I know, I know. Any idea who?"

Mom was speaking now, "It was a flat ear, sir. One of those blasted new nanotech designs that chameleons onto whatever it's stuck on. It's on the main computer terminal in the room; we actually found it by accident when we had to adjust the monitor's angle to see it better. Then we just followed protocol, sent you the flag, and got out of there. You're the only other person who's been in there, sir. We have no idea where it came from."

Roger already knew in his heart who had placed it there. He knew that soon the world would be given the "real story behind the *Magellan* Incident." A reporter had outsmarted him, and he hated it.

"OK, time for damage control. I'll get a team in there to remove our little ladybug," he almost smiled at his creativity in the name, "and sweep the room for any other surprises. Don't you people worry, the blame for this rests solely on my shoulders. That room should have been swept in the first place."

"What do you want us to do, Dr. Hand?"

"Mom, I want you to get back in there like nothing has happened. Don't try to spin anything for our nosey neighbors, but don't let anything else new be spilled as you learn it."

"Yes, Doctor," was the only reply.

Isn't it odd, Roger thought, *that the cost (or rather one of the costs) of command is that the one in charge always gets all the glory and has the choice to share that. But when it comes to receiving the blame, leadership is a very lonely and sometimes very cold world.*

CHAPTER 31

ME AND MY SHADOW

The EVA was progressing nicely as the two astronauts worked from the bow of *Magellan*, circling the entire ship and taking readings of the hull and exterior ship's systems with their handheld scanners. The scans were being fed directly into *Magellan*'s massive mainframe that was nestled between engineering and the bridge. All of the scans were being fed to LGD visuals as the crewmembers inside the ship watched for possible problems.

The two spacewalkers were now separating, each taking one of the engine canons for themselves.

A full two-thirds of *Magellan*'s length was dedicated to the twin-engine propulsion system with the drive sled located roughly halfway down the canon drive. As the two worked alongside the ship's canons, *Magellan* continued to glide along silently in her orbit of the ringed giant of the night sky.

Cathy Parker was on the port canon, Charlie Hodson scanning the starboard one. As they worked meticulously toward the drive sled, Cathy noticed one of the smaller moons arcing around its Saturnian orb along a path that would place it directly between the canons just a few degrees above the sled. Thinking that this would be a great photo op, she focused the vid feed on the area and waited as the brilliantly lit disc came into position. Slowly passing the port canon, then seemingly coming to rest above the drive sled, Cathy was shocked to see the magnitude of the moon decrease by half as it passed into the direct line of the IGS platform, then regaining its brilliance as it went off-axis. A creepy, unsettling feeling began to shake her psyche.

She just about jumped clear out of her suit when her com beeped.

"Hey, Cathy, your vitals are going way off the charts. You OK?" It was Jon Armone on the line.

"Jon, did you see that?" was all she could get out.

"What Cathy?"

"The moon, as it lined up with your little IGS device-it—" Cathy was trying to articulate vocally her mental picture and was coming up empty. "It faded."

"We're running the sequence now, Cathy, hold on."

"I'm going to look at IGS."

"No, Cathy, just hold on a second."

Cathy was doing all she could to obey the command, but the need to know was beginning to take its toll.

Inside *Magellan,* all eyes were on the LGD visual as the sequence was looped and repeated several times. No one said a word as they watched the small moon fade as it went past the line of fire of the IGS engine drive system, only to brighten again as it came out of direct line. Outside the ship, Charlie Hodson was keeping a close eye on his shipmate. She was roughly a hundred feet away from him, her silhouette a sharp contrast to the banded world behind her. He knew her well enough to know that at any moment, she was about to bolt straight to the IGS platform, so he spoke up.

"Hey Cath."

"Yeah, Charlie."

"I missed the spectacle, but I know we'll be able to see it when we get back inside, so, uh, don't get too gung ho on me."

"Charlie." She sounded very excitable to him, and that had him worried. "There's something up with IGS; I *know* it."

"Well, tell you what," he said as he unhooked his tether and fired up his booster pack, "let's take our time and check it out. Mark your position now, and then we can come back when we finish the complete scan and check it out together."

"Charles, Cathy, it's Simone." The heavily accented voice almost seemed out of place in their headsets. "Do me a favor—don't touch the IGS sled, front or back. Don't use any flash or lighting for video feed, and don't use your thrusters; use the ION puffs only. OK?"

155

Charlie was only about twelve feet away from Cathy, and he could see the dislike she had for Simone even in the semidarkness of space.

"Sure thing, Simone, what is it you suspect is up?"

"I think we might have a, oh how do you Americans say—a hitcher?"

For the first time in many hours, there was the sound of laughter onboard *Magellan* as Dr. Armone chimed in, "That's hitchhiker, Simone"

"Yes, that." She ignored the laughter and then said, "Just be very careful." Simone was beginning to sense an ominous dark cloud forming over their adventure.

"Roger that, Princess," Cathy spat out. Charlie had never seen his friend take such a dislike to anyone so quickly before.

She didn't give him a chance to question her as she started a slow, deliberate trek toward the sled system.

—

Smitty Smithton could melt into any crowd, any situation, and never be spotted. He was actually having a good time at the interpretive center at the mounds site, walking from display to display and gathering all the information he knew he'd never need about the culture of the mound builders.

He was standing in the open space of the entryway of the museum looking at a large fresco depicting the mounds area at the peak of their civilization. That's when he heard her. Sound and in particular voices were a hobby of Smitty's. He could remember a voice for years and place it to a time or person. He nonchalantly glanced over to see a man and woman talking as they walked from display to display. He'd already done his homework. The man was Bob Mengersi, the site manager at the park, and the woman, dark hair and all, was definitely Jessica Vandale. Under his breath, he muttered a few expletives and then turned and exited the building.

—

Ralph Marlow was going over the *Magellan* transcripts (the ones that were released for the public) from the past twelve hours when his cell rang.

"Hello."

"Hey, Ralph, ya busy?" came the greeting from Roger Hand.

"Just reading what you guys let our public see, why? You got something for me?"

"Let's go get some lunch. Where are you?"

"I'm at the studios working up a storyline for *Magellan*."

"Good; that little bistro still open next to the studio?"

Ralph started laughing "Mickey D's? Sure, you better be buying, though."

"You're on, buddy. See ya in twenty?"

"Roger, Roger."

All Ralph heard before the connection was terminated was the hearty laugh of his friend.

If Roger Hand was laughing, something was up.

This could turn out to be an interesting lunch—a very interesting lunch indeed.

CHAPTER 32

SELF-DESTRUCT

It was just after noon when Martin got to the mounds. He decided to forgo the usual pleasantries over at the center with his longtime friend, so he parked on the north side of old business forty. A small parking lot sat nestled on the eastern side of mound thirty-eight and was dappled with a few visitors' cars. Martin pulled into a parking spot facing the mound, and turning off the motor, he simply sat in his truck staring at the mound. Then, reaching under the seat, he grabbed the small package that he had nearly forgotten at his house the day before. Putting the item in his trousers in the rear waistband and certain it was covered by his old faded blue-jean jacket, he stepped out of the truck and made his way to the mound.

There was a gravel and dirt walkway that meandered from the parking lot to the southward-facing end of the mound where the large stairway to the top began. Martin went on past the stairs, left the footpath, and continued on around the mound. The prairie grass was already beginning to turn a lively green and resemble small ocean waves as the early spring breeze gently blew. He was in no hurry. Where else would he go? All his life he was mesmerized—no, enchanted—by this place and the mystery of its builders. He walked over where the original museum used to be located; only those people who remembered the old adobe-type building would be able to spot the location of where it used to sit. Martin remembered the park as it used to be, with swing sets and teeter-totters scattered around a paved parking lot that also no longer existed.

He was on the western side of the mound now, looking up the grass-covered manmade hill. He remembered the days when children and adults alike would be climbing all over the mound, not limited to manmade paths. But that was a long time ago when only a child's imagination was the limit. As he continued to walk around mound thirty-eight, he found himself remembering just how big this mound was. Covering about fourteen acres at its base and on very uneven ground, Martin found himself tiring before he was much more than halfway around. Off to his left, the cars on the interstate were passing by seemingly without a care in the world. How many lives were passing by? How many other lives were intertwined among those lives? Why did he even care? Truth was, he didn't. Just ahead of him was the blockade area, so he wandered over to it. On the other side were two digs he had been overseeing last summer. The familiar square holes were dug into the land, with a simple string marker around them. He felt a tear coming down his cheek.

"No!" He said it aloud to no one but himself. He had already decided he would not cry today. In fact, he was not going to ever cry again. Why would God make him lose everything? What great, evil sin did he commit to make the Almighty so angry with him? What did he do to become an enemy of God? Funny, that thought seemed wrong. God wasn't his enemy, and he knew it. But he sure felt like he was God's enemy. Or was God his enemy? Was there a difference? Does it matter who is whose enemy? What hope is there for a man when the God of the Bible has turned against him? Can one fight against God?

"This is stupid; I'm just wasting time." Funny, now he didn't even care if anyone was around to hear him talking to himself. That thought made him smile. He left the blockade and headed once again toward the stairs. It took a good five to six minutes to reach the bottom of the stairs from where he was. All along the way, his eyes were scanning to and fro to see if he was alone, and he could also see there was no one up on the top of the mound, so then he looked back to where he had parked and saw that his truck was now the only vehicle there.

"Good." Martin then walked to the front of the mound and began the climb up the large stairway to the top.

Once he got to the top, he walked over to the western side of the mound. He could see the city of St. Louis some eight miles away, the Gateway Arch sparkling like a jewel in the sunlight, a helicopter flying past, looking as if it were a fly about to land upon it. He looked down at the area where he was just walking through and for a moment imagined the laughter and voices of little children as they played in the park so long ago. A hundred yards to the west of the big mound was a small, gently rolling mound that he remembered rolling down with his brother and sisters when they were children. They would just lay down in the grass and let gravity do its thing. Those were good days, except for the day that his incredibly brilliant brother decided to stand in the swing and go as high as he could. As a little boy, Martin was terrified when he saw all the blood that came out of his brother when he fell and the swing smacked him in the head. It was nothing serious, his brother's head being too thick for any real damage to occur, but a terrifying ordeal for a seven-year-old to witness nonetheless. And then there were all the picnics. Martin still loved to picnic even to this day. *This day*; that simple thought brought him back to the present.

Martin found himself sitting in the grass on top of Monks Mound, mound thirty-eight he reminded himself, with nothing left to live for. The breeze was gently blowing, and the sky was the most beautiful blue he had seen in a long time. It all seemed so surreal; he was tired of all the hurt, the pain of living life, and yet he was surrounded by beauty. Everyone, everything in his life he had ever cared for was now gone, and even the God that he thought loved him had given up on him and turned a deaf ear to his cries; he was so tired of living this life. He reached behind his back and pulled out the small package he had hidden in his trousers. He didn't say anything; he didn't think anything. He simply took one last look at the panoramic view from atop Monks Mound, and then he took the old .22 caliber pistol, cocked the hammer, and put the short barrel of the gun into his mouth.

CHAPTER 33

DUCK AND HIDE

"That's about it for the center. Would you like to go on a hike?"

It's about time, Jessica thought to herself. "Sure, it's a beautiful day. Why not?" *There's that smile again.*

Opening the glass door that led to one of the hiking trails, Bob Mengersi motioned with his hand, sweeping before him, and said, "Ladies first."

Jessica stepped out of the center onto a concrete porch and then continued onto the grassy pathway that led toward the west, parallel to mound thirty-eight. In the early afternoon sun, the shadows of the huge oak trees were short on the ground, and as they passed through the shadow of a large elm, Jessica could feel the coolness of the spring air when the sunshine was momentarily blocked. She had to admit, this place was incredible. All around her were the mysterious icons of a long lost bygone era, and she felt as if she had actually stepped back in time as she walked past the twin mounds that abruptly rose some forty feet into the air. Even at an eighth-mile distance, she could tell that mound thirty-eight was enormous, easily dwarfing the twins that she was now admiring. Bob was still talking away, mainly to himself, and Jessica was lost in another world, not paying one bit of attention to anything the site manager was saying.

Bob Mengersi had noticed the look in her eyes and recognized it immediately.

"Do you want to go over to the big mound, Jessica?"

Jess was still lost in another world, but her ears did pick up her name. Snapping out of her wonderment, she said, "Hum, ah, I'm sorry, Bob, I just can't get over the intrigue of this place." *If he only knew.* "What were you saying?"

"Mound thirty-eight, would you like to go over and see our baby?"

"Yes I would. I'd like that." She was smiling again as they turned and headed back toward the center.

"We can take the truck over. Don't want to wear you out on your first day." Now he was smiling. Jessica thought he seemed to be a nice enough man, and she decided to try to play him a little easier. *Who knows, maybe he is even aware of some dark secrets, or obscure legends, of the Mississippians.* She decided to play the angle.

"Are the mounds all that there is here, or oh, I don't know, are there any legends or secrets to this place?"

Bob chuckled out loud. "I wish I had a dollar for every time I was asked that question."

"I'm sorry Bob, I just—"

"No, no, it's quite all right." He was laughing lightheartedly. "There really isn't anything here but these big, beautiful hills of dirt. I know it sounds corny, but I've got to tell you, I love this place. The only real mystery is the people themselves."

"The Mississippians?"

"Ah, you were listening!"

"No reason for them to just pack up and go away huh?"

"That's just it, Jess, we just plain don't know."

They were getting near the rear parking lot as a dark sedan was pulling into the park. Jessica's senses immediately came online as she recognized the type of vehicle that was coming toward the center. It was one of those ordinary-looking cars that always looked a little too ordinary, and her nose was smelling trouble. As the car was nearing the center, a man waved to the driver and the car slowed, then stopped, allowing the man to get in. Jessica was standing talking to Mengersi and positioning him between her and the other visitors. Then as Bob went in to get keys to one of the vehicles, Jessica stood by a small maple tree and watched carefully as the car parked and the two men remained inside of it talking. These were two of the men she had seen at the hotel, and she now knew for sure that the race was on. She couldn't let them see her. Disguised or not, she couldn't take the chance. She had to get out of there for now, and she couldn't let Mengersi suspect anything.

"Here we go." She jumped as Bob came up behind her, catching her off guard.

"Oh, Bob, you are such a sweetie." *Time for some charm.* "I just realized I need to get back to the hotel and do some com work. Gotta let the network know how I'm spending their money." She was smiling, bringing some levity into the situation. "You know I want that tour of mound thirty-eight. Can I come back this evening?"

"Sure, Jess." She could detect the masculine disappointment. "That's not a problem. Just look me up. I'll be here."

"Thank you so much, Bob. I really appreciate it. So, see you this evening?"

"You got it."

"Bye, now."

"Good-bye."

Jessica was watching a tour bus pulling up as she was excusing herself, hoping that it would park in a convenient spot, and yes, it did! The bus had stopped directly between her and the two agents. This was her chance, so she quickly made her way to the Humvee and pulled away from the center. As she left the parking lot, she saw the two men getting out of the sedan making their way to the center. She had gotten away undetected, but she wondered what kind of conversation would be going on in a few moments with Mr. Mengersi. She had no doubt that in a few hours she would find out, one way or another.

—

Roger and Ralph were sitting outside underneath a rather large, happily painted umbrella enjoying a particularly intense lunch. It was a lunch punctuated with some very direct questioning from Roger Hand.

"Look, Roger, Jessica took a sabbatical, something to do with some family problems. Hey, buddy, what's up with this kind of interest in our star reporter anyway?"

"So you haven't heard from her in, what, about twenty-four hours?"

"Not a squeak. C'mon, we go back too far for this kind of drilling. What's going on?"

Roger was tapping his fingers on the metal picnic table anxiously peering around his surroundings. Then, looking deeply into his friend's eyes, he said, "Is she on special assignment?"

"No."

"Are you sure?"

"Positive."

"Could she be on one and you not know it?"

"Highly unlikely." There was a slight nervous pause, and then he said, "But certainly not out of the realm of possibilities."

Roger could tell a bluff when he saw one. He was no rookie when it came to interrogational procedure and response, and the truth was, he saw no hint of deviant behavior from his friend.

"If you're trying to get one over on me, Ralph, I swear I'll have you locked up till the sun burns itself out."

"Fair enough. So tell me, what's going on?"

"Your little Jessica has been spying on our *Magellan* command unit."

"So? You drill me with an Uzi for what? Improper reporting procedure?" Then it dawned on him.

"Oh man, there must be a little more to our *Magellan* thing, huh?"

"A lot more." Then, carefully eyeing his surroundings once more, he leaned forward and began to speak in a much softer, less abrasive tone.

"Look, Ralph, we have been friends a long time. Truth is, we might be sitting on one of the biggest discoveries mankind has ever uncovered. Now, I can't tell you any of the details, but I have to know where Jessica would come up with one of these."

As he spoke, he tossed the flat ear across the table to his friend.

"Whoa, Jessica did this?"

"You betcha. Found it in the hot seat area on one of the monitors, and she was the only one that had been in there, so ..."

Ralph was discreetly scrutinizing the small piece of modern technology.

"I've never seen one of these, but I sure have heard of them—uh, unofficially, that is."

"We scanned it and then bypassed the sensory unit. She's only getting what we send her now."

"Hey, Roger, this would be too covert or stupid for the network to be behind."

"I was wondering 'bout that. You could all lose your jobs over this one."

"No kidding. Did you trace the signal?"

"Thought you'd never ask. Wanna do a little undercover snooping for your country?"

"What can I do?"

"This thing was feeding her home terminal so ...uh, well I don't know if you have a key to her place, but I can get you in if you want to help me out. I don't have time for this kind of stuff but—"

Without any hesitation, Ralph Marlowe spoke very distinctly, "I'm in. Tell me what I'm looking for."

It was just then Roger's cell beeped at him.

"Dr. Hand speaking. Yes, all right, I'm on my way." He slapped the phone shut and then looked into his friend's eyes. "I gotta go, Ralph. I need to know everything. I'm trusting you on this one, buddy. You might be finding out some interesting stuff. Don't share anything with anybody. Here, use this. Just stick it on the modem of her computer toward the rear where it won't be as easily noticed. As soon as it is attached, it will activate all on its own. Got it?"

"Got it."

Roger had gotten up from his lunch and was turning to leave when he heard his friend.

"Hey, Roger, one more thing."

"Yeah?"

"I was ordered to ditch her in the ocean. The brass wanted to know if she'd float."

Roger Hand laughed all the way back to his Jeep. As he got in and pulled the door closed, he realized that, with Ralph sharing his biggest secret, they both knew they could trust each other. And Roger desperately needed someone he could trust right now.

—

Stalker Conrad had contacted every newspaper and every television studio in the St. Louis area and found out no more than he had already known. Something had definitely happened in this area yesterday, but he had no better idea now what it was. He found himself driving back over to St. Louis on an invitation by the local NBC affiliate to return to the studio and look at more videotape of the massive pileup on the interstate that had just come in. He had just passed the mounds area as he was speeding his way to St. Louis when his phone rang.

"Hey, Stalker."

"Yeah."

"What'cha got?" came the voice of Daniel Blackstone.

"Nothing new. On my way back over to St. Louis to look at some videotape of the interstate mess that one of the cameramen forgot to unload yesterday. That's about it."

"OK, I want to give you a head's up on something. It seems we've got some nosey neighbors coming around."

H. C. Beckerr

"Oh?"

"Jessica Vandale is in the area, and she's playing our game. She's hiding underneath some dark hair, but Smitty is sure he saw her at the mounds a few minutes ago, so keep your eyes open, buddy."

"You got it."

Stalker had driven about two minutes further when he noticed to his right a massive dirt hill that made the mounds look like tiny, miniscule ant hills. Along the foot of the hill were pipes coming up out of the ground, and flames were spewing from some of them. This had to be one of the largest landfills he had ever seen.

Stalker laughed out loud as he spoke aloud to no one. "All this money spent at that mounds thing to see what it is, and two miles away is the answer! If we could only learn how to tap into what's underneath the trash, we'd have fuel and power till doomsday."

If he only knew how close he was to the truth.

CHAPTER 34

LET'S DIGRESS

Blackstone and Smitty were playing tourists when they spotted Bob Mengersi coming out of his office. In a nonchalant, roundabout way, they intersected his path.

"Hi," Blackstone said to the site manager as he came close by.

"Hello," came the noncommittal reply.

"This sure is some place you got here, sir."

"Thank you. Are you two gentlemen from around here?"

"Oh no, we're from the west coast. We're in St. Louie for business and heard about this place. Thought we'd check it out.

"Well then, welcome to the Midwest." A more pleasant, professional smile was now coming on the face of the director. "What kind of business are you gents in?"

"Satellite software; uplinks and downlinks, crossload transmission technology, data sharing. Probably nothing like you would need here, though."

Daniel Blackstone was good; he was really good at his profession, and Bob Mengersi was playing right into his hands.

"You may be surprised, but we've used a fair amount of satellite technology around here the last couple years. Still can't get some of the hardest questions answered, though."

"Really? Like what?"

A feigned answer if I ever heard one, Smitty was thinking to himself.

"Well, the biggest question of all is," he paused for impact, "where did the mound builders go? Satellites can't tell you that. You need a different scope of science to peer down that corridor, and we've got some of the best archaeologists in the world visiting here all the time trying to answer that very question. We even have our own local college professor who spends most of his spare time right here on site. In fact, I just saw his pickup pull in over at number thirty-eight and park not twenty minutes ago."

"You don't say." Smitty was well ahead of Daniel and knew they needed to find out what little Miss Vandale was up to, so he spoke up.

"How come we never see anything on TV 'bout this place?"

"You just need to know when to look, my friend. Lots of people are interested in this place. Unfortunately, they're always looking for some kind of space or alien connection. That's a waste of time."

"Why's that? Seems like the whole world's lookin' for ET." Smitty was offering up a chuckle as he spoke.

"There's nothing here to do with space or ET, nothing really mystical at all. But I will tell you, there's a lot of history and mystery 'round these parts."

As the men were chatting, a page came over the PA for the director.

"Gentlemen, please excuse me. If you have any more questions, I will probably be right back but," he continued with a smile, "if ET's phoning me home, it might be a long winter's night till I'm back on earth."

The two men laughed and offered up handshakes and excused themselves as well as the director turned and disappeared behind two wooden doors.

Blackstone was looking at his watch "Why hasn't Harry called?" As if on cue, his cell beeped. The two men turned and headed out of the building with Blackstone tapping his cell and speaking as the two massive entry doors closed behind them.

"Watcha got for me, Harry? OK, I'll take a look. Oh, he's with me now. We'll get back to ya."

Blackstone smartly snapped his cell shut and then spoke to Smitty. "I had Harry do an Omni scan on the campus system. Seems they didn't want to talk much about their archaeology professor."

The men got to the car and sat down. Smitty opened the glove compartment (at least it looked like a glove compartment) and activated a small crosslink receiver. Blackstone opened up his cell and keyed to the receiver and started scrolling through data.

"Seems there's a lot of personal drama going on with our elusive professor."

"Oh yeah, like what?"

"Got fired yesterday, wife left him awhile back. Says here she took everything but the house and his truck." That's when some bells went off in both men's heads. "He's here," Blackstone said as he started the ignition and headed to the other side of the highway.

"Here," he said as he tossed his cell to his partner. "Find out his license plates and truck type; hurry."

"Got it," Smitty said as they pulled across old Business 40 and headed into the other parking lot.

"That's our boy, all right," he said as he saw Martin Sherfy's truck.

The two men got out of the car, took a quick look at Martin's unlocked truck, and then stood looking at Monks Mound before them.

"It's a lot bigger than the pictures make it look."

Blackstone was just standing there silently, and then he spoke up. "This place is incredible," was all he could say as he began to make his way toward mound thirty-eight.

CHAPTER 35

CROSSROADS

Roger Hand pulled up to Johnson Space Center just as one of the tour busses was driving out of the gate. He looked up and smiled at beaming faces lost in the dream of space travel. It looked like a junior high or middle school tour. *Future astronauts; future hope,* he thought to himself. As he approached the large glass doors, he saw one of his floor technicians nervously awaiting his return. Nodding as he entered the building, he spoke to the lieutenant.

"What's up with our adventurers?"

The lieutenant seemed extremely agitated as he looked around to see if anyone was within hearing distance; then, seeing no one, he spoke in a hushed, darkened tone.

"There's been an incident, um, I mean an accident at *Magellan,* sir." He spoke as he handed the doctor a manila envelope marked, "Classified." The two men spoke very softly as they began walking rather briskly toward mission control. Roger Hand stopped in midstride as he read, "Spacewalk aborted after accidental death of astronaut Cathy Parker." Then he hastened into a double-time gait as he continued toward the control room. As he came upon the doors leading into mission control, he noticed two armed guards standing in front of the door. Noticing his ID tag marked "All Access," they silently stepped aside, one to the left and the other to the right as the two men approached them and then entered the room.

As Dr. Hand stepped into mission control, he entered a scene that he did not expect to find awaiting him. It was silent. He had been around these parts during the later years of the shuttle program and was here during the *Columbia* disaster and had seen his share of sorrow and sadness in this place. This, however, was different. There was a sense of horror, no, terror, on the floor of his beloved control room. All eyes had fixed on him and tensely waited his command.

"Run the tape," was all he said as he stood down toward the front of the control room. Some of the people turned away so they would not have to watch the sequence of events all over again. Roger sensed that more eyes were on him than on the large screen on the wall before him.

He saw first the sequence of Saturn's moon Rhea as it passed directly (how far away he could only guess—maybe thirty or forty thousand miles) behind the drive platform containing IGS. He squinted his eyes as if to see better (or understand what he was seeing) when the reflected light of Rhea was sucked away from it. It almost looked like a vapor had left the moon and was sucked into the IGS drive. It somewhat reminded him of a wind tunnel, with the smoke that is used to see the results of aircraft aerodynamics. But this was no wind tunnel; this was the vacuum of space. And it was no smoke that he saw being drawn into the engine system; it was light.

He was becoming very uneasy as he stood stoically before the screen. He heard the conversations between the ship and the spacewalkers. He heard the warnings and commands from the commander as the two spacewalkers came slowly closer, closer to the drive sled. The two astronauts' suits were aglow from the combined lighting of the sun and the ringed giant behind them. They passed the sled platform on the Saturn side of the ship. Then, as they got to the end of the aft engine canon, they were about to tether themselves to the hull. As the first astronaut made the secure click onto the tether ring, he reached out his hand to his partner. She had allowed herself to drift slightly away from the engine hull and was trying to peer into the IGS core when it began. Almost as if melting wax was floating away in water, the reflected light of her suit began to drift or stream toward the sled. The vid cam caught the incident in horrifying clarity as the face of the young woman began to distort in the face shield of her suit. She began to scream an agonizing screech as her whole person seemed to turn to a sickening, xanthous stream of light and disappear into the IGS drive chamber some sixty feet away. Her partner was trying frantically the whole time to reach her, but as his gloved hand came close to her, it began to disintegrate as well, so he had to literally jerk his hand back as if he had touched a hot object.

"Stop tape." Deafening silence had enveloped Roger as he tried to contemplate what he had just seen. The sound of a gentle, soft sobbing was coming from somewhere behind him, and it began to slowly bring him back to the moment.

"Get me *Magellan* on the line."

—

Jessica Vandale had a suite atop the Marriot on Houston's Beltway just south of the George Bush Intercontinental Airport. Ralph Marlowe had been there once before as he was assigned to escort Ms. Vandale to a formal shindig, as the Texans put it. He knew her pass code, so it was no problem getting past the security in the lobby. There was no need for questions as he simply walked up to the outward-facing Plexiglas-enclosed elevators and punched in her personal code. Within three minutes, he was in her suite. That was the easy part; now he had to think of what to look for. That's when he heard it, the soft whine and click of a modem and processor working in tandem. He went just through the doorway into her bedroom, and there it was. It was Jessica's very own workstation, plugging away with (at least now) false data from mission control. He approached carefully, noting whether or not she had a webcam mounted on the screen. He really didn't want to be caught by her snooping around in her room. If she was in this deep, it was hard telling what else she would be capable of.

The screen was alive at the moment telling him that Jessica (or at least somebody) was cross-linking over and downloading all files. He was tempted to simply unplug the blasted thing but fought the temptation and simply sat down and started to read the screen.

Ralph felt a very cold chill up and down his spine as he realized all the information on the screen was in Arabic.

"Oh, Jess, what else have you gotten yourself into?" he sighed as he gently slapped the routing tapper onto the modem.

Ralph pulled out his cell and called Roger.

"Hand here."

"Roger, hey, it's Ralph. I'm at Jessica's suite. Man, you won't believe this, but all the info is encoded in Arabic."

Roger was cursing on the other end with an endless plethora of profanity.

"I've got the routing tapper on now. No, nothing showing; wait, hold on." There was a two-second pause that seemed like an eternity to Roger. Then he heard, "Signal feed going to two places. One is Tehran and the other is … Collinsville, Illinois?" he said rather incredulously. "The Collinsville one is Jessica's personal feed. What is she doing there? Where is there anyhow?"

"Look, Ralph, I've got a situation here right now with *Magellan*. Get anything else you can and get outta there ASAP." He paused for slight half-second and then added, "Tell you what, c'mon down to control, and I'll give you a story for your own self. Got it?"

"Got it. Be there in fifteen or twenty."

Ralph never even heard the phone call end. The phone just went dead in his ears.

"Wonder what that's all about?" was all he said as he started to do a little more snooping.

CHAPTER 36

THE INTERNAL DARKNESS

Charlie Hodson was in shock when he entered the decompression chamber. He barely made it back inside *Magellan*. His entire body was soaked with sweat and trembling, his mind clouded with fear and panic. The inner chamber door opened with a surreal clang as his crewmates pulled him back into the safety of *Magellan*'s berth. Everything seemed to be in slow motion. All he could utter, almost incoherently, was, "I tried to reach her—I, I tried …" His eyes were frantically going back and forth to the all the ones surrounding him; he was looking deeply into each of the faces of *Magellan*'s crew, searching for an answer, searching for some help for his troubled soul. "He's in shock," he heard from someone, the voice sounding as if it were coming from down a long corridor. He couldn't even tell if it was male or female.

"Get him out of that suit," came another distant voice. Then came the relief of darkness. Sinking into a deep, morphine-induced delirium, he whispered one last time, "I tried—"

Commander Moore looked up and said to everyone, "We have to go." He then turned to Dr. Armone. "I don't know if we should even try IGS, Doc."

"I can run some simulations, Commander, but we're not gonna truly know unless we try."

"It's that or ten months of interplanetary travel. At least that's relatively safe. I think."

"If we can even achieve escape velocity away from this planet, Commander, you know that we will probably need to do a slingshot escape, which means another extra orbit," Captain Wilkerson said.

Commander Moore was well aware of all those details, so once again he looked at Armone.

"Get on with those simulations, Doc. Captain, let's get working on the slingshot logistics, just in case."

—

"I sure hope you're a good shot, Professor," was all Martin heard as he sat on the ground with the gun barrel in his mouth. How long had he been here? Who was talking to him anyhow? He realized that he had not been on top of the mound for more than five, maybe ten minutes trying to work up the nerve to pull the trigger, so he slowly opened his eyes and to his left saw a rather imposing, well-dressed black man standing holding a large handgun by the barrel.

"I've seen the result of people who don't know how to use guns, let alone use a little pea shooter like you got there. Never know what that tiny bullet will do. Ricochet round in your head, bounce off a metal filling in your mouth, and BAM! You're wounded for life. No sir, if you want to do it right, here. This is a government issue .40 caliber handgun. Take most of your head clean off of your shoulders. That's what ya want, isn't it, Dr. Sherfy?"

Dr. Sherfy; it had been years since anyone had called him that. He was still sitting with the gun in his mouth, and he was beginning to feel a little, oh, stupid.

"Who are you?" he mumbled through the metal barrel in his mouth.

"How 'bout putting that gun down so we can talk, sir. We're here to talk about your little incident yesterday."

Then the man put his gun back into a holster under his coat. As he did, Martin saw the glimmer of some kind of badge on the holster. The man was about five feet away and started to squat down so he could talk eye to eye with Martin. Slowly his own .22 caliber came out of his mouth, and he simply laid it on the grass before him. Now he could speak English a little better.

"Who are you?"

Taking a deep breath the letting it out in hushed rush, the black man spoke as his eyes were clearly surveying his surroundings.

"Professor Sherfy, my name is Daniel Blackstone, and this is my associate, Mr. Smithton."

Martin hadn't even noticed the other man who was on his right. As he looked over to him, he saw his .22 handgun in the man's hands. Smitty simply smiled and said, "Howdy."

Martin sat there and buried his chin into his chest. He had never felt so humiliated in his life!

"I don't know what you want, but I don't think I'm interested," was all he could say.

"Oh, I don't know about that. From what I gather, you're one of the top dogs when it comes to this mound. Your friend over at the museum said so, your academic transcripts say so, and even your former employer says so."

"You've been at the campus?"

"We've been looking for you, sir," Blackstone said as he stood, sweeping the grass from his pant legs. Then he offered his hand to Martin.

Looking up into his eyes, Martin said, "You still haven't told me who you are."

"Let's just say we have a mutual interest, sir. We're standing on it, in fact." Then Daniel Blackstone looked deeply into Martin Sherfy's eyes and said, "There's a secret under this mound, and I need—actually, sir, your country needs your help."

"That's, without a doubt, the most cliché line I have ever heard in my life. I can't believe you said that."

At that, Blackstone began to laugh and then admitted "I know; it's the best I could do and besides," he now stopped laughing and slightly raised his eyebrows, "it's true."

"Who are you guys?"

—

"All systems have been checked again. IGS seems to be nominally safe."

"Excuse me, nominally safe, Doctor?" came a rather gruff retort from Mike Beck. "That thing out there has killed one of our own crew!"

"Doctor Armone, do you have any idea what happened out there?"

Clearing his throat, the doctor replied, "Actually, no, but I think—no, I know there is an explanation, but I don't know what it could be."

Now it was Simone's turn. Since the visitation in her room, she had noticed a severe shift in the crew's attitude toward her. No one except Jon Armone would seek her out to be with. Well, maybe Matt Moore as well.

He had seemed to show some interest in her faith. Maybe that was just professional courtesy …

"I might have an answer. It seems a little outlandish even to me, but as I said, maybe we have a hitchhiker," she spit the phrase out slowly so she'd get it right this time.

"When IGS engaged, maybe it took a piece of the black hole, or should I say its properties, with it. Maybe IGS opened the door for the grav properties to split like an amoeba. That could explain what has happened."

"Great, that's what we need, our own little black hole."

"Now wait a minute, Deb, she might have something here."

Commander Moore continued weighing in on the dialog. "Would it be safe?"

"I truly don't know right now, but in all honesty, it may be truly safe to use as a drive system provided no one gets close to it again." Simone was sitting now on the back of a chair, her feet planted on the seat .

"I'm willing to give it a whirl. We need to get home ASAP. Anybody got any problem with that?" The commander stood, looking into every crewmember's eyes. No one spoke.

"It's settled. We leave in eight hours after our next orbit around the dark side. I want everyone to use the next six hours to get some shut eye. No exceptions." He was speaking sternly now. "Carl, Mike, and myself will each take two-hour watch duties, so any last questions?"

"Yeah, I do." The mission specialist speaking up again. "Who's gonna watch our little Simone?" He turned to look her in the eyes. "Sure would hate to find a real hole in our hull instead of some stupid religious crap burned into it."

"That's enough, Mr. Beck," Moore barked. "You know as well as I do that she couldn't have done that."

"Well, do me a favor, Simone; kindly ask Jesus to keep his paws off of *Magellan,* would you please?"

Simone returned the man's gaze eye to eye and answered with a soft intensity, "If He did keep His hands off of *Magellan,* we probably, in all likelihood, would be dead right now, Michael." Then she turned and quietly left the room.

CHAPTER 37

THE VISITORS

Jessica waltzed into the Holiday Inn and went straight up to her suite. After swiping her pass key and going into her room, she sensed she was not alone as the door clicked shut behind her. She quickly pulled her little friend from its berth in the back waistband of her pants, and like a predator stalking its prey, she began to enter further into the suite.

"You really don't need to bother, my sister," the raspy Arabian voice came from the left corner of the room. Stepping out to where she could see him, her visitor stood smiling, hands folded in front of him.

"We are here to offer our assistance, Miss Vandale," another voice came from behind her. *How did I miss that one?* she thought to herself.

"My brothers, it is good to see you. However, I'm not sure any assistance is needed as yet." As she spoke, she lowered her weapon, tucking it back into her pants.

"What you have stumbled upon is a very large operation, is it not? Surely you don't expect to go it alone?"

"No, I don't. It's just that I still need information, which," she paused to turn to the agent behind her and eyed him as he joined the other man's stance in front of her, "I should have by the end of the day."

"Very good, Ms. Vandale." *At least one of them respects my wishes,* she thought.

"We will contact you in the morning."

Bowing her head, she said, "May Allah be praised," as she spread her hands out before her. With a soft click, she heard the door close behind her, and looking up, she saw that the visitors had left the room.

Ralph Marlow pulled up to the large gate on the western side of Johnson Space Center and noticed several extra security personnel meandering around the perimeter. It was then as he watched these men that he realized this whole *Magellan* thing was probably much bigger than he realized. *And what does Jess have to do with Tehran?* he wondered. *How in the world does this all fit together?*

"Mr. Marlow, sir. Dr. Hand is expecting you. Please wear this tag." The man was walking up to his car as he sat waiting for the gate to open. "We'll park your vehicle, sir. Would you come with me please?" Ralph got out of his car and was handed an "All Access" badge to wear. He refrained from saying something stupid like, "Wow," when he realized the implications of his newfound status. He followed the guard into a small side door marked "Maintenance" and found himself in an elevator going up three floors. When the doors opened, he was just down the hall from mission control.

"Wait here please, sir," the guard commanded and then walked off to the control room door. He disappeared through the door, and almost immediately Roger Hand appeared, coming out of the door toward him.

Roger wasn't smiling as he approached. Then he proffered his hand toward the door leading into the hot seat area. Ralph didn't know what to say as he stepped into a room that was anything but civilian friendly. Finally Roger spoke. "So, tell me what ya got."

—

In the six- or seven-minute walk from the top of Monks Mound to the parking area on the eastern side, Martin Sherfy had been told the entire story of the *Magellan* incident and the possibility (*or impossibility*, he thought to himself) of a black hole residing right under very his feet. It was also made quite clear to him the sensitive nature of what he was being told.

"So what do you want with me?" he asked as they opened the car door for him.

"Think, Doctor. You're an archeologist; find us a way in."

"A way in?"

"Yes, sir, a way in. There has to be a way to get into that area underground. A cavern, tunnel, something."

Martin got into the sedan dumbfounded. *These guys can't be serious. They would have to be a couple drunken idiots to think there was a way to saunter their way one mile down beneath my beloved mound.* That's when he smiled. Something about "drunken idiots" triggered a memory of an old story or more accurately, a local fable he had heard years ago.

"Do you find something amusing, Professor?" Daniel Blackstone asked him as he narrowed his gaze in an uncomfortably menacing way.

"Go straight up this road to the left. It will take you to Main Street."

"And what will we find there, Professor?"

"Collinsville Public Library. I want to do a little digging. Um, no pun intended, guys."

The two men in the front seat both laughed as they turned east on old Business 40 and headed back toward Collinsville. In less than ten minutes, they were pulling up in front of the library, and Daniel looked at Martin and spoke in a hushed, ominous tone.

"May I remind you, Dr. Sherfy, the information you are privy to is truly classified. We will be watching and listening to everything you say and do, sir."

"Who are you guys, really?"

"We are your best friends in the whole world, sir. Or we are your worst nightmare. It all depends on you, Dr. Sherfy."

Martin was sitting in the back seat behind the driver. He slid over to the passenger side and said, "Look, fellas, I don't believe this black hole story of yours for a minute, but I do think you could be on to something here"

"Is that a fact, Professor? Why is that?"

"Do you know that this area's main source of income at one time was coal mining?"

At that, both men turned their full attention to their newfound professor friend. "No, we didn't know that, but please go on, sir."

"Well, it seems to me that when I was a little guy growin' up, there was a story about a couple of men that started a mine and then just a couple of days later shut it down and moved to another area of town and started another mine. To this day, no one knows where that original mine shaft was for sure."

"So, you think this old shaft could be our way in?"

Martin continued, "These two men got drunk one night and told the people at the local tavern that their original shaft led straight to the gates of hell."

With that, Daniel threw open his door and said "Let's go visit your library, Dr. Sherfy."

PART III: DEVIL'S HOLE

CHAPTER 38

CONNECTIONS

Simone dreamed of a desert, and she could feel the heat zapping the strength away from her very soul. A hot blast of desert wind flung sand into her face. She swiped at the grit and then lifted her arms to ward off the wind's attack. As she leaned into the oven's blast and squinted in the unmerciful light, she saw a horde of people before her. Some were standing, some kneeling, all facing in her direction but staring past her. As she tried to make some kind of sense of what was before her, a mighty peal of thunder rumbled from behind. It was thunder so intense, so powerful that it made the very ground shake beneath her feet. It was unlike anything she had ever heard or felt before. The multitude before her fell prostrate, trembling and mumbling. While intrigued, Simone curiously felt no fear; actually, she sensed a feeling of familiarity. Who was this large mass of people, and what were they looking at? Simone turned around and saw a mountain. It was at that moment she understood and whispered reverently, "Israel, the children of Jacob." She now realized they were staring at Mount Sinai, the mountain of God.

She too now found herself watching, studying the mountain. Although it was midday with the sun directly overhead, darkness shrouded the top half of the mountain like a cloud that resisted natural light. Soon an unnatural light beaming with an unusual intensity began emanating from within the cloud. Simone smiled and excitedly clapped her hands. "The burning bush," she shouted as she found herself jumping up and down. She lifted her arms to the heavens in praise. "Moses. The Angel of the Lord. Jehovah God, the Ten Commandments."

Instantly she found herself standing in the mighty brilliance of the dark cloud, at first alone, and then a man appeared before her cradling two pieces of stone. Simone's mind was screaming out, "The Ten Commandments, the very handwriting of God." Although her voice was temporarily gone, momentarily parched by the ravaging desert, she did manage to whisper as her eyes met his, "Moses?"

The man nodded, his face remaining solemn. He briefly studied Simone and then inched closer to her. He placed his right palm on her left cheek.

Tears slid from Simone's eyes and washed over his hand. "The Ten Commandments?"

The ancient prophet of God nodded once.

Simone tentatively stretched out her right hand and touched one of the tablets. Although she could plainly see it was stone, it felt as smooth as Crysteel.

Moses turned to leave.

"I'll see you again, my friend," Simone said in a hushed tone.

Moses turned around and once again looked deep into her eyes. "Before the throne of our God, Simone Sytte, we will rejoice together on that day."

—

Commander Moore had been on duty for about an hour and a half. The quietness of *Magellan* and the vastness of space were beginning to unnerve him. He started to remember the old space epics he had seen as a child. The scary ones, the ones with aliens popping viciously out of people's bellies and space ships getting sucked into black holes and finding alternate universes that weren't exactly user friendly to human kind. That's when he laughed out loud. "This adventure blows 'em all away," he said to the silent Saturnian orb before him. It seemed to him that once again, truth really was stranger than fiction.

—

Simone fell to her knees and began to weep profusely. Why was this happening? Why was she here? As the sobs began to grow weaker, her sensory perceptions returned and she began to smell a nauseating stench, and it seemed to envelop her. Hashish; she recognized the stench of the drug immediately. She began to hear voices around her growing louder until it was a raucous noise that seemed to swallow her up. Simone opened her tear-stained eyes and instantly winced at the smoke's attack.

She was in a large room; no, it was more like a hall or meeting place of some kind. She heard a voice that rose above the noise of the crowd commanding the attention of all. She turned and saw what appeared to be a king of some kind on a throne bedecked with gold and jewelry. Instantly following the sound of the voice, three men and a woman left the gathering and scurried out a side door as if on a mission of sorts. Then, almost as soon as they left, they returned carrying golden goblets and bowls and laid them before the throne.

This was all somewhat familiar to Simone, and yet she couldn't quite put her finger on what was going on.

—

Commander Moore was going over the telemetry readouts before him seemingly in midair as the sound of a door hissed open behind him. He turned as the voice of Carl Lewis filled the control room,

"So, did ya manage to stay 'wake?" he jovially said to his commander in the phoniest Scottish accent he could muster.

"Course I did. I had to fight off all those mean, ugly aliens that always seem to attack when the crew's sleepin'."

Both men grinned, yet there was an underlying tension present, and they knew it, felt it. They were silent for a moment, standing in front of a rather large window that Moore had the computer restructure in the hull so they could see the planet's pyrotechnic night side.

"What a view."

"Yep."

"So, we gonna make it home in one piece?"

"Yep."

There was silence again for a few endless seconds. Then Lewis asked, "You been keeping an eye on our little princess?"

"Nope. Look," Moore was visibly searching for the right words to say to the communications officer, "for what it's worth, Carl, I still trust her."

"With your life?"

"No." He placed his hand on Carl's shoulder. "With our lives."

Carl Lewis was assimilating his thoughts on Simone Sytte as he spoke again. "Better get some shut eye, Commander."

"Yeah, I know." Taking one last look and slowly shaking his head, he uttered, "Man, Saturn." Then he turned and walked out.

—

Women who were barely dressed were slopping wine into the golden bowls and goblets when a solitary, terrified scream pierced the hall. Twenty feet from Simone, a redheaded woman was standing, staring, pointing over to a wall past Simone's right shoulder. Simone's eyes followed the direction of the woman's gaze, and she saw a large hand, with no body, writing on the wall with its index finger. Now the room was quiet. The only noise was the sound of the hand writing on the wall. This also, was too familiar; now Simone understood where and *when* she was. She returned her gaze to the king, who was as white as a ghost.

"Belshazzar," she hissed, and then incredulously added as she took in the panorama all around her and put it all together, "Babylon!"

—

Martin Sherfy's fingers were flying over the computer keyboard in the library's reference section while Daniel Blackstone stood beside him, watching the archeologist sweep through the library database in a blur. Smitty was off to one corner discreetly flipping through the latest edition of *National Geographic*. It was already well past two in the afternoon, and Blackstone was about to give his "time's a-wasting" speech when Sherfy spoke to him in a hushed, illicitly excited tone. "I think I've got it!"

Somehow from twenty feet away Smitty heard him and shifted positions, locking eyes with Blackstone.

Before Blackstone could ask any questions, the professor had already printed several pages of information and jumped up from the console in such a hurry that he almost knocked the chair over. He walked up to the librarian's counter, inquired how much the time and printed material would cost, and then turned to Blackstone.

"I need three dollars and sixty six cents, please." Blackstone simply gave a short huff as he reached into his wallet and pulled out a five. Handing it to the librarian, he said, "Keep it" and turned toward the door. Smitty had already made his way out of the library and was eyeing the neighborhood, making sure no one was keeping tabs on them.

The three men got into the sedan and pulled onto Main Street.

"This is incredible!" Sherfy could barely contain himself; for the first time in what seemed like a long, long time, he was once again enjoying life.

"And what would be so incredible, Dr. Sherfy?"

"Martin, guys, just call me Martin."

"OK, Martin it is. I feel all buddy-buddy now. So, whatcha got?"

Martin was on a roll. "Turn left up here at the light, go over to the next block, and go left again."

"And where are we going, Dr., um, I mean Martin?"

"A little town five minutes away called Caseyville."

"And why?" Smitty was getting in on it now, his hand making the rolling "tell me more" gesture as he turned around from the front passenger seat to face Martin, who was sitting in the middle of the rear seat leaning forward like a teenager out for an evening ride. In the rearview mirror, he could see Blackstone's eyes taking turns watching him and watching the road.

Smiling ear to ear, he read bits from the papers he held in his hands.

"1873, John Saul and William David built the mine in Caseyville. You know, the one I told you about. I think we may have found a piece of the puzzle, gentlemen. The mine was called, get this, Devil's Hole."

"How do we get there?"

"Make a left on 157. We need to do a little snooping."

As the sedan pulled onto Illinois 157, Daniel prodded his newfound friend, "So tell us more."

"OK," Martin mumbled in a "I'm trying to read this first" tone.

"Here it is, wow! I've been told this story a dozen times when I was a kid. Just thought it was a, you know, a story that older people tell little kids."

"We're waiting," Smitty chimed into Martin's soliloquy.

"Saul and David opened a mine here in Caseyville, and according to the report, there was an accident that caused the mine to collapse. Now, the interesting part is, they only had the mine opened for three days."

"So?"

"Well, they didn't even hire anyone to work for them yet."

"And?"

Patience was not one of Smitty's strong points. Daniel Blackstone was a little more discreet with his annoyance.

"Martin, we are trained at putting puzzles together, but not when someone else holds all the pieces," he said, trying to smile.

"I'm sorry." Martin tried to begin again. "They claimed that their shaft was over a mile long when it collapsed." Martin paused. Blackstone and Smitty instantaneously got his point.

"They found a tunnel or cave system," Smitty spat out. "One that led to the, what'd you call it, the gates of hell?"

"Exactly. Now we need to find out where the entrance is, or was."

"And I hope you have an idea, Mr. Sherfy."

The car was going over a viaduct that spanned across a set of railroad tracks. St. Louis could easily be seen from this vantage point to the west, but Martin Sherfy was looking the other way down the tracks, to the east.

"I think I see it."

"What, Martin, see what?"

"Turn left at the base of this viaduct. There, Old Mill Road. We need to follow that road back along the railroad tracks."

"And what are we looking for?"

"Irma Saul, John Saul's granddaughter. She lives in the original house that her granddaddy built. Rumor has it that it somehow conceals the entrance to the mine tunnels—least that's how the old fable goes."

—

Funny how, in a dream you can understand what people are saying when they speak in a foreign language. But to Simone, this was more than a dream; her very life depended on what she was experiencing, and she knew it. She could taste the reality of her surroundings.

"Get me Daniel the Hebrew prophet. *Now!*" she heard.

—

Roger Hand was tapping the top of the desk at the rear of the hot seat area. Holding a phone in the other hand, he was anxiously awaiting the person on the other end to speak.

"Yes sir, that is correct. She needs to be stopped, sir."

Ralph Marlow was sipping coffee, taking in the sights. He knew satellite surveillance hardware when he saw it; after all, he was once NASA material. *Once NASA, always NASA*, he reminded himself. What was in this tiny room, however, rivaled all of mission control down below him. He felt like a kid who just stumbled into Santa's workshop.

"I need a Quick Jet, sir."

That got Ralph's attention. Last he heard that technology was still five to ten years away. It was aircraft that can do Mach twelve, get you where you're going, and then return to a normal jet aircraft speed before G-force sets in. It had vertical or horizontal take off and landing. This was getting really interesting.

"I won't let you down, Mr. President. Good-bye, sir." Roger disconnected the com link and then turned to face his old friend.

"Seems our Ms. Vandale was interested in more than learning about *Magellan's* nuclear reactor."

The look of interpolation on Ralph's face spoke myriads to Dr. Hand. Continuing on, he spoke in a more hushed tone.

"Seems Jessica has a double life, Ralph; she's hooked up with the Persian Element, and they're looking for some new weapons armaments. Man, she's gotten herself in over her head."

"What're you gonna do?"

"You stay here and work with these folks, stay on top of *Magellan,* and keep me informed if any new developments arise. I'm going to go get our Ms. Vandale."

Ralph looked around him once again and began to surmise the enormity of this situation.

"I'll do my best, Roger."

"I know ya will. I'll be back as soon as possible. *Magellan's* trajectory should put her in com range in about four hours or so. I hope to be back by then."

Roger Hand stood up and walked toward the door. It swooshed open, and he quietly disappeared down the exit corridor.

"Oh, Jess, what have you gotten yourself into?" Ralph worriedly whispered as he realized the impending implications awaiting his longtime friend.

—

Daniel's phone rang as they turned onto Old Mill Road and started down a rather bumpy country lane.

"Got it. Now get back here and go to the hotel and stay with Harry till you hear from us." Daniel smartly shut his phone with a loud snap.

"Doesn't anyone ever say good-bye anymore?" Martin asked.

"Stalker found some interesting footage of our deer parade yesterday on the interstate, but nothing that seems to be of any use to us," Blackstone answered. "I certainly hope Miss Irma Saul has more for us to go on." He was looking ominously in the mirror at Martin as he spoke.

"Me too," was all Martin could reply.

—

All Simone could hear was the hushed voices of the guards at the doors, and then she heard a loud click as one door was unlatched and opened. "Daniel," she spoke to no one but herself as the elderly man was ushered into the hall, bringing with him a sense of nobility and honor. She watched this man of God keenly, noting his complete contempt and disgust as he saw the temple utensils being perversely used as tavern instruments. He was escorted (Simone wondered as she watched the parade develop before her who was leading whom) to the king's sofa, where Simone could hear the anxious voice of the king explaining the situation to the prophet. She smiled as she noted the look of annoyance on Daniel's face. She moved closer. She was now only a few yards behind Daniel as he gave Belshazzar a quick history lesson on the Lord's dealing with his forefather, Nebuchadnezzar.

Daniel's voice dripped with contempt, a subtle, respectful contempt that had nothing to do with political correctness; in fact, he seemed to be scolding Belshazzar as he would a wayward child. Then, slowly, he walked over to the wall, and running his fingers along every Hebrew letter, he solemnly announced the edict of God.

"Time's up, mister," Simone couldn't help but say with a slight grin.

"You must come here." The prophet spoke not to the king but to Simone. She sheepishly made her way to the opening in the hallway where the message had been written.

Daniel was looking at her, studying her. It seemed no one else in the place had even noticed her but Daniel. His face softened, his voice sweetened. "Touch this; it is the handwriting of the Lord, the Holy One of Israel."

Simone reached out to touch the tan-colored wall of sandstone. She ran her fingers over and into the Hebraic etching, and then she caught her breath as she realized the smoothness of the stone where the finger of God had touched felt just like the writing on her wall onboard *Magellan*.

"You know this handwriting, don't you, my sister?"

"Yes, Daniel, I do."

As Daniel turned away from her to leave, Simone could detect a sense of sadness in the man of God. It must be hard to be all alone in a world that hates the living God and to stand for His Word when no one wants to listen. Simone was thinking these thoughts as she turned to face the wall of stone one last time. Then she too made her exit from this place of human depravity thinking, *Isn't it amazing that a nation can go from being the mightiest nation in the world to being a cesspool of humanity in only a generation or two?*

—

Later that afternoon, Jessica had a date with destiny that she had no intention of missing. But it was still early afternoon, so she opened her laptop to see what new information she could glean from her little spy. Nothing really new jumped out and grabbed her, so she shut down the link and started going over all the data she did have. She thought to herself the oddity of the fact that, for a while, info was coming fast and furious, and now hardly anything was going on. Somewhere in the most remote places of her mind an alarm was going off.

—

Slightly larger than an F-15 Eagle, the Quick Jet began to power up as Roger was inputting instructions into the onboard computer as he prepared for his flight. With a gentle lift, the aircraft silently (was it really this quiet or is the cockpit's soundproofing that good?) began to hover in the hangar at Houston airport. All flights in the immediate airspace had been diverted for a few minutes to give Dr. Roger Hand a launch window that would not be easily visible by passers-by. Gaining a slight forward momentum, he inched toward the hangar door. Behind him a launch wall had popped up to give the thrust something to work against, much like on an aircraft carrier. All systems flashed to green, and then Roger said "Let's go for a ride." He put full power to the thrusters and shot out into the Texan sky. Less than three minutes later, he was powering down for landing at Scott Air Force Base, minutes away from St. Louis. He wanted to use the vertical landing function, then decided against that, and used the military runway so he wouldn't attract as much attention. The Quick Jet stealthily pulled into a remote hangar marked "tool shed." Roger was smiling ear to ear.

"I gotta get one of these," he said to himself as the aircraft's wings automatically folded underneath the fuselage of the jet, much like a bird of prey would settle down to rest after a long flight.

191

Two men were waiting at a car parked outside the rather large "tool shed."

"Dr. Hand?"

With a nod of affirmation from Roger, the man continued, "We have a room for you in the Collinsville Holiday Inn. We will be glad to take you there if—"

Roger broke in, "Does the car have GPS guidance?"

"Yes, sir."

"Then I won't be needing a chauffeur, gentlemen."

"Very good sir." The two men remained motionless beside the car, and then the other one spoke up.

"Sir, we are to inform you that there is an ops team also quartered in your hotel headed by a ..." He searched a small handheld. "A Daniel Blackstone."

Smiling, Roger said, "Thank you very much. Now if you'll both excuse me, I really must be going."

"One more thing, sir."

"And that would be?" Roger spoke with obvious annoyance at the two MPs.

"Your trunk, sir. It's loaded with state-of-the-art field weapons, ah, should you get into any kind of ..." he paused, delicately searching for the right word, "situation, sir."

The other spoke up again. "Here's the keys. The panic button is the only way to get to the weapons, sir, and there's also this." He was reaching under his coat and surveying the immediate area as he handed Roger a nine millimeter with a double resonate silencer. "Washington wants you armed at all times, sir."

"Got it. I really must go, gentlemen. Anything else?"

"No sir."

Without a word, Roger jumped into the white Chrysler and headed off base. As he neared one of the gates, a chime went off, and he saw a pass light go on the overhead readout above the gate. Roger headed for the interstate and then down to Collinsville. He flipped open his phone and hit the auto dial.

"Blackstone."

" Hey, I just thought of something; I thought you retired?"

Daniel began to laugh. "I tried too, but they said they'd have to kill me to make sure I didn't tell any secrets. Are you local?"

"Yeah, I'm here. Just got into town and am checking into your hotel in about ten minutes."

"So, what brings you in on this? I mean, besides the obvious *Magellan* link, why are you here for covert ops?"

"Jessica Vandale."

"Oh yeah, we've spotted her around down by the mounds. Saw you with her the other night too. What a pair."

"Oh please don't remind me. By the way, you guys are slipping."

Laughing again Blackstone queried "What're you talking about slippin'?"

"She has a suite down the hall from you guys."

"Gotta hand it to her, she's good."

"She's a lot more than that, Daniel." He paused and then added, "She's a member of the Persian Element."

"You're kidding."

"Listen, give me an hour to get set up then meet me back at your room."

"You got it."

Daniel slapped his phone shut.

Martin shook his head as he watched Daniel end his phone conversation. "Nobody says good-bye anymore. I'm telling you, it just isn't polite. Ho, whoa, slowdown, yeah, this is it. Turn right."

The car bounced over the holes in the driveway and pulled right up to Irma Saul's front porch. The door opened as the car came to a halt and an elderly woman heartily stepped out to see her visitors.

Blackstone said to the other two men, "I'll handle the intros."

—

Simone stealthily stepped out into the sand and rock-packed street. She didn't know how she knew, but she knew she wasn't in Babylon any longer. She walked down a narrow street, turned the corner, and froze in her tracks as she saw the temple before her. She smiled, and then she lifted her hands in praise to the living God.

"Thank You, Lord Jesus, for letting me see this," she said and then began to run toward the temple. It was massive in grandeur and in size, and exquisitely pieced individual stones made it all the more impressive. She ran up the steps and entered into the outer court; the court of the Gentiles. She heard a commotion off to the far side, and after making her way toward the disturbance, Simone had no problem seeing over the heads of the people gathered together. What she saw frightened her. It was not as danger frightens a person; no, it was more like an apprehension one feels when one goes to meet a famous person or leader. Beyond a small group of noisy men, she could see a woman lying on the ground half-naked. Just past her was a man kneeling on the ground, and He was writing in the sand. For the first time in her life, Simone Sytte could put a face with the name that is above all names.

"Jesus."

She made her way around the angry mob of Pharisees and positioned herself, just off center, alongside Jesus and the woman. Simone knelt down, face to the earth, and wept in the presence of her King.

CHAPTER 39

SENTINEL

"Irma Saul?" Daniel politely questioned as he eyed the elderly woman standing on the porch before him. As he closed his car door and took a step forward, he noticed the ancient but deadly looking sawed-off sixteen-gauge shotgun leaning against the door frame. Two more doors closed behind him as his fellow companions exited the sedan.

"You boys must be cops or something."

Daniel smiled and then answered, "Why's that?" He remained close to the car; he didn't want to alarm the old girl.

"No one calls me Irma, least, no one 'cept the law or politicians." She eyed the men with a slight suspicion, but it was clearly evident she wasn't in the least bit fearful of them.

"So, what should we call you?"

"Miss Saul will do for now." She waited, patiently looking over the three men, and then said to Martin, "Ain't you one of those mound diggers?"

"I'm Professor Martin Sherfy, ma'am. I teach archaeology at the university."

With that, Blackstone shot a subtle glance over to Martin, a definite hint to end the explanation. The look was not missed by Irma.

"So, what do you boys want?"

"Miss Saul, Martin here tells us that your grandfather once had a mine somewhere around here."

"Grandpa had a few mines," she said as she raised her eyebrows, waiting for the next question.

"We're looking for the one called Devil's Hole."

"Why?"

"We're investigative writers, and we're doing a story on lost American folklore. We saw the story about the mystery of Devil's Hole and thought it would be worth checking into."

"Sounds good," she replied, "but I don't buy it for a minute." The men stood for a second exchanging a quick, playful laughing glance at each other. Martin realized just how good these guys were at lying and once again wondered, *Who are these guys?* Before anyone could say anything, Irma continued. She was playing now; she leaned up against the door with both arms folded across her chest and asked, "Since when do investigators for newspapers wear guns?"

Daniel was caught off guard by that one. "Ma'am, it ain't safe nowhere anymore," he offered with both hands raised at his side, palms up.

"Oh, I believe that. Truth is, it ain't safe here neither." And in one lightning move, she grabbed her shotgun and pulled back the hammer, rested the butt of the weapon on her hip, and aimed it in the general direction of the three visitors.

Daniel continued to hold his hands out to his side and said, "Miss Saul, I work with the defense department. We didn't mean to alarm you. Truth be told, we've been interested in this area for a long time. We need to find safe underground refuge areas in case of any incidents or attacks on our country."

"Still don't buy it, sir." She was holding her ground, and Martin was more than just a little bit nervous since he hadn't had a gun pointed in his direction for quite a while.

Daniel stood there for a moment silently studying the face of the aged American before him. Finally, he looked over at Smitty, who simply shrugged his shoulders then looked back at Martin and then looked back at Irma.

"We do work for the defense department, ma'am, but truth is, we just want to know if there is a way to go underground to Monks Mound from here. Really. We think there's something hidden down there."

"Really? Like what, gold? Uranium? You trying to make more of those big blasted H-bombs?"

She had lowered her gun but hadn't set it aside. "Got a badge or something?"

Daniel smiled as he pulled out a defense department ID.

She looked at his ID, and then Smitty offered up his to the woman to see.

"Wish you government types would just tell the truth the first time 'round. Sure would save a lot of trouble." She opened the door and started to walk in. "C'mon, I got some lemonade made up. Might as well share it with you boys. Besides, been a long time since I had a gentleman caller. Fact is, never had three at once. This could be fun."

The three gentleman callers all started laughing at once and then laughed even more once she set down her shotgun.

The troupe walked into a parlor that had large windows all around, giving it the appearance of a much larger room than it actually was.

"Grandpa liked lotsa light. Hated workin' in the dark," she said from the kitchen as she poured lemonade over ice in blue carnival glasses. She was an elegant hostess, setting the glasses on a crystal tray and then walking carefully to the men, who were all waiting in the parlor.

"Please sit down, fellas," she said with a playful twinkle in her eyes.

The room was full of antiques; in fact, the whole parlor was an antique. The afternoon sun was bouncing playfully all around the room from every imaginable angle, bouncing off one glass object and then another in a hauntingly magical symphony of light; it seemed the whole room was a prism of sorts. Irma saw the men looking at all the light beams and then began to speak again.

"Grandpa used to say that God lives in the light and the devil lived in darkness. Said that's what the Bible always said."

Blackstone checked his watch. He had about thirty minutes before he had to leave.

"Miss Saul," he began slowly, "I really don't mean to be rude, but I really need to know." He paused. "Is there a way to get underground to the shaft or to ..." he seemed to be stumped for the proper terminology

"The tunnel?" she finished for him.

"Yes, the tunnel. What do you know about it?"

"Been guarding this secret for better part of a century, and here you come one afternoon and want to know it all." She was shaking her head. It seemed to Martin that she was weighing her options, so he spoke up.

"Miss Saul, I just met these two men down at the mounds. I began to tell then the legend of—" he didn't get to go any farther

"Legend?" At first she seemed angry, but she simply began to laugh.

"The American dream, get rich, own your own business. Ain't gotta answer to nobody. Let me tell you boys something: my grandpa loved this country, loved this here neck of the woods, he did. Said it was special." She leaned forward as she began to majestically unfold her story, lowering her voice to practically a whisper—a very intense whisper.

"Said this is the place where heaven and hell collide. Said he saw it himself. He found the tunnel after a big rain came through one day. Opened up a sinkhole, it did. Looked down into the hole and saw a bigger hole; a tunnel. He had a friend here in town, old William David. His whole family's gone now." For a moment, the men thought Irma would drift away on another memory, but she shot right back.

"Anyways, Grandpa, he ran down the tracks to the David's farm a-yellin', 'I found a mine.' Old William was a-plowin' in the field, so he finished up his work and left to go with Grandpa down into the tunnel."

For a few moments, the walls, the large windows, the antiques, even the wrinkles on Irma Saul disappeared. The men were transfixed, mesmerized by the orator and engulfed in the story, the story of a day gone by, a lifetime away.

"They spent five or six hours just lookin' 'round. Said they'd found enough coal to fill an entire train, so next day they ran an ad in the paper sayin' they'd hire the first twenty men who showed up at the tracks by town on the following Monday. Now, long 'bout Saturday afternoon, Grandpa and William came runnin' out of the tunnel yellin' and screamin' like a whole nest of yeller jackets was a fixin' to chew 'em up." Irma paused just long enough to take a nice long drink and then continued.

"They came into town and went down to the old dry goods store and got a keg of black powder. Then they went back to the tunnel and was gonna blow it to smithereens." She stopped again and looked at Blackstone and said, "Now, that was the days you could trust a man with explosives. Fact, Grandpa used to take his shotgun to school with him so's he could do some huntin' on the way home." She laughed and answered the unspoken question. "Yeah *that* shotgun. Sure is a different day now, ain't it? Grandpa'd cry his eyes out if he saw what has happened to the good ole USA." She stopped again to collect her thoughts. Then, wiping away a single tear, she continued the story.

"It was getting evening time, so the two men took the keg, punched out the seal to let it bleed out, and then rolled it down the hole. Didn't know how far it went, so they lit the powder trail and ran as fast as they could.

"Next thing they knew, they were pickin' dirt and grass outta their hair and teeth, and the next thing they saw was a second hole going down to the tunnel. Grandpa said must have been something the Good Lord wanted to leave open, so they just left good enough alone and went back to town and got all drunked up. Started telling people 'bout how they saw the gates of hell and all that stuff. Folks all thought they were drunk and crazy, so they never paid it much mind. Grandpa figured since he found one hole and then made another one, he was kinda responsible not to let anyone else go down there, so he hid the second hole and filled in the first."

"Do you know where the second hole is?"

Blackstone's voice ushered quietly through the rays of sunlight.

"Well, I tell ya, the first hole was right there." She was pointing to her flower garden just outside the window. "And you're sitting right smack-dab on top of the second hole, Mr. Blackstone."

CHAPTER 40

THE KING'S AUDIENCE

Simone knelt on the sand and stone floor silently weeping. It seemed that all of time had halted around her, enveloping and caressing her. How long had she been there escaped her grasp; she simply wanted to remain in the King's presence. Her tears were falling silently to the ground, making a small puddle of sandy mud. She gradually began to look around, first to where the woman had been; she was gone, nowhere to be seen. Then she looked toward the accusing Pharisees, and likewise, they were gone. Panic and disappointment began to grab her thoughts as she realized He might be gone as well, so she turned to face the position He had been at. He was sitting with His legs drawn up, knees in His chest, looking at her the way a loving parent would look at their child.

"I'm still here, Simone," He gently said to her. She felt as if she was about to faint, but then He reached out His hand, touching her shoulder ever so gently. She gathered her strength and attempted to speak through her sobs. "L-Lord Jes, Jesus," was all she could seem to get out. She once again lowered her gaze, but He took His hand and gently lifted her face so she could look into His eyes. *His eyes!* she thought. *The eyes of Jesus!*

"My daughter, you are so special to Me" He began softly. "I have given you gifts so that you could serve me. You have been a very faithful servant, my child." And then He took her by the hand. Simone thought to herself, *I'm holding the Lord Jesus' hand!* He turned and smiled the biggest smile Simone had ever seen. "Yes you are, Simone. But don't forget, it is I who holds your hand and ..." He paused to look deeply into her eyes. "I will never let you go!"

"My Lord and my God," she said to the King.

"Come, I must show you something," Jesus said as they stepped over past where He had been writing in the sand. She read what it said, but she knew she could never tell anyone; it would be a secret between her and her Lord forevermore.

"You have been shown much this evening for a very good reason, Simone," Jesus said. Simone loved to hear the Lord Himself speaking her name.

"Simone, watch and learn the meaning." Jesus positioned Simone so that the writing was at her very feet. Then He smiled at her and knelt down, and with one breath, He blew away the message that had been scribbled in the sand. The sand began to twirl like a miniature dust cloud or tornado. Simone was absolutely transfixed by the scene. Then the sand began to spread out and rise up before her like a curtain. A curtain of stars.

—

None of the men knew what to say. Daniel had jumped out of the chair like he had felt something moving underneath him. Irma laughed.
"You're kidding me!" He managed to at least sound calm.

"No sir, would you like to see it?"

"Ma'am, if it's here, we need to see it."

"Tell you what, you quit calling me 'ma'am' and 'Miss Saul' and we can make a deal."

"What do you want us to call you?"

"Sunshine," she smiled and said. "S'what Grandpa used to call me. He built this room with all the windows in it to keep out the darkness, and he started callin' me sunshine."

All the men were standing, smiling back at an old woman who didn't seem so old anymore.

Daniel laughed. "Sunshine, that's absolutely wonderful!"

"Grandpa said that someday somebody might come a lookin' for the tunnel, said that I would have to listen to my heart and I would know what to do." Saying that, she got up, reached under the chair and the men heard a click. Then she walked over to an old cuckoo clock that wasn't working and pulled the weight chain, swung the pendulum, and made the hands of the clock go to twelve o'clock. The cuckoo started cuckooing, and the entire floor section that the chair sat upon began to swing backward out of the way, revealing a very dark hole with an old wooden ladder going down into it. The musty smell that attacked their senses seemed ancient, adding to the mystical magic of the moment.

—

Stars! "Oh Lord, they're beautiful!" Simone said. Then she realized she was back on *Magellan.* No, wait, this looked a lot like *Magellan,* but it was somehow different. For one, it seemed empty. There were no voices, no one hurrying about. There was no planet before her, only a vast array of stars. They were stars and constellations neither she nor any other human had ever seen before. She placed both palms onto the window and then leaned her forehead on the Crysteel bulkhead before her trying to make sense of the scenario she was engulfed in.

"Captivating, is it not?" the voice came from behind her. It was a voice she had longed to hear for over ten years now. "Poppa," Simone said as she turned around to face her father who had not been there just a few seconds ago.

"You have seen things very few people have ever seen, my precious one," he said as he came alongside her and faced out the giant viewing area. He stood tall and strong, both hands behind him in an almost military stance as he too looked into eternity's sky, the stars seemingly beckoning him onward.

Simone quietly came nearer to him and laying her head on his shoulder, simply said, "I know, but I don't understand, Poppa." His head gently touched over to hers, his arm reaching around her, and holding her tightly, he began to speak again.

"Tell me, my baby girl, what is engraved on *Magellan's* wall in your room?"

"Psalm 46:10."

Smiling, he said, "No, more than that, Simone, think. What did every episode of your vision contain?"

Vision, she thought, *not dream?*

"The handwriting of God, at least in one form or another."

"And that is what *Magellan* contains, does it not?"

"Yes."

Her father could tell she was still at a point of confusion in the matter, so he guided her along.

"Do you remember what Psalm 46:1 says?"

"Of course, you used to sing it to me when I was but a small child. In fact, I never told you this, but it is one of the verses from the Word of God that wooed me into a love affair with Him. It says, 'God is our refuge and strength, a very present help in times of trouble.' I learned to trust Him because of that verse, Poppa."

"You need to trust Him ever more, sweetheart. Look, out of the three times God Himself wrote a message to someone, how many of those messages are still readily available to be seen?"

Simone thought for a few seconds. She knew the answer was none, but she still couldn't figure out her part in this scene.

"None," she said blankly.

"The Commandments are held securely in a secret place by the Lord Himself, Babylon was destroyed, and you yourself saw what the Lord Jesus did with His message."

The father-daughter duo simply stood silently before the view field for a few moments, and then David Sytte kissed his daughter on the head and said, "You're a bright girl. You'll figure it out. Just promise me you will always remember that 46:1 passage. You have a busy life ahead of you."

Simone looked up to see her father's eyes, but he was gone already. Once again, she found herself crying, kneeling on the floor. She raised her hands as if to grasp onto all the stars before her and said, "Behold the maidservant of the Lord. Let it be unto me according to Your will, oh Lord."

—

The men knelt down, staring into the ink-ish abyss before them.

"Don't know if it goes to Monks Mound, but I do know that it heads west, boys."

"Incredible. All these years …" Turning to Irma, he said, "You ever … eh?"

"Go down *there!* No way. Rather shoot my way outta Hitler's Germany than go where you boys want to go."

Blackstone looked at his watch then over at Smitty and then at Martin and said, "I gotta meet up with someone. You boys can take a look, but don't go far. I'll be back in, oh, probably less than an hour with some equipment." He was forgetting his manners, so he looked once again at Sunshine and asked if it was OK for those two to remain while he left. Getting her permission, he hurried out the door as he heard the words "lanterns" and "rope" being mentioned behind him.

—

Carl Lewis was toying with some theoretical black hole algorithms, trying to be creative and pass the time all at once. The idea of smashing the speed of light to smithereens all the while staying in the physical realm would have probably made Einstein pull his hair out. He laughed as he thought maybe that's why his hair always looked like that in the first place. Not getting anywhere with creative mathematical engineering, he turned his thoughts to *Magellan*, then to Simone; then almost automatically to the writing on the hull of *Magellan* in her room.

All logic could do for him is to point to Simone as some kind of religious lunatic, yet all the evidence seemed to scream that she was innocent of all guile in the matter. Carl allowed his mind to wander for a moment.

"What if it's true?" he reasoned aloud. After all, he'd be alone for another hour …

"What if there is a God?" He stopped for a moment and then added, "And why would He want to talk to Simone, or even us?"

As Carl Lewis looked toward the gigantic planet before him, its night side display too beautiful to describe, he could have sworn he heard a gentle whisper deep down in his soul, "I'm here, Carl, and I love you too."

CHAPTER 41

IN MOTION

Ralph had no idea how he could be of any assistance to the folks, so he simply asked, "Is there anything I can do to help?"

The three team members looked at each other and then smiled, and one of them said, "We could sure use a bite to eat."

"Yeah, and how about some *real* coffee?"

Ralph felt a little agitated at the thought of being a gofer, but he went ahead and promised to be back as soon as he could with some food and coffee. *Isn't it funny,* he mused, *that at a time like this, the human body still wants some of the pleasantries, not to mention the staples of life. No computer, no system of any kind can run without electricity, and no human can run without fuel.*

Ralph walked out into the warm Texas sun and headed for his car. Pulling out his cell, he hit speed dial for his favorite Italian eatery. He ordered enough pizza, spaghetti, and pasta con broccoli with garlic bread to last until Judgment Day. As he jumped into his car and headed toward the main gate, one of the guards walked out to meet him.

"Heading out, sir?" came the gruff but polite voice of the marine.

"An errand of mercy." Ralph smiled and then added, "Can I get anything for you, young man?"

The marine eyed him with what seemed to be a mild annoyance and then said in a short, tense voice, "No sir, I'm fine, thank you." He had the gate open before he was finished speaking.

—

"You putting on weight there, Roger?" Daniel Blackstone was smiling, genuinely glad to see his old friend.

Roger was looking at his watch, grunted, smiled to acknowledge the remark, and then abruptly replied, "3:45. Tell me whatcha got."

"Well." Daniel was surprised to see the matter-of-factness his friend was exuding.

"We might have a way to get under mound thirty-eight; in fact, I've got two men looking into a tunnel right now not ten minutes away from here. The rangers at the park haven't got a clue as to what we are up to or even what they're sitting on top of. How 'bout you? How's *Magellan?*"

"OK. There was a death a few hours ago during a space walk. Other than that, we hope to high heaven they're coming home soon as they round Saturn's dark side, which, by the way, is anything but dark."

"Really, I'll have to see the pictures some day, but right now," Daniel was unceremoniously eyeing his surroundings, "I need to know what's up with your reporter friend. Why is she here anyway?"

Roger didn't even blink

"She's got a dirty little secret; seems to be a member of the Persian Element. Been spying on the whole blasted event. Bad thing is, I let her in the door."

"Oops."

"Yeah, you can say that again. Speaking of our friend, I can't believe you guys didn't even know she was your neighbor. Gotta hand it to her, she is pretty good, man." He sounded exasperated. "I just don't understand why a woman with her knowledge, connections, and money has anything to do with terrorists. She has everything anyone would want."

"Evidently not. She's always leaned toward eastern religion."

"You know this—how?"

"I know everything, Roger. Don't forget that."

Both men were laughing when they saw her walk out of the hotel and get into her Humvee.

"Doesn't exactly stay low key, does she?"

"Like I said, you guys didn't even know she was your neighbor. Look, you get what ya need for your little tunnel trip and I'll follow little miss phony. Be careful. We've already lost two men and some pretty expensive hardware."

"Roger," Daniel feigned surprise, "I never knew you cared."

"I do, old friend, but this is possibly the biggest assignment either of us has ever been on."

"You be careful too. If she's hooked up with these Middle-Eastern thugs, she's probably packin' some heat."

"Don't worry, so am I." With that, Roger hopped into his rental and made his way up the avenue toward the stoplights less than a block away. Jessica was just now turning toward the south on the highway, so he took his time coming up to the stop. Watching to make sure she didn't get on the interstate, he pulled out onto Illinois 157 in pursuit of destiny.

—

Ralph pulled onto NASA Boulevard and then onto Highway 1 and headed toward the little town of Seabrook that was settled by Galveston Bay. Ralph loved to drive along Clear Lake, especially as the days started getting longer and warmer. The late afternoon sun was now almost behind him, casting the shadow of his car ahead of him. He was lost in thought, primarily about his closest media associate, Jessica. *What is she up to?* He wondered if she was on a secret assignment, and it wasn't the first time that thought had crossed his mind. He hoped, even longed for, that to be the case.

He was just coming up on Clear Lake when he saw a car behind him that, for no apparent reason, caught his attention. "You're getting paranoid, old guy," he mused aloud to himself. All the while, his internal alarms were sounding. He slowed his speed a little. Didn't matter much, Seabrook was only ten minutes away. Checking his rearview he noticed the car behind him seemed to have slowed as well so, he sped up; purposely, noticeably faster. Two minutes down the road, he noticed the car was getting even closer now. He laughed out loud. "Probably someone Roger had tailing me to keep me safe and sound," he mused and then looked again. Now the car was only a few car lengths behind him, and it looked as if there were two people in the car. Glancing again just in time, Ralph saw the passenger hanging halfway out of the window, pointing some kind of weapon his way.

Ralph was not one to be shaken too easily, so he said, "OK, let's play," as he slammed on the brakes. The would-be assailants smashed into the rear of his car, propelling him forward and at the same time forcing them off the road and down into a small ravine. Picking up the phone, he dialed Roger's number. It only rang half a time, and then he heard, "Hand."

"Hey, Roger, it's Ralph. We got new players in the game." He proceeded to tell the entire story of the last five minutes.

"You all right?"

"Oh yeah, don't know if they are or not, and quite frankly don't care. Hey, who's payin' for the damage to my car?"

"We'll take care of it."

Then laughing, he said, "I know, just like to hear you say it."

"Ralph, I'm following Jessica right now. Looks like she's going down to the mounds thing. I gotta go, buddy. Watch your rear."

"Roger that one. Be careful. Guess I don't know her as well as I thought."

"You're not the only one." There was a slight click, and Roger was gone.

Looking in his rearview mirror, he smiled and then said, "You guys really shouldn't mess with an American fighter pilot." Then he thought, *Wonder if they crashed into the lake? Guess I need to call in a report.*

—

Martin was standing at the foot of the old wooden ladder reaching up for the lantern as it was being lowered to him. The sound of water dripping was alluring him onward, but he needed to wait for Smitty, who was still being showered with equipment by Sunshine.

"Martin."

He heard it as a slight whisper. Goosebumps were rising up all over his body. It was like when you're just about asleep and you hear someone whisper your name. Problem was, Martin wasn't asleep, and he definitely heard a voice. It was about at that instant he realized that he was no longer on a scientific adventure; he had stepped into the unknown territories of the supernatural, and he needed to watch over those who would be accompanying him.

"Father, I know that I have failed You today. I thank You, oh Sovereign King of the universe, that You kept me from so great a sin. God, I was going to kill myself! And yet, You spared me, oh Lord. I ask for Your forgiveness, Father. I ask for Your protection from whatever or whoever is down here. Guide me, Lord God. It's You I trust with all I am, and Lord, protect those who You have placed alongside me in this, this, adventure." Martin knew that he wasn't done talking with the Lord, but Smitty was noisily making his way down the ladder, so he simply added, "Let the blood of Your Son Jesus cover me. Let Your Spirit guide me. Father, into Your hands I commit my Spirit."

"Who're you talking to down there, Martin, the rock?"

"No," he said, exasperated, "I was talking to my Lord Jesus. We're gonna need His help on this one."

"Oh yeah, like when we found you on top of thirty-eight with a pea shooter in your mouth?"

"I deserved that one," Martin muttered under his breath and then turned to face Smitty, who had just reached the ladder's bottom rung and jumped firmly to the floor of the cavern. His whole body was clanking noisily from all the hardware their newfound friend had lavished upon them. Smitty held a lantern up to see his surroundings and then examine the professor's demeanor.

"You know, life doesn't always go the way that one thinks it should, Smitty."

"Yeah, I know. I also know this is America and there is always tomorrow to use to change one's life around."

Martin started to speak of knowing about one's tomorrow, about the fact that our tomorrows are never guaranteed, but he held his peace, as Smitty had already passed by him and was checking his compass.

"Looks like we're going this way," he said as he proceeded down the darkened corridor that was only partially illumined by the primitive oil lantern.

"When Blackstone gets back, he should have some better lighting. We won't go far, so don't you fret, Professor. I just want to get a feel for our immediate surroundings."

"Martin."

There it was again.

"Shh! Did you hear that?" Martin asked.

"Hear what?"

Not wanting to add more fuel to the Looney Toons fire, Martin simply said, "Nothin', just thought I heard something."

"Well, I didn't. Maybe God's trying to get your attention there, Professor." The cynicism was dripping from every word.

"It's not God's voice I'm worried about," he muttered, mainly to himself.

—

"Been about an hour and a half since I relieved our brilliant com officer," Mike Beck was recording on the ships log. "Everything's nice and peaceful here at Hotel Saturnia. Should be seeing the first coronal evidence through the planet's outermost atmospheric layer in 'bout, oh, forty or forty-five minutes." He paused the log and started checking for any movement anywhere onboard *Magellan.*

"Good, looks like everyone's still being have themselves." He said as he checked the thermal imaging collector in Simone's room and saw the red/blue signature of a partially clothed human.

"You just stay right there, lady."

—

Daniel Blackstone was in the hotel room briefing Harry about the tunnel when Stalker walked in. They both turned to see a middle-aged man sucking on a partially melted bomb pop.

"Ice cream truck," was all he mumbled. Then, seeing his two comrades shaking their heads disdainfully, he added, "Hey, I was hungry."

"All right." Daniel started once again telling of the tunnel and about their neighbor.

"One of us needs to find out exactly why she's here," he said as he looked at the youngest member of the team. "Yeah, you. She's gone now, and Roger Hand is tailing her. He'll call if she starts heading back this way so—"

"I'll go, I'll go," Harry was already saying. After stuffing an electronic device the size of a small cell phone into his pocket, he left the suite.

Daniel looked at Stalker, who had a blue ring around his mouth, and said, "I need to get back to the tunnel. You stay here and monitor the situations. Whatcha got for spelunking?"

"Should be a bag of toys down at the desk. Had some stuff sent UPS while we were on our way here."

Daniel looked at him quizzically.

"Don't worry, it's labeled HAS, Houston Archaeology Society." Smiling, he added, "Let's go to the toy store."

Daniel really enjoyed working with creative people. In fact, he was smiling ear to ear as they left the room.

—

Simone woke up once again fully refreshed. However, this time she felt as if time were running out. She needed to do something but had no idea what that something was.

"What a dream," she said as she swung her legs off her bed and planted her feet firmly on the floor. In the darkness, her feet stepped on something on the floor that her senses told her was quite out of place.

"Little Shepherd."

"Chirp."

"Room lighting-one third."

"Chirp."

The lights came up slowly, allowing her eyes to adjust. She was staring at the floor unable to tell what she had stepped in.

"Room lighting eighty-five percent, please."

Simone Sytte sat on her bed, smiling at the floor.

"I love You, Lord Jesus," she softly said as she looked at the handful of sand strewn around her bed on *Magellan's* floor.

"Wake up, sleepy ones," came Mike Beck's voice over the ship's intercom. "It's another day in space, and hey, it's time to go home. Coffee's on in the galley. Nothing new to report; all is well." You could literally hear him smiling as his voice was lilting through *Magellan's* rooms and corridors. "Time's a-wasting, oh great astronauts, and we've got work to do. Breakfast in fifteen." Then there was silence.

CHAPTER 42

THE BOND OF DARKNESS

In all the years he had been with covert ops, Daniel Blackstone had never felt the sense of apprehension that he was now feeling. Even when he worked in the NSA, he never had the uneasiness that he was experiencing at this moment. Although he could not put his finger on any one cause for alarm, his senses were heightened, and he felt as if he were ready for anything.

He pulled up to Irma's house. "Sunshine," he kept reminding himself. She was waiting at the porch door, lemonade in hand, shotgun within reach, leaning against the porch rail.

"At least I feel that I'm welcomed this time," he said as he got out of the car and walked back to the trunk. Opening it up, he pulled out a large nylon duffel bag and then slung it over his shoulder.

"May I come in, ma'am?"

"You are hereby always welcome at my house young fella," she said with a mischievous twinkle in her eyes. Then she added, "Course, I can't speak for the Devil's Hole. You might not be welcomed there." Daniel was lowering the bag down to the floor of the tunnel when Sunshine started to pray.

"Oh Lord, me and You ain't been talking much lately, but I sure hope You'll listen to me now. God, if this tunnel takes 'em where they want to go, they might not like what they find. Fact is, it could get a might dangersome down there. Please keep 'em safe, Lord. Don't let the old wretched devil have his way with 'em."

Daniel waited patiently for the old girl to finish her invocation of protection on the small band of men. *Does she know something else that she hasn't told us?* he was wondering as he began to speak.

"You may hear some explosions, some noises. Don't let it worry you. We may have to blast our way through any cave-ins. Oh, here, it's a two-way radio."

"Looks like a phone to me."

"It is, eh, essentially. You can talk with us by pushing this button, and we can call if we need help. Now if you don't hear from us ..." his voice trailed off for a second almost unnoticed, "for twenty-four hours, push this green and black button." He was showing her the face of the phone so he knew she would understand which button. "And help should get here pretty quickly, OK?"

"Got it, young feller."

"Thanks, Irma. Keep your eyes and ears open, sweetie."

"You talk to me like that and you're gonna take me out for dinner, young man."

Daniel laughed. "You know what, you're on!" He kissed her playfully on the cheek and headed down into the darkness of the tunnel.

—

Ralph had made it to Pascaloni's Pub and was headed back to Johnson Space Center in record time. As he came around one of the long bends in the road, he saw numerous emergency vehicles and police cars up ahead. He slowed as he approached the scene and scanned the immediate area and saw the car being pulled up from out of the lake. The two would-be assailants were leaning, with their hands cuffed, on one of the highway patrol cars. He saw two troopers examining what looked like one of the modern automatic weapons he'd only recently been hearing about. Shifting his gaze back to his assailants, he noticed that they had seen him and were staring menacingly at him. He smiled as big as he could and waved to them as he continued on his way.

—

"So, you're saying that we should only do a three point five–second burn instead of a five-second burn?"

"That's right, Commander. Simone and I have run simulations, and I, um, I mean we agree that to be on the safe side, we should only engage IGS for three point five seconds."

"So, according to your calculations, where would that place us?"

"Just about twenty-four hours away from terran orbit, Commander—that is, if *Magellan's* engines are at eighty-five percent or better."

"*Magellan's* engines are at ninety-five point two, Doctor," chimed in *Magellan's* pilot.

Matt Moore had received all the information he needed, and he acted upon it.

"OK, sounds reasonable enough to me. You all have one hour to get ready to go home. Anyone have any problems with that?"

No one voiced any opposition to the plan, so Commander Moore made it official.

"Very good, one hour. Let's make it right, folks. Let's move it." He faced his communication officer and spoke in a more subdued voice.

"Carl, let mission control know we're coming home."

"Yes sir, gladly." He spun in his seat and started the communication linkup. His commander had walked up behind him, and speaking in a hushed tone, said, "I also want you to set up a priority one secure line in my quarters for, oh, fifteen minutes from now. Is that a problem to arrange, Carl?"

"No sir, not at all." He turned to look into his commander's face to see if there were any other instructions.

"No one is to know of this, Carl," was all he said as he slapped him on the shoulder then walked off to check with the rest of his crew.

—

"So, how 'bout that hike to mound thirty-eight?"

"I was wondering when you'd be back," Bob Mengersi said to Jessica as he walked up and took her hand. "Tell you what, we're gonna be closing up shop here in about," he looked at his watch, "thirty-five minutes. How about I buy you a cup of coffee," he said as he led her to the quaint little café that was tucked away in the back corner of the center, "and you can scroll through these archives. I'll be with you before you know it."

He had handed her a laptop file reader labeled "Historical Research" and she sat down, eyeing him as he walked over to the counter and then returned with a rather large cup of cappuccino.

"Thanks."

"I won't be long. There's actually some pretty interesting stuff in there," he said as he walked away.

Roger Hand was parked out in the farthest area of the parking lot so he wouldn't be noticed by Jessica. It also gave him a good vantage point to watch all the exits out of the center. Roger was one to always make the most out of his time, so he started to go over the file he had downloaded labeled, "Jessica Vandale: Level-One Only."

—

"Hey, where are you guys?" Blackstone said loudly into the darkness ahead of him. He hadn't lit any of the light sticks yet. He was still standing at the bottom of the ladder. Just then, some faint light appeared off to his left. Then it grew brighter, and he realized he had been staring at, and talking to, a side wall of the tunnel when he announced his presence in the lightless void of the subterranean chamber.

Smitty and Martin popped into view ten feet away. "Hey, boss." Smitty was smiling. "Our professor has the creeps down here."

"Can't say I blame him," Daniel replied as he took in the sights. "You can put those lanterns out. We've got toys." As he spoke, he opened the bag he was carrying and took out what looked like soap on a rope. Taking the bar, he smacked it on the side wall, and it began to glow a dull white light. Five seconds later, it had the brilliance of a thousand-watt halogen bulb. The rope allowed it to be hung around Daniel's neck. The very design of the light bar projected the light away from the small band's leader.

"That's nifty. What else ya got in your bag, Santa?"

"All kinds of stuff. Right now let's get our direction right." His voice trailed off as he engaged a small laser compass into operational mode. "That's the way," he said as he pointed ahead.

"So what kind of weapons ya got?" Smitty asked as he automatically patted his side to make sure his pistol was still in place.

"How's radiation pulse grenades for a start?"

Smitty let out a long, low whistle. "I've heard of them bad boys. Melt a tank in one three-second pulse."

"And then there are these," Blackstone said as he handed Smitty a rather fat-looking snub-nosed pistol.

"Energy frequency pistols—nice." Smitty was smiling ear to ear now. "Let's go, Cap'n."

Now it was Martin's turn to speak up.

"I hate to say this, guys, but um, I get the feeling those weapons aren't going to help much down here if my instinct is right."

"What, pray tell are ya talking about, Martin?"

Looking Daniel Blackstone in the eye, he matter-of-factly said, "I don't think this battle is going to be against flesh and blood."

Daniel thought for a couple of seconds and then said, "I don't buy into any of your religious stuff, and quite frankly, I wonder if you even do. Two hours ago you were about to blow your brains out, and now you're 'onward Christian soldier'? Just what in the name of Sam Hill are you talking about?"

"Maybe this really is the Devil's Hole"

"And maybe it's ET's mommy, Professor. Anyway, it turns out, we have to find it, OK? You in, or do you want to go stay with Sunshine?"

"I'm in."

"Good, let's go find our little black hole."

—

Jessica loved searching historical archives, so she didn't mind waiting for her personal tour guide. She started at the earliest records, and then an idea struck her. She broadened her search to include the local area, not just the mounds site. She started at 1800 and began scrolling forward just to see what this neck of the woods had tucked away. That's when she saw it. The local paper that heralded the two mine owners who, in a drunken binge, blew up a tunnel they had found because they said, "It leads straight to hell's doorway."

Interesting, she thought, so she entered the names of the two men into the search engine of her palm top, and in about fifteen seconds, she was looking at the address of a person called Irma Saul, a granddaughter of one of the two drunken miners. She entered the region, then state, then city, and finally the address for Irma into her GPS uplink and almost instantaneously was looking at a picture of a small house taken from space. It was a small house that had a very familiar sedan parked in front of it.

"Great," she muttered about the time that Bob walked up.

"Hey, I can go get lost if you want." He was half-smiling.

"No, not you." She sighed mainly just to buy time for a line or two. "It's just, well, I'm having trouble with the story I want to do, Bob."

"Can I help?" he said as he grabbed one of the high-back café chairs and sat in it backward, leaning his chin on the back of the chair, studying his newfound friend.

Jess had to go out on a limb. Time was running out, and she needed to make a move and get to the little gem that was, supposedly, tucked away right under their very feet.

"Look, Bob, um, can I trust you?" She was really pouring on the charm now.

"Sure, Jess … I, I guess so. Trust with what?"

"Well," she toyed with her spoon and cup, "I wasn't entirely truthful with you about why I'm here."

That made him sit a little straighter.

"So, why are you here?"

She was looking around. There were still a few center personnel finishing up, and she was using that as an excuse to give her more time for a bigger, better lie. "D'ya have somewhere we can talk?"

"I've got just the place. C'mon." He jumped up, took her hand, and walked around the corner, through two huge copper-looking doors and down a hall to his office.

"It's probably not as fancy as what you're used to, but, welcome to my office. No one will bother us here. Hold on a sec." He picked up his phone

"Hey, Judy, look, I'm back in my office. Yeah, last-minute stuff. Hey, can you lock up for me? Good, thanks, Judy. Good night." He hung up the phone, folded his hands in front of him on his desk, and then said, "So, Ms. Vandale, what can Cahokia Mounds offer you?"

—

Roger was totally engulfed in Jessica's background file when his cell rang.

"Hand."

"It's Ralph. Hey, *Magellan's* going to break orbit in a couple minutes and head home. Any instructions?"

"No, you know protocol. Just keep me posted. Hey, by the way, anything else on your highway buddies?"

"Funny you should mention that." Ralph began his abbreviated version of what he saw on the way back to Johnson Space Center.

Roger was laughing as he ended his phone call. He could just see his old friend driving by two would-be assassins, waving, smiling, and probably even saying, "Na-na, ya missed me."

—

The scene on board *Magellan* was tensely subdued. "Let's leave a view port open this time," Dr. Armone requested.

"Not a bad idea, Doctor. Are we ready?" His ears were attacked by several voices all at once saying, "All systems go," and "Drive parameters nominal"

"Three and a half seconds, Doctor."

Simone chimed in, "IGS online and ready to initiate drive."

"Thank you, Simone. It's your show now Dr. Armone. Just remember, we have about a ten minute window to do a sling-shot escape if we have to."

All eyes were fixed on Jon Armone as he began the sequencing countdown.

"IGS will engage in five, four, three, two, one."

CHAPTER 43

THE DARK HALL

"How long have we been down here?" Blackstone asked as they rounded yet another bend in the tunnel.

"Twenty-three minutes, Cap'n," came the reply from Smitty. "Hey, Professor, whatcha know 'bout these tunnels?'

"Know? This is all new to me. I thought it was just an old local fable, but," he reached his hand out to touch a trickle of water as it meandered down the wall on his left, "I never even dreamed I'd be here."

Blackstone was leading the small troop slowly down the ebony-slated corridor. He was in a hurry, but he knew at times being in a hurry could get you killed. "We're still on course, it appears," he said as he checked the compass. The walls seemed to breathe around them, encompassing the small troupe in the ancient underground lair of darkness. One moment the pathway was barely wide enough to walk through single file, and then the next, wide enough for the men to walk side by side.

"This is creepy," Smitty said.

"Yeah, I'm not liking it a whole lot either, but hey, so far no one's been shooting at us."

As they came around another bend single file, Blackstone stopped dead in his tracks. Martin winced as he heard the blasphemies emanating from the man.

Then he simply said, "Gentleman, it seems we have a cave in." Without saying another word, he held his right hand out, palm up, and waited as Smitty planted one of the grenades into his ready hand.

"Boys, I suggest you get back a few dozen yards. We're gonna melt some rock."

Martin had never even heard of radiation pulse grenades before, but when it detonated, he saw a faint swish of green light that he knew he would never forget. The funny thing was there was no sound of an explosion, no rocks flying through the air or crashing down, nothing, save the faint almost-iridescent green flash.

"What about radiation?" he found himself timidly asking.

"No residual radiation, it's all fused out of existence the instant it pulses," Blackstone answered. "Let's see if we made an impact."

They got up from their crouching positions in unison and peeked around the bend.

"Wow, now that's cool!" Smitty said as they looked at the newly opened corridor, its rock walls now glistening in the artificial light like highly polished marble. "Jules Verne would be so proud."

As they started to continue on their quest, their attention was drawn to a light, cold breeze that came at them.

"That's weird," said Smitty.

"No, what's weird is that we are on our way one mile beneath the surface of earth to look for a black hole," Martin replied.

"I agree. This all seems, oh, I don't know, just, just plain weird, doesn't it?" Daniel said.

As they walked, the ground began to abruptly descend beneath them to the point that it was hard to walk at a normal speed. Another bend, and Daniel stopped dead in his tracks again and this time whistled.

"Wow, this is cool."

The path was now a single rock a yard wide stretched out for about thirty yards with pools of water on either side. Daniel didn't move for a moment and turned to make sure the other two men were stationary then he turned out the light.

The water was alive with a pale blue glow. Within it were swashes of orange and yellow as subterranean fishes darted to and fro. The glow from the water was almost bright enough to light their way, but Blackstone turned his light back on, sighed, and said, "I think we're getting close. The sub saw blue light just before it, uh,… vanished."

"Sub?" was all Martin could spit out.

"Look, Professor, in some aspects of our little adventure, the less you know the better for all of us."

That statement did not make Martin any more comfortable at all.

"So, have people died?"

Sighing, Blackstone answered, "Two fine men, soldiers; worked with 'em both on more than one occasion." He stared at the scenery in silent reverence.

It was just about this time that the reality of this situation was beginning to sink in even deeper to Martin Sherfy's soul.

"I'm gonna pray for a minute."

"Need a gun to put in your mouth to help you talk to God?" came Smitty's snide remark.

Martin stared them both down. "Look, I'm a man. I'm also a Christian who believes in the God of the Bible. Now, that doesn't make me perfect. I got tired of life, fed up with stupid crap just like everybody else does. Don't you find it odd, even just a little bit, that you happened to find me when you did? Isn't it also a little strange that we're here now because I just *happened* to remember an old fable? Look, I don't give a rip about what you think of me, but I get the intense feeling that I need to talk to the Lord. So just deal with it." He stood there for a few seconds in silence and then said, "Father, I—no, *we* need Your help and protection. In Jesus's name only I ask. Amen."

Martin didn't know what to say when both men quietly said "Amen" as well.

"Let's go," Daniel said as he unbuttoned the holster that held his pistol and began to walk slowly across the surface of the rock bridge.

Smitty and Martin waited for Blackstone to reach the end before either made a move forward.

"You go; I'll keep rear guard," Smitty said.

"Hey, Daniel, was it slick?" Martin yelled to his leader.

"Didn't seem so. Just take your time, though. Don't really know what those little fishes like to eat."

Martin inched out onto the rock jetty. He was thinking that it resembled a small whale when a light wisp of cold air hit him in the face.

"Martin."

There it is again, he thought

"What did you say?" Daniel said. "I thought someone said Martin."

"I didn't," Smitty grunted

Daniel was looking around him now. "Almost sounded like a whisper."

221

Martin was ignoring the conversation; he had spiritual battle on his mind. *If Daniel heard it too,* he wondered, *is that a good thing or a bad thing?*

"Jesus, You are my Shepherd. I am walking into enemy territory, and I ask that You deliver me—I mean us—from evil." He was slowly, cautiously making his way along the rock path, now better than halfway to the other side. At that instant, his soul was ignited by his unseen God. His spirit aflame with power from on high. He stopped right where he was and lifted both hands up high above his head. Then speaking, no *shouting,* at the top of his lungs, he said, "Yea, Lord, even though I walk through the valley of the Shadow of Death, *I will fear no evil.*" Then somehow he sounded twice as loud when he proclaimed, *"For You, oh Lord God of Israel, are with me! Whom shall I fear? What shall I fear? You alone are God of heaven and earth, and I belong to You!"* With that, Martin dropped his hands and began to laugh like a child playing in the back yard as he finished his trek to the other side.

"Very dramatic," Daniel said as the sound of one man's applause echoed from the other end.

"I was beginning to wonder if we would ever hear the 'Valley of the Shadow of Death' thing in our adventure." They could hear the smile in Smitty's voice as he approached. Then he crossed over to them and slapped Martin on the back and said, "Thanks, buddy, believe it or not, I needed that."

"We all did," Daniel said as he reached his hand out to shake Martin's, not as a leader or a commander, but as a friend.

"Sure wish I coulda had a video cam for that one."

"It was no act, guys."

"I think we know that now, Martin," replied Blackstone.

"Martin."

All three men heard it that time. They both looked at Martin, and Smitty asked, *"Spiritual* warfare, eh?"

"Yep, I got the feeling we're up against the very forces of hell or at least some of them. By the way, when we find this black hole thing, what are we supposed to do then?"

"This is strictly recon, Martin, we don't do anything yet," Daniel replied.

"Recon?"

"Reconnaissance, Professor," Smitty chimed.

"Take pictures, buy the T-shirt kind of outing?"

"That's the ticket."

"Anybody ever tell you two that you're crazy?"

"All the time," Daniel said, smiling.

"Yeah, that's why we get the interesting jobs."

"Maybe you'll tell me some stories sometime."

"Maybe, but not today. C'mon, let's move." Daniel turned his attention to the task at hand and then stopped again and looked at Martin, his forehead furrowed as if in deep thought.

"Why do we keep hearing your name whispered? We're the, um, dangerous secretive government types. So why you?" Daniel asked.

"I don't think you want me to preach to you guys, but," Martin silently, secretly, quickly asked the Spirit of God to help him as he looked into both men's eyes, "I'm Satan's enemy. I belong to the Creator of all things, and he knows that. Now," Martin knew he didn't have much time, so he condensed all he could, "if you guys have never been what is called *born again*—that is to say if you've never asked God to forgive your sins through His Son Jesus and accept the gift He alone offers—you're not the enemy, so to speak, of the devil. He couldn't care less about what you do. In fact, you could be playing a part in his scheme and not even know it."

Daniel put up his hands and said, "OK, I asked, and now I know. That's enough."

He turned and started along the corridor once again.

The three men walked in uninterrupted silence for about fifteen minutes. All the while, Martin was praying silently for the two men he was with. "God, I don't know if I did it right. These guys might even die today. Please, God, open their hearts to Your love, Your forgiveness."

"Hold it," Daniel said. He was standing at a fork in the tunnel. "Listen." All three men heard it. They put their hands on the wall before them, and they could feel it pulsing on the other side; the underground river.

"So, which way do we go?" Smitty asked.

Getting out the compass and then frowning, Daniel said, "Well, we would go south, but since the compass isn't cooperating, we need to be a little more creative." He saw the questioning look on Smitty's face, so he tossed him the compass. Smitty started laughing and then tossed it to Martin. Martin held it up in the light so he could see it and was surprised to see the compass spinning like a fan blade.

"That's a new one to me," he said and then tossed it back to Daniel, who stuck it back in his pocket.

"S'not unheard of. We've seen it happen before around strong mag fields and even around nuclear reactors."

Daniel fell silent for a moment as he laid both hands on the wall before him, trying to feel the direction the water was going, but to no avail.

"Let's split up," he abruptly announced. "You two go that way for ten minutes and then return here. I'll go the other way. Maybe we will get lucky."

This sounded reasonable to the other men, so Smitty and Martin took the right corridor while Daniel headed down the left; it was almost amusing to see the two agents both pull out the fat little pistols at the same time and begin to walk away from each other.

Martin and Smitty were only on their trek for maybe two minutes when Smitty announced, "I don't buy it, I just don't buy it." He looked over his shoulder to a somewhat baffled Martin Sherfy and then continued with, "The Jesus thing, sounds kinda goofy, Professor."

Martin was praying silently again for direction. This was a God-appointed conversation, and he knew it.

"I don't understand it myself, Smitty, but …" he was searching for the right words. *So, help me God!* he prayed. "I know it's all true. Look, the Bible's never been wrong about anything, and there's hardcore science and biology in it—astronomy and astrophysics, things that couldn't have been known by people when it was written. Then there's doctrine, teaching of right and wrong, not to mention all the prophecies. Those that have been fulfilled were fulfilled exactly as predicted."

"So what about our little black hole?"

"What'dya mean?"

"Surely something this big would be mentioned, wouldn't it?"

"Not necessarily, but maybe it's part of the end-times scenario. Maybe it is there, and no one sees it. Besides, it's not that big of a deal to the One who spoke the universe into existence. I'll tell you what is a big deal to God, though."

"Oh yeah, what's that?"

"You, Smitty; you're a big deal."

Smitty just snorted as they began to notice a slight inclination of the causeway.

"If you die today, do you know where you'll go?"

"Nope; don't much care neither."

"God cares."

"Right."

"Really. Look, if you were the only person on Earth, God would have still come and died to pay for your sins."

"OK, so what about the old walkin' outta the tomb deal? Where's the proof of that?"

"Let me ask you a question."

He saw Smitty would acquiesce, so he continued, "Somewheres about 1992 or '93, an American blew up a federal building in Oklahoma City. Remember the story?"

"Yeah, course I do. Required study for our kinda job. You're talking about Timothy McVeigh."

"That's right. Do you remember what evidence they had against him? Watch your head," he added as Smitty narrowly missed smacking into a stalactite that appeared out of nowhere.

"Yeah, real piece of detective work. All the evidence was circumstantial. Not one shred of physical evidence to link him to the attack, no eyewitnesses placing him there. What's this got to do with your Jesus, Professor?"

Smitty had to duck around another stalactite and its accompanying stalagmite formation as he was asking the question. "The resurrection; there were eyewitnesses and all kinds of circumstantial evidence. Truth is, eyewitnesses can lie, but it's hard to concoct circumstances, right?"

Smitty stopped and leaned against another mineral deposit the size of a small evergreen tree.

"Circumstantial evidence sometimes speaks louder than words." Smitty was curiously eyeing the stalagmite forming coming up from the ground as he spoke. He glanced up ahead and then said, "We need to turn around and go get Daniel. I think we're on the right path."

"How do you know?" Martin asked

"Stalactites and mites. There's water 'round here dripping down to cause these formations. We must be really close."

"Let's go get Daniel, then."

They turned around and were heading back, and Martin was asking God to get the conversation going again. About that time, Smitty spoke up.

"So, what circumstantial evidence?"

"If the resurrection was a hoax, don'tcha think the leaders and government people would have had the ability to prove it? They never did find the body of Jesus, ya know."

"Yeah, but it coulda been pulled off."

"OK, so why did the officials just fade away? What about ten or eleven men who died horrible deaths, and all they had to do was 'fess up' and they coulda lived. Ouch!" Martin just cracked his head on the first stalactite they encountered on the way in. It was obviously better hidden from this direction. He was rubbing his forehead as he continued, "Then there's the local people who saw Jesus.

"No one ever contradicted them. Not even on their deathbeds did they admit to lying. But I tell you," he was speaking most earnestly now, "to me, the most compelling evidence is the Jews themselves who abandoned Judaism to follow their Messiah. Jews don't give up Judaism. It's who they are."

"We're back," Smitty abruptly announced and stopped. No sooner had he stopped when they heard Daniel coming up to meet them. Smitty stood tall and proud, smiling from ear to ear as he asked, "Any luck?"

"No, starts going down deeper, though. What about you two?"

"Bull's-eye."

Daniel understood and simply said, "Let's go."

Without so much as another word, the three men headed down the path. In a matter of moments, they began to pass the stalactites from above, having to duck hither and yon and cautiously make their way past the stalagmites on the ground.

"This is about as far as we got, no wait. This is farther, it looks different." Martin announced.

Daniel looked around somewhat confused and then asked, "How do you know it's the right way if this is as far as you guys went?"

"The rock formations, man!" Smitty loved to play teacher. "Water is close. That's what's causing all cavern formations." He put his hand on the wall alongside him, expecting to feel the pulse of the underground current but instead felt nothing. "That's odd, no water running here." It was just about as those words came out of his mouth the three men heard a drip. *Doink!* Loud as you please. As if on cue, the three men looked up. They hadn't noticed, but the ceiling was now more than fifteen feet up.

Smitty jumped up on one of the larger stalagmites and started to climb upward. Martin was amazed at the man's agility. He looked like some large primate playing in the forest. In no time at all, he was reaching his left hand up to place it on the cavern's ceiling while securing his hold on the rock formation with his other extremities.

"Well I'll be!" he exclaimed. "We're underneath the river!" Scurrying down most of the way and then jumping the final four or five feet, Smitty landed on his feet and said, "We must be getting close. I could feel the pressure of the current against the rock, and it is flowing..." He paused, smiled, and then pointed and said, "That-a-way."

"Let's go, boys." Daniel was obviously excited. His pace was more like that of a twenty-year-old than that of a man in his sixties. They came upon another bend in the road and were about to round the corner when they heard it again.

"Martin."

A wisp of hot air blew in their faces as they heard the voice. Then they smelled the most awful aroma of rotten eggs.

"I was at Old Faithful there in Yellowstone once. It smelled just like this," Smitty said as he scrunched up his face in disgust.

"Sulfur," Martin said matter-of-factly as the three men paused; Daniel had turned around to face them, which put the bend in the tunnel behind him. That's when Martin noticed it. He thought at first his eyes were simply adjusting to the light now pointing at him instead of away in from him.

"Turn off your light, Daniel."

"OK, but why are you whispering? Seems like the bad guy already knows we're here," Smitty said as he leaned over to speak to Martin, who was standing next to him. Three men who were about to make one of the greatest discoveries of all time (if not the greatest) stood for a moment and laughed uncontrollably.

As Daniel turned off the light, they saw that there was a soft blue light coming from around the bend in the tunnel, and somewhere in the distance, they heard the sound of a waterfall.

CHAPTER 44

MAGELLAN'S CUP

Before any alarms sounded, before any fear arose, a single computer-generated voice announced, "Impact in seven minutes."

Then the chaos erupted as the moon grew menacingly before them .

Amidst the clang and clamor of sounding alarms, Matt Moore's commanding voice was heard loud and clear, "Stations, report. Helm?"

"Breaking jets did not fire, sir, and helm is not responding, Commander. Repeat, helm is not responding."

Unshaken by the helm report, Matt systematically turned next to his navigation officer

"Navigation report?" he queried

"We're headed nose first into the dark side, sir." There was a slight pause, and then he said, "But just barely. I'm estimating a six-degree latitude impact site from the line of solar demarcation."

"Great. Carl, how's the com link?"

"Negative, Commander, as long as we are in the dark. Chances are no one knows we're even here."

"What about IGS, Dr. Armone?"

"I'm on it, but I don't think we have time for programming any sequencing," the doctor said as he worked at his keyboard.

"Will somebody please tell me something that we can use?"

"Impact in six minutes," almost on cue the computer announced.

Matt Moore was about to speak to Simone when he noticed the vacant, inexpressive look on her face

"Simone!" he yelled over to the scientist. Just as if someone had slapped her or splashed ice cold water on her face, she became animated once again.

"Now I understand," she said to no one.

"What, Simone?" Moore was almost frantically crying out, "Understand what?" The commander now stood before the woman thinking she had an answer to the current dilemma. He was totally unprepared for the next statement from her.

"Aren't there explosive decouplers on the sled, Commander?"

"What!" He didn't know what to think of this girl now. "What are you talking about, Simone?"

"Commander." Simone now looked deeply into Matt's eyes and spoke in a very controlled, almost dreamlike tone.

"I cannot take the time to explain, but I believe *Magellan* is doomed. However," she stopped for a second to look once again at our moon that was looming ever larger before them, "there need be no loss of life."

Commander Moore wouldn't let her continue. "What is wrong with you, Simone? What are you talking about?"

"Commander, if we plunge nose first, there will be no survivors, but if we blow the sled, maybe we can alter our trajectory enough to come in on our belly."

"She may be right, Matt," chimed in *Magellan*'s pilot. "We have no control here." He lifted his hands in surrender.

"But we must act fast, sir," Simone continued. "Before we get any closer to the surface, and maybe we can get just enough push to get into a line of sight mode for communications to be operable."

All eyes were on the commander now

"Go, go, go! We blow it." Then turning to his pilot, he said, "Do we even have pitch on your control?"

Magellan was spinning slowly on her flight to the moon.

"Negative, sir. I can't explain it; it's like someone just shut the whole blasted ship down."

"OK." Then, turning on the internal com system, he looked over and said, "Simone, you and Dr. Armone go to the sled pad on the port-side cannon down the access shaft to junction C. I'll keep in touch on the com.

"Roger," was all they said as they both ran out of the bridge.

"Impact in five minutes."

—

Jessica and Bob were about to get into a deep discourse on mound thirty-eight when the office doors were kicked open. Two Middle Eastern men came in with weapons drawn. The larger of the two spoke to Jessica.

"Go, you are done here. We are the ones who are doing Allah's work now."

"I don't think so," she protested as the other one grabbed her by the arm and threw her out of the room. She jumped up and started to come back toward the man when he pointed his pistol at her. She stopped and, without saying a word, turned around to leave. That's when she saw all the blood still flowing from a woman's lifeless body not ten feet from her. Jessica had never been so angry in her life, but she continued out the doors, which had never been locked.

"What do you want? Who are you people?" she heard Bob's frantic voice from behind her as she left.

—

Roger was still reading her file when movement in the parking lot caught his eye. He watched Jessica walk up to her Humvee and pound on the side and then turn to look at the building she had just come out of. She didn't move. It looked to Roger as if she might be planning her next move, so he quickly got out of his car and started very quietly to come up behind her. He had a good hundred feet or so to go, but he was trying his best to sneak up on her unaware. Fifty feet; she still hadn't moved. He could now hear her cursing someone. Thirty, and then twenty feet to go. He was almost upon her when, for no reason, she turned around and looked right into his eyes. The woman had the strangest look of complete surprise on her face.

"Well, Roger Hand," she said almost in a convincingly innocent tone. "What are you doing here?"

—

"Shut up." The large man said ominously, "We will ask the questions."

Bob Mengersi was terrified. "What d-do you want?"

"The passageway—where is it?"

"What are you talking about?"

"Do not play games with me," the man said as he aimed his hand gun at Bob's face from less than three feet away.

"You tell us how to get beneath the large mound *now.*"

"Are you guys nuts? I have no idea what you are—"

Bob didn't get to finish his statement as the handgun exploded before him. At the same instant, he felt pain like he had never felt before. His whole face was on fire, and then instantly he saw, as if he was above the scene, the large picture window behind him becoming splattered with blood and brain material. Everything fuzzed out around him into a thick darkness, and Bob Mengersi screamed into the void as he felt the fires of hell envelop him. He had been lonely in his lifetime, and now all he would ever know is loneliness; loneliness and the eternal suffering of damnation.

—

"We're at the terminal, Commander," Jon said over the com.

"Four minutes to impact"

"Man, that's getting on my nerves," Matt said to no one in particular. Then he said to the doctor, "Pull the two red pins out of the junction box. That will release the firing mechanism."

Just as Simone and Jon Armone each pulled out a pin, a new alarm sounded.

"That's impossible!" Simone screamed her objection to the alarm she had designed. Then they heard the computerized voice say, "Containment field breach; system will go critical in twenty minutes."

—

Roger Hand was a dozen light years past angry; before him stood a traitor of the highest magnitude. He honestly wanted to kill her on the spot. For an instant, he even entertained that very idea, knowing full well it was within his authority to do so, no questions asked. Instead, he reached out with the velocity of a cobra and latched onto her upper arm and said, "C'mon, young lady, you're going with me."

He never saw the mace container in her other hand. She pulled the arm he had grabbed into her upper torso to pull him nearer, and then, emptying the small canister into his face, she escaped his grasp. As he brought both hands up to his face and eyes, she spun around and brought her foot crashing into the side of his head. Roger had been knocked to the ground and for all general purposes was as useless as a screen door on a submarine.

Jessica hopped up into the Humvee and, turning the ignition key as fast as she could, threw the vehicle into drive, making her getaway.

As she went past the two large entryway doors to the interpretive center, she saw the two men coming out. They in turn saw her and began to head to their vehicle. As they made their way to the car, they heard coughing coming from the rear parking lot. Looking over, they saw a man lying on the ground apparently trying to catch his breath. The two assassins had no idea who the man was and, quite frankly, didn't care. They jumped into their car virtually unnoticed by Roger and sped off down the center's drive.

—

"Matt, the pins are out," came Dr. Armone's voice over the com. As he spoke, a small, cylindrical post arose from the console.

"Good, now, turn the large round cylinder to the left—counterclockwise till it clicks and then stops."

"I'm doing it." Jon was turning the shaft till he heard (and felt) a click. Then the cylinder would turn no more. Instantly the console turned a pale yellow and the shaft glowed with an orange hazard color. "OK, it's done, and I've got color."

"Listen, Doctor, you two are right under the blast area. The sled is mounted right above you, so when it blows—"

"Three minutes to impact"

"I wish that thing would blow itself," came the exasperated cursing from the commander.

"Matt, Simone and I are ready; we're running out of time."

"OK, wait till I give you the signal and then blow that puppy. We need to wait till we roll one more time." The pause seemed like an eternity. Simone and Jon Armone both were entangling themselves among pipes and conduit, not knowing what kind of force would be emitted from the blast but trying to be ready for it.

"Steady, steady, a little more—now, Jon!"

Jon Armone pushed the cylinder back into the console. The entire console turned to orange as the overhead locking bolts blew apart. A secondary charge underneath the sled forced it away from *Magellan*, its blast equally moving *Magellan* into a different trajectory.

The force of the blast shook the entire ship, knocking half her crew to the floor.

"I've got some thrusters responding, sir!" exclaimed *Magellan's* pilot. Our vector is a little steep, but I might be able to steer this lady a little."

"Keep at it," barked Commander Moore. "Jon, Simone, get up here, and—no, wait, go to engineering and see what is up with the reactor."

"We're already on our way, Matt."

"Two minutes to impact."

"I wonder why it's always a female's voice on a computer voice card telling people bad news," Jon innocently said to himself out loud. Simone started to laugh and then said, "C'mon, Jon, we've got work to do."

The door at engineering was flashing a warning light as the two approached. "No hint of contamination yet," Jon said as the two entered through the door.

The room seemed in perfect order. There was no hint of any danger.

"This is bad, Jon," Simone said quietly.

"What, Simone? I don't see anyth—oh no!" He spotted the problem and instantly knew what had caused the damage.

"Fluxural feedback. The reactor wasn't shut down enough when we initiated IGS. The sequencing caused a slight magnetic shift in the harmonic frequency regulators." Simone was all business now. Not even looking at Jon as she spoke, Simone laid one hand on the top of the reactor core as if she were trying to soothe a dying child.

"She is burning herself up."

"And us with her, uh, if we survive the crash, that is."

"Crash or not, she is gonna blow. I know that we needed to have the main engines on line, just in case IGS failed, but we should have at least partially shut down the reactor. How could we have been so careless, Jon?"

"Don't go blaming yourself, girl. This is space, and in space, things go wrong."

Just then the com came to life.

"Jon, Simone, talk to me."

"Commander, the reactor is going to go critical," Simone said stoically.

"One minute to impact."

Matt Moore spoke to everyone now. "Get helmets and strap in. It's going to get bumpy, folks."

"We're going to make it, Commander. The Lord is with us," Simone said as she strapped Jon and herself into the padded chairs along the wall of engineering.

Matt wanted to say something to Simone, but he let it go. He looked at his crew as he strapped himself in and gave the thumbs-up signal. Everyone had gotten their suits on and were breathing their own oxygen as Captain Tom Wilkerson spoke into their earphones

"Impact in thirty seconds." *Magellan* shuddered violently, and everyone's eyes looked twice as big as normal.

"Whoa! Braking jets are firing—we're slowing down! I've got aft and belly thrusters at forty percent power … we just might make it folks!" The captain actually sounded excited to be crash landing on the moon some quarter of a million miles from home.

Just then a blinding light filled the bridge. "Daylight! Impact in five, four, three, two, one."

The sound of *Magellan* crashing onto the sterile lunar landscape was unbearable inside the craft. Outside there was no noise, only debris and metal flying everywhere. The dust that was kicked up by the airplane-style belly landing simply rose up above lunar surface and seemingly hovered in the sunlight as *Magellan* finally came to rest some twenty feet from a crater wall.

"Get mission control and tell 'em we need help," Matt said to Tom.

CHAPTER 45

SUBTERRESTRIAL

Daniel pulled out another toy from Santa's bag, as they dubbed it.

"Hey, I had one of those spy things when I was a kid. Took thirty cereal box tops and six weeks of endless waiting to get it," Smitty said as he looked over the newest addition to their arsenal.

"This one cost a little more, buddy," Daniel said with a chuckle. He held it in one hand as he entered commands onto a small keypad. With a small whirr noise, the periscope came to life, unfolding itself into what resembled an L shape—perfect for looking around corners.

"I've set it for normal light; let's just see what we have." Daniel was talking as he knelt at the edge of the corner and positioned the viewing instrument against the wall. Then he slowly moved the lens around the corner. Martin and Smitty stood silently by as Daniel attempted to see something, anything, apparently with little or no success. He pulled the unit back and entered a different command and then went back to looking. After about a half dozen attempts, Smitty spoke up.

"Why don't we just peek around the corner?" he asked. Daniel gave him a disgusted look, and then, with a slight huff of exasperation, set the unit down and lowered himself onto the base of the tunnel with the side of his head resting on the hard cold floor. He inched his way to the wall's edge. His memory filled with the story of the astronaut on *Magellan* who was sucked into a much smaller version of this thing. He wasn't prepared for what he saw, nor could he explain it.

"Great God of Creation," was all he could utter.

—

Jessica was driving with one hand and getting a satellite dump on her handheld with the other. Following the directions she had just seen on screen was easy. Losing the two maniacs behind her—well, that proved to be a little harder than she anticipated. She didn't even want them around the house she was headed for. She saw the soccer fields coming up on her right and she had a slight inspiration, of sorts. "After all, this is a Humvee isn't it?" She laughed to herself as she power slid into the empty parking area and headed across to the fields.

Just about a football field behind her, the two Arabic agents were in hot pursuit. Leaving the gravel area and bouncing into the field, her vehicle seemed so far to be all it was cracked up to be. She was actually enjoying the ride. Then her mind went back to the dead body on the reception room floor just five minutes ago, and somehow the fun turned quickly into primal fear. She looked in her rearview mirror and saw she had gained a little lead on her pursuers, but not nearly enough. Up ahead she saw a drainage canal, so she pushed harder on the accelerator and aimed for what she hoped was going to make for a good jump ramp. As she hit the bottom of the small ridge, she buried the gas pedal and hoped for the best. The ditch itself was a little wider than she had realized, a good thirty or thirty-five feet across. Amazingly, she landed past the dune on the other side and kept on going. She looked back just in time to see the pursuit car hit head on into the far ditch wall.

"Guess you're not as good as you thought, huh, fellas?" she said aloud as she headed for a small park just ahead of her. She had to go up and over some railroad tracks without a crossing, but after what she had just done, that was no problem at all. She pulled up onto one of the park's access roads and leisurely pulled to a stop beneath a spread of maple trees that were just beginning to show signs of new life. Jessica wondered about Roger. She really did like him. He was a real man who would always stand out in a crowd of little boys pretending to be men. She felt a twinge of sadness as she knew in her heart she would never have the opportunity to nurture any kind of relationship with him again. After all, she did give him the mace-in-the-face routine. With a deep, longing sigh, Jessica Vandale put all these thoughts aside and now began to focus on a house and a woman.

Irma Saul.

—

"We're venting atmosphere," was one of the first things Matt Moore heard as *Magellan* came to a crashing halt. On impact, all of the lesser critical programs and systems shut down, a precautionary measure to help ensure against fire. So, for the moment, the only light from within *Magellan* was emergency lighting, a soft red glow from incandescent lines built right into her hull. However, the light on the outside was brilliant and beautiful.

"Where are we venting?" came the request of the commander.

"On all lower decks—all our quarters, in fact. That's where the most damage has been done, at least for now."

"All right, people, we need to move it." At that statement, all eyes were on Matt, and they were asking the same question.

"Move it where?" was finally asked from an anonymous space-suited astronaut in the rear.

"Out people, out there, away from this space craft. If she blows her core, there's going to be a mighty big crater where we're standing, and I, for one, do not intend to be here at that very critical moment."

Even as he spoke, Commander Moore heard the sound of hatches de-pressuring.

"Reactor core breach in fifteen minutes."

That simple computer-generated statement did more to get everyone moving double time than anything Matt Moore could ever say. Knowing they were preparing to leave, he headed for engineering.

—

Panting for breath, gasping aloud, Daniel pulled away from his corner vantage point. His eyes were like two giant saucers. Smitty and Martin looked at him in the dim blue light and then at each other. Neither one was able to understand the look on the older man's face. The only noise they seemed to hear now was not the distant waterfall, but rather the sound of a man who was almost in a state of complete panic.

"It's—it's not a waterfall," he repeatedly stuttered out incredulously. His whole body was now shaking fiercely, a state of shock was rapidly setting in. Smitty was afraid for his friend, so he bent over and began to help him up. Martin took his cue and began to help. Both men were rubbing him down, first his arms then legs as they felt he could now stand on his own. The quaking had passed, but the fear was still very, very tangible in the elder agent's eyes.

"You'd think he just saw Medusa," Smitty said.

"I think he saw something a lot scarier than an old fable," Martin said in a hushed knowing tone.

Then, out of nowhere, when they never expected it, Daniel spoke. His voice was clear and steady, but it was also as cold as any icicle had ever dreamed of being, "It's sucking the water right out of the air."

Both Martin and Smitty now had to take a look for themselves. They sat Daniel down on a large rock and went to the corner; one man down on his knees, the other standing over him. Two men peaked around a corner and saw something that very few men in all of history had ever seen—let alone live to tell about.

Smitty could only curse in disbelief. Martin quietly exclaimed, "Lord Jesus, what do we do with this?"

—

Jessica hammered on the handheld processor as fast as she could.

"Got it," she exclaimed happily as the GPS upload logo came on screen. Entering a few swift strokes, she ran her fingers through her hair as she awaited the reply from her server. The unit beeped twice and then started spitting out directions. Jessica smiled defiantly as she realized she couldn't be much more than five minutes from Irma Saul's home. She entered a few more strokes then waited patiently for the response, checking constantly her mirrors to ensure no one would sneak upon her unaware. Beep! Beep! She looked at the small one-inch ultra high-definition screen and saw the identical scene at the Saul residence. The dark sedan was still parked outside the home, and she could see what looked like an elderly lady walking in the yard.

"Hmmm," she said as she began to think aloud. "If that's Irma, where is her guest—or should I say guests?" That's all she needed for an incentive to resume the quest. The Humvee came to life, and she pulled away from her temporary oasis. She was careful to observe all the traffic laws. The last thing she wanted right now was to be stopped by the police for speeding or running a stop sign. Occasionally glancing down at her live satellite GPS feed, she could see exactly where she was and where she needed (or wanted) to be. Pulling up to a stop sign, she saw that she needed to turn left and head north. Checking both directions. she pulled out onto Illinois 157. She hadn't gone much more than two blocks when she saw the sign marking her direction.

"Old Mill Road, there you are." Jessica was getting excited but was still constantly looking over her shoulder. She was on the road for a lot less time than she expected when she came around a curve and saw her destination. She pulled into the driveway and parked next to the sedan. She glanced down into the passenger area just to see if she could glean any info. *It really is quite handy being in one of the tallest vehicles made,* she thought. Seeing nothing (or no one) there, she began to exit her vehicle.

"Howdy there, young lady," came an old-sounding voice from the house's porch.

"Well, howdy yourself," Jessica said as she turned on the charm that had helped make her famous and deadly. She slung her purse onto her shoulder as she started to approach the porch steps. She began to talk as she took the first step forward.

"I'm here to do a news story on a lady named Irma Saul. Would that be you, by any chance?"

"Maybe, maybe not."

Jessica stopped before she stepped up onto the second step. "Well, I must be at the wrong house, 'cause you look way too young to be Irma."

That caused the woman to laugh, and she said, "I usually hear that line from those blasted cable salesmen that come out here to sell me cable service. You do look familiar, though." Irma was eyeing Jessica, and Jessica was eyeing the shotgun propped up against the house.

"My name is Jessica—"

Before she could finish, Irma finished for her, "Vandale, that's who you are, all right. Girl, what did you do to your hair?"

"Oh, that." She ran one hand through the rumpled, tangled mess. "Trying to not be noticed everywhere you go can get hard to do sometimes."

"Well, you don't fool me none, lady."

Then with a big smile, Irma said, "Come on in. I got some fresh lemonade."

—

"Is there anything you can do, Simone?"

"No, not unless you have several thousand gallons of water to flush the coolant systems. Then that would only buy some time. Our problem is a whole lot bigger than we can fix here."

Matt Moore looked at Jon Armone, who simply gave him the *that's the way it is* look.

"How far do we need to get away from ground zero?" he finally asked in a hushed, severe tone. Simone had a pen in her hand, tapping fiercely on the table that was between her and Matt.

"That's a little tricky here in a reduced grav situation.

"One thing in our favor is the fact that we are practically lodged against a decent-sized crater wall; that will help deflect the initial blast in one direction." Looking up from the pen into the commander's eyes, she continued, "We need to go the other way, and we need to go now, Commander."

—

Jessica loved to play cat and mouse, but this time she didn't have the luxury of time on her side. She was sitting in a rather large chair, undoubtedly an antique, sipping happily on a glass of the best lemonade she had ever tasted. The house around her was full of antiques, she quickly noticed, so she used that as her opening line. "I love this house, Irma. This is a real piece of America. Does the cuckoo clock still work?"

"Oh, once in a while," Irma said with a smile. "Mainly only when it wants to."

"How long have you lived here?"

"All my life, sweetie. Ain't never been married, but I did have a song written 'bout me once."

"Really." Jessica feigned interest. "What was the name of the song?"

"'Coal Miner's Daughter,'" Irma delivered the punch line, and both women burst into laughter.

"I didn't even see that one coming," Jessica said as she rose from the chair to stretch her legs and walk over to the large picture window that displayed a garden off to the left and the parking area of the driveway off to the right.

"So, is that your car?"

"No ma'am," Irma said matter-of-factly.

"Oh," Jessica said in a nonchalant manner, her head feeling a little tired, probably from all the excitement. She looked around the room, and then it dawned on her there was no TV in the house.

"Irma, don't you have a TV?"

"Nope, and that's what I keep telling those cable folk. Ain't never had one, ain't never wanted one neither." Irma was smiling.

"But well, how did you know who I was?" Jessica asked.

"Daniel," she answered matter-of-factly.

"Daniel?" Jessica was sensing something wrong now.

"Yes'm, Daniel Blackstone. He told me you might be by, so he asked me if I could make lemonade for you."

"What?" The visitor's mind was suddenly fogged, dazed, and confused.

"Yep, and he gave me some special sugar to sweeten it with too."

At that, Jessica collapsed onto the large sofa, sound asleep.

"Bet'cha didn't even see that one comin' neither," Irma said with a knowing smile.

Irma walked over and arranged Jessica's body more comfortably on the sofa. Then she laid her hand on the woman's shoulder and prayed.

"Heavenly Father, this here girl's all messed up. Please protect her and watch over her. Help her to see that the stuff she's involved in is all wrong, Lord. I ask this in my Savior Jesus's name. Amen"

CHAPTER 46

SETTING LIMITS

"I'm OK now, guys," Daniel announced abruptly. Then he said, "Did ya get a load of that thing?"

"Yeah," both men answered simultaneously.

Smitty asked, "So what's the protocol?"

"Protocol?" Daniel laughed. "Go introduce yourself to it."

"I'll pass," Smitty answered.

"Have you guys noticed something?" Martin asked.

Both men looked at him, and without them saying a word, he could see that they didn't have the slightest idea what he was asking.

"We haven't heard my name for a while."

"Maybe it knows you're here already," Daniel said.

"No, that's not it. I don't think it has a personality."

"So what're you getting at, Doc?" Smitty asked.

"I think we need to get done with whatever you guys need to do and get out of here ASAP."

"I'll go for that," Smitty quickly agreed.

"OK, we need to measure that thing, but from a distance."

"Yeah, no kidding. Man, can you believe it? There's a black hole right on the other side of this wall. I thought they sucked in everything around them," Smitty said as he opened up Santa's bag and got out a few odd-looking toys.

"Truth is, no one knows anything about them," Martin said.

"Until now, there wasn't any absolute proof they existed," Daniel said.

"Well, if anyone needs proof, there 'tis," Smitty said, smiling, pointing with his thumb in the direction of the anomaly.

Daniel was completely himself now, taking full control once again. "Let's start with a one-second UV scan and see what happens." Then he added, "By remote, of course."

They set up a small tripod device no larger than a four-inch flower pot on wheels and programmed the instructions into it. Once that was done, they pushed it with the periscope out around the corner just a few inches.

"Here we go," Daniel said as he hit a button on a remote control, wincing as if he were about to get slapped by an angry parent.

The instrument whirred gently for one second and then stopped. The men looked at each other and then decided to pull the scanner back to themselves just as the pressure wave hit them. It came out of nowhere and built in intensity like the sound of an oncoming train. It was hard to explain, almost as if the air in the cave was actually pushing down on them.

"Blackie knows we're here," Smitty whispered.

"I hope that's as bad as it gets, but we need a picture of the entire chamber over there. Then …" he paused and looked at his two comrades, "we leave."

"Um, you gonna use a flash?" Martin asked.

"Yeah," Daniel said as he prepared a small, remote-controlled camera.

Just like the measuring device, they set up the camera, and using a remote, handheld screen, they positioned the camera and adjusted the viewer till the whole chamber was in view. From above, they could see what looked a spider's web coming down to the small (or was it large? They really couldn't tell) sphere, giving it the appearance of hanging above a great chasm in the room. Then there was the river. That was creepy. It sounded and looked like a waterfall, only horizontally falling into the sphere from across the chasm. Then there was the faint blue light. All in all, a very surreal, even nightmarish, setting.

"OK, we're ready boys," Daniel said

"Lord, watch over us," Martin prayed

"Maybe we shouldn't use the flash," Smitty added as Daniel held up his hand and silently counted down with his fingers—five, four, three, two, one—and he pushed the camera's remote.

—

Back at mission control, Ralph Marlow was shocked at the transmission from *Magellan*. This was trouble with a capital T.

"Get me the white house," he said sternly to the ground communication officer.

Ten seconds, later he was handed a small black phone.

"Mr. President?" he inquired and received his answer.

"This is Ralph Marlow." He paused for a second. "No, ah, no sir, Roger is not back yet. In fact, sir, we have a situation that needs immediate attention."

As he spoke, he made his way to the back of the control room, and climbing the stairs slowly, he made his way to the hot seats.

—

In glorious sunlight unfiltered by atmosphere, seven astronauts traveled along the lunar surface as quickly as they could. Before them the stars shone in majestic splendor, and the earth hung before them in silent majesty.

"Carl," Matt Moore said as he huffed his way along, "did you get that message out?"

"Yes, sir, and a response."

Moore was caught off guard by that one.

"Response?"

"Yep, we need to go to a solo channel, sir."

Matt knew the protocol that was inferred by that statement. One on one, no other ears to hear. He surprised his com officer by saying, "Negative, Carl; we are all in this together"

Matt thought to himself, *we won't survive this ordeal anyway; what would it matter if someone heard something that might be labeled top secret?*

"You got it, sir. Well, there is a rescue underway. It should be here in less than an hour."

At that, Moore stopped dead in his tracks, and grabbing Carl by the arm, stopped him as well.

"An hour, how?"

Simone turned around to see the two men had stopped, so she hurried them along with one simple statement, "Gentlemen, the reactor core will go critical in less than two minutes; every yard away from ground zero will help."

At that, the two men started to walk, even jog slightly. From up ahead, the voice of Mike Beck was heard calling out, "Hey, guys, I think we've got some cover." He had walked up onto a small crater maybe a hundred meters across and ten meters deep.

Jon Armone caught up with him and said, "Yeah, this ought to do nicely."

"Are we far enough? What about radiation?" Deborah Dean asked and then wished she hadn't. They were immersed in more natural radiation just strolling along the lunar surface than anything *Magellan* could produce. Sheepishly, she added, "Oh yeah, guess it's not the radiation we need to worry 'bout; it's the blast and shock wave."

"Exactly," Simone said as she and the other astronauts caught up to them. The rim of the crater had one area that had a gentle slope, so they all quickly descended into the bowl.

"Thirty seconds," Simone announced

"You're starting to sound like the stupid computer," Moore answered the announcement, and as they spoke, a glimmer of reflected light streaked across the sky. Everyone looked up and stared in disbelief at the spectacle above.

"The sled," Jon said quietly.

"It's headed straight for *Magellan!*" Moore said

As the lunar pilgrims watched the missile head for its target, the horizon before them erupted in a blinding flash—then was gone. No blast, no nothing.

"What the … ?" Commander Moore spoke in a slow drawl.

Simone watched the whole episode quietly, contemplatively. The nuclear blast took out *Magellan* and the sled, and its own little black hole took out the blast.

"Lord, You are incredible!" she finally manager to utter. Simone knew in her heart that the Lord had dealt with the situation. In one deft blow, He had erased His message and protected them from a blast that was far bigger and deadlier than they had expected.

—

The cavern walls began to shake—no, more like pulsate—from the camera flash

"Blackie's mad again," Smitty said as he pulled the camera and tripod back from around the corner. Pieces of ceiling were beginning to crash around them. A low-frequency hum and vibration coming from the anomaly was causing the situation to escalate from bad to worse in a heartbeat or two.

Daniel was looking at a small monitor and saw the picture come up. He yelled above the noise, "Leave the equipment. Let's go!"

The three men were scrambling to make headway as if they were in a wind tunnel. The air pressure was so great they could barely walk, let alone run. This was worse than those dreams you have when you know you're in danger and can't move. The only problem was, this is no dream, and the danger was very real. Just then part of the cavern wall blew out, spewing rock and debris at the men. Smitty was stuck by a flying stalactite, and it tore through his upper torso with such force that it virtually ripped his body in half. He was dead instantly, and the other two men knew it.

"Leave him, go, go!" Daniel screamed

They both turned away from the corpse and started to head away when, instantly, it was over. The pressure wave left so quickly that both men fell on their faces as their muscles had overcompensated to the immediate lack of resistance.

"Don't look, Martin," Daniel said as they regained stance. Ignoring the advice, Martin looked back at Smitty, at least what was left of him. All he could see was the upper torso and bloodied face of a man grotesquely twisted into a very unsettling posture. "Oh, God," Martin sobbed, "I don't think he knew You."

"C'mon, Martin; we need to go"

"Wait a minute, will you? Don't you care?"

"Martin," Daniel said in a hushed, controlled tone, "Smitty knew all the risks. He knew—"

"Knew! Knew! How in creation could he have known what we were up against?"

"Martin," now Daniel said louder and more directly, "Smitty was a member of an elite group of men who face death regularly. He knew the risks."

Martin just stared at Daniel and said nothing as he began to head back to exit at Irma's house.

—

Roger was furious as he headed back to the hotel. If he found that woman, he promised himself that he was going to put a bullet right into her skull. He pulled into the hotel parking lot and scurried right up to the Blackstone Suite, as they dubbed it. He had his own pass key to the suite, so he walked right in. What he didn't expect to find was Harry Armstead sitting over in a corner, his knees folded up to his chest and tears streaming down the young agent's face.

Roger bypassed all the computer equipment that was still busy compiling data and went over to Harry.

"Harry," he said in a soft but still commanding voice. The young man still remained stoically silent, so Roger spoke his name once again a little bit louder

"Harry."

Harry looked up at Roger and simply said, "She's gone."

"Who's gone?" Roger asked as a knot began to fold upon itself in the pit of his stomach. Harry was again looking blankly at his knees and slowly began to answer.

"*Magellan*, Commander Moore, Simone." When he spoke Simone's name, he began to sob once again.

"What do you mean gone, son?"

"They crashed on the moon as they were heading home," was all he could manage. "No survivors."

Roger spun around and started toward the computers that were scattered, seemingly haphazardly, around the room.

Roger Hand began to curse silently as he read over the still-incoming reports.

—

"So, how much air do we have, Cap'n?" Carl asked as they climbed up from their lunar haven.

"Just as much as you need, Carl; these are the new biosuits."

It was clear that Carl wasn't quite up to snuff on the latest space suit apparel.

"Huh?" was all he said.

"These babies make their own air. Biologically engineered filters take your carbon dioxide and turn it into oxygen. So, we're good for air. It's everything else I'm worried about." Captain Williamson was just about at the crest of the crater's rim as he spoke. Some of the rocks gave way under his foot, and he began to slide back down into the crater. It was Simone who grabbed him by the arm and stopped his rather awkward descent.

"Careful, Captain." Then she spoke to Carl. "You said help is on its way; from where?"

"Well, it seems there is a top-secret lunar base up here. Guess we'll have to promise to keep a lot of secrets to ourselves if we ever want to get home."

While she never spoke it aloud, Simone was getting a very bad feeling about their rescue. But even as the feelings of apprehension began to filter into her mind, an unexpected wash of peace and tranquility flooded her soul. Once again, Simone Sytte knew she wasn't alone or unprotected. Her God was God, and wherever she was, He was always there.

"Look! Over there, three o'clock," Deborah Dean yelled in excitement.

All eyes were looking across the barren lunar landscape, and in the distance they saw movement coming toward them, flying just above the ground.

Looks like a demon in flight, Simone thought to herself as their rescuers got closer.

CHAPTER 47

HIDING THE TRUTH

"So then, where did she go, Irma?"

"Sweetie, I just plain do not know," the old woman was standing at the window watching the two FBI agents looking over every inch of the rented Humvee that was parked out in front of the house.

Daniel Blackstone was frustrated, trying to put together a puzzle.

"So, let's go over this again," he said as he heard both Irma and Martin moan. It had been three hours since the two came up from the tunnel and found a drugged woman, who was supposed to be on the couch, gone.

"I'm telling ya, I heard a noise out back, so I went to look—"

Daniel broke in, "Did you take your shotgun?"

"No." She thought for a moment. "No, I didn't go out front at all."

Before she could say anything else, Daniel had gone out on the porch, and seeing the ancient firearm propped up against the home wall, he grabbed it and went inside and handed it to Irma.

Irma started to mumble something about bringing a loaded shotgun into the house as she took the weapon from Daniel and popped the barrel open to take out the shell.

"Hey, it's empty," she said in astonishment. That's when Daniel knew that more than just Jessica Vandale had come a-callin' today. He was about to say something to Irma when the two FBI agents walked in and tossed him a bag with a small magnetic cylinder in it.

"Tracking device," the shortest one said.

"Yeah, and pretty sophisticated too," the other one added. "Tied into her GPS system. Somebody knew where she was every single moment."

"Yeah, but the question now is, where is Jessica Vandale?" Daniel asked as he gently tossed the bag up and down in his hand.

—

As the small, rather odd-looking lunar taxi landed before them, the remaining crew of *Magellan* made their way into the craft. There was barely enough room for everyone and not a pilot in sight. That's when the com came to life and fed audio directly into their suits.

"Welcome home, *Magellan*. I am Mark Manski, the commander of Lunar Base Alpha. As soon as the pressurization of your compartment is complete, you will see the green safe light come on, and you can remove your helmets. The shuttle you are on is completely automated; in fact, it's being flown from right here at Alpha Base. So just sit back and enjoy the scenery. You should be arriving back here in about ten minutes. Just save all your questions for then. See you soon."

Before Matt Moore could say anything, the com went silent and the green safety light came on. Their taxi lifted off smoothly and headed in what seemed to be a southerly direction.

Matt was the first to disconnect his helmet with a sharp snap as he twisted it to his right. He smelled the air and gave a thumbs-up. Within seconds, all of *Magellan's* crew was breathing air from a fresh new source. Two minutes later, all of the astronauts were beginning to fade into unconsciousness. The air was tainted with a quick-acting, coma-inducing airborne drug. Simone was the last one to slip into unconsciousness. As she began to sleep, she heard the voice of the One she had finally got to meet speaking softly to her.

"I will never leave you nor forsake you, my daughter. Sleep for now, Simone. I will awaken you when it's time. There is more work for you to do."

Simone Sytte could hear her own voice answer, as if in a dream, hearing it from a distance, sweetly speaking her Savior's name as if she were saying goodnight, "Jesus."

—

Roger Hand had complete presidential authority over the situation. He watched the plane taxi down the runway as the three remaining members of the situation team left for their debriefing at the Pentagon. He still had two remaining loose ends to deal with, namely Martin Sherfy and Jessica Vandale. Martin was easy. He placed him in charge of the Cahokia

Mounds Historic Site since he already knew all he needed to know about its history and secrets. Jessica was another story. He figured she would show up sometime, and that thought worried him.

Roger drove from St. Louis International Airport and went to see Martin at the interpretive center. He went into the center as Martin was just finishing up a speech to his new subordinates and was walking to his office.

"Hello, Dr. Hand," Martin said as he opened the large doors that led to the interior of the building where the offices were. With a sweeping gesture of the hand, he offered an *after you* motion.

The two men walked silently for a few short seconds and then stopped outside of Martin's new office. Martin opened the door, and both men entered the room. Martin let out a long, drawn-out sigh.

"I can't believe what has happened to me in three short days," he said as he poured a cup of coffee for Roger.

"You do realize this could be a dangerous position, don't you?" Roger countered

"I trust God, Dr. Hand." Then, with shrugging shoulders, he added, "Whatever happens, happens."

Roger handed him a small business-type card "Here's a number that you can always reach me at. We'll be adding some of our security people to your staff: janitors, groundskeepers, and the like. The federal government will be adding a substantial chunk of change to your expense account. Use it wisely, Martin. I needn't remind you that everything you have seen and experienced the last few days is classified as top secret. You work for me now, Martin, and you answer to me alone."

"Understood," Martin simply replied.

"Look in your top left drawer."

"What?"

"Look."

Martin opened the drawer and saw a brand new .38 caliber handgun. He didn't say a word.

"My question is," Roger continued as he sipped his coffee, "if push comes to shove ..." He then looked up from his cup and stared into Martin's eyes. "Could you kill someone if you had to?"

Martin didn't hesitate in his answer. "To just simply kill someone, no. But to protect the people under me as well as to keep Blackie a secret, yes. No question about it."

"So, I know about your religious convictions. What about the old, 'Thou shalt not kill' thing?" asked Roger.

"Actually, Dr. Hand, it's more accurately translated, 'Thou shalt not commit murder.' Big difference between murder and warfare."

Roger put down his coffee cup and stepped closer to Martin.

"That's what I needed to hear." He offered his hand to Martin.

"Welcome to the team, Dr. Sherfy," He said. Martin didn't say a word; he just half-smiled and turned to look out the window behind his desk. A hundred yards away, he noticed a small herd of deer in the field grazing. He said softly, "I wonder what other surprises we'll run into."

"Don't be in a hurry to find out, Martin. This thing is just starting." He looked at his watch and then spoke again, "I'll be in touch; you keep your eyes open, Mister." Roger Hand simply turned and walked out the door, leaving Martin alone with his thoughts.

"So what are we supposed to do with this thing, Lord?" he asked quietly as he reached over and turned on the TV for the local news.

"On the western shore of Horseshoe Lake, a woman's body was found today. There was a single bullet wound between her eyes. Her front teeth were also knocked out with a blunt object, possibly the butt of the gun used to kill her. The major case squad has been called in to investigate."

Martin suspected deep down in his heart that he knew who the woman was and said to no one, "It really is just beginning"

Epilogue: Away from the Darkness

Kobi-ona looked across the great river before him and then turned to face his people behind him. It had now been ten years since his brother went into the underground waters, and he knew he would never see him again. The day Kobi-nana went into the darkness, the ground heaved in anger, and the deer all ran away in fear; they had never returned, and now his people were starving. Already half his people left before the first snow and went south to a land far away where they'd heard of great stone temples being built. Kobi-ona was taking the remainder of his people and was heading into the setting sun. An uneasiness was stirring in his soul as he felt as if he was being watched, and it was quickly turning into a deep-seated anger as he could swear he heard a dark, sinister laugh coming from the temple mound, floating across the prairie—a laughter that mocked and enraged him, a laughter that could never have come from a friend. Kobi-ona knew neither he nor his people were ever to return to this place. And personally, he didn't care; this place was evil and defiled. The day was almost spent, and the remainder of his people, the Mississippians, were heading across the river and off the pages of history. Forever.